Still Life with Pistol

Still Life
with Pistol

ROGER
ORMEROD

CHARLES SCRIBNER'S SONS
NEW YORK

This novel is a work of fiction. Names, characters, places and incidents are either the prod-
uct of the author's imagination or are used fictitiously. Any resemblance to actual persons,
living or dead, events or locales is entirely coincidental.

Library of Congress Cataloging-in-Publication Data

Ormerod, Roger.
   Still life with pistol.

   I. Title.
PR6065.R688S75   1986   823'.914   86-11877
ISBN 0-684-18728-0

First American Edition

Printed in the United States of America.

Dedicated to my friends at The Hill Residential College, Abergavenny, because the many happy week-ends I have spent there have influenced the atmosphere I have tried to create. Not that I have ever encountered murder, assault or seduction there, nor have I ever met any of Bruno's students, but I'm sure that any time they like to come along they will be made welcome at The Hill. Those that are left.

Still Life with Pistol

I

Amelia glanced sideways at me. 'We needn't have come, Richard, if you're going to be bored.'

I made no comment, concentrating on the road surface ahead.

'If you don't fancy being here a whole fortnight, you could have said.'

I changed down for the swing into the drive. I did want to, anyway, or at least as much as I wanted to do anything else. Neither for nor against, which was the trouble. But I was annoyed that it had shown.

'It was me fixed it up,' I reminded her casually, at least hiding the annoyance. She was looking at me with that frown of doubt I'd seen so often lately. Amelia is too perceptive.

'All the same . . . I can read you like a book.'

But so many of my pages were still uncut. 'I'm quite content,' I offered. 'Besides, I did want to see what Bruno's done about the security.'

'Which'll take you about an hour.'

'More than that.'

'Well . . . so long as you're happy, Richard.'

I smiled. Happy? Yes, very happy, and had been for the past year. Just being with her and hearing her voice, that was the strength of my happiness. Content, even, if that's what you want. The trouble was, I was beginning to doubt that I did. Truth to tell, I was missing the effort, the moments of triumph, even the doubts and fears and failures. I was drifting along a level track of contentment.

'I shall haunt you,' I warned her. 'At your shoulder every minute, pointing out your mistakes. I'm going to have a grand old time.'

'You dare!'

'I might even have a go at it myself.'

5

'Now *that's* a good idea.'

'Hah! It was a joke.'

The drive up to Fillingley Manor was narrow and rutted and the surrounding trees had been allowed to encroach. Bruno Fillingley had run out of money. Poor chap, my heart bled for him. When his father and elder brother had died together in a car crash, there he'd been in Vienna happily pigging it on a large allowance and painting away merrily with none of the desperation and poverty of the Impressionists whom he so much admired. Then suddenly he was the owner of the manor house and about eight hundred acres of woodland, river and lake and, after taxes, without a couple of tenners to rustle together for maintenance. So what had he done? He'd turned his home into a painting school. For a sum that had startled me, you could enjoy his hospitality for a fortnight, basking in country manor luxury and at the same time receiving expert tuition in whichever branch of the creative arts attracted you. You pick it, and he'd done it. He was the resident genius.

More than that, Bruno was the most expert art forger I had ever encountered. I hoped Amelia would be amused.

The invitation had been extended six months before, when I'd been to the manor, alone, to advise Bruno on security. His problem had been unique: not breaking in but breaking out. I'd been glad to do the job for nothing. Don't tell Amelia, but it'd been a small upsurge in the interest line. But, advice over, Bruno had relaxed and we'd chatted, and I'd told him about Amelia's artistic endeavours. She had confidence in oils but not in watercolour. So then the invitation had been made, both of us as his non-paying guests for one of his fortnight courses in June. Fine. It'd be a break, and just the sort of thing Amelia would wallow in. Between you and me, she's better than she claims, and perhaps her expectation was as much for warming praise as for constructive criticism.

All the same, even with the excitement flushing her, she had not lost sight of my welfare. Was I perhaps regretting my retirement from the police force? Just a little bit, Richard?

I wasn't going to admit it. I twirled the wheel, dodging the worst of the potholes, and chatted desperately.

'Don't be surprised when you see it. Fillingley Manor sounds very grand, but from the outside . . .'

6

We burst from the trees, and were confronted by the acre or so of oval, immaculate lawn, surrounded by neat gravel drive. The manor house sat beyond it, part Tudor black and white, part ugly Victorian restoration, ivy and wistaria rampantly softening the worst of it. The house spread sideways, all angles and different levels and towering slim chimneys, with hideous buttresses taking the sagging weight. The original windows were leaded, but the extensions had sash windows and heavy, curved bays. The door was a massive, studded slab of ancient black oak.

'Richard!' she squealed. 'Stop! Let me look. Oh . . . it's beautiful.'

I stopped. In the eye of the beholder, they say, so I suppose that was why Amelia was the artist and not me. All I could see was a hodgepodge of clashing styles that I found quite painful. Perhaps she was referring to the setting which was spectacular. There was a glimpse of sparkling water to one side, beyond the clock in the stable tower, and a grand sweep of birch trees around the back. In the expanse of oval lawn was one of those splendid old cedars, which must have been there when the original house was built.

There was already one car parked out on the gravel, nose in to what I knew to be the library windows.

As I drew in to park my Triumph Stag beside the blue Escort, Amelia said: 'I wonder where the red Fiesta's disappeared to.'

She had noticed that the lane from which we'd turned to enter the drive went nowhere. After twenty yards it was a dead end. So . . . where was the Fiesta? I shrugged, not particularly interested.

Bruno was in the doorway, all welcome and shining charm. The setting framed him well, the two massive black pillar beams of the porch at his shoulders, the studded door open behind him, the brass coach-lamp matched to his sports shirt. This was not the Bruno I'd met before, the casual businessman with the sharp thrust of efficiency behind his grey eyes. This was the Bruno you'd expect to see if you were coming to meet Bruno the RA, Bruno the landowner, your host. He was an inch or two over six feet, golden haired, an elegant forty-five or so, now in slim, beautifully-tailored chestnut slacks, silk sports shirt, and with the artistic concession of a silk scarf at the open neck. His strong bronzed hand reached forward.

'Richard. How splendid to see you again.'

A brief pressure from his fingers, nothing too effusive. Then, for Amelia, a hand to each shoulder, a twinkle from his eyes, the tiniest flicker of a smile of approval.

'And this is Amelia . . .'

Then, not one kiss but two, carefully planted one on each cheek just brushing her lips in passing, followed by the extended arms and the artist's appraisal.

'You must allow me to paint your portrait. No . . . I insist . . .'

All this was ruined, fortunately before it ran away with itself and embarrassed Amelia too painfully, by the sudden intervention, from behind Bruno, of a short, meagre man, scuttling on his hurried way out.

There would have been room to slip through between Bruno and the framing upright beam, but this was not a man with a balanced control in his life. Dark and urgent in his nervousness, his eyes hunting everywhere beneath a shock of black hair, he tripped over his own fumbling feet, caught Bruno's arm with his shoulder, and darted away towards his Escort, his toes kicking up gravel and his arms flying. He buried his embarrassment inside the rear door, and seemed to be tenderly raising a small child from the seat. His concentration held me. His entire body was unified into that single action. I realized that behind me Bruno was silent, he too fascinated.

The dark head emerged. It was not a baby he was cradling in his arms, but a plain, white vase, perhaps a foot tall. He turned, and retraced his steps, at first controlled, but then, when he realized our attention, abruptly disorganized again.

'Oh dear . . .' he said, his voice reaching into the higher register. 'Sorry. Yes. Must get this inside. You see . . .'

He stumbled towards Bruno, who moved hastily to one side, then he disappeared with a sharp pitter-patter into the darker recesses beyond the door. I stared at Bruno. He shrugged. Amelia gave a small, tight laugh.

'That was Bert Inskip,' said Bruno. 'Don't ask me . . .' He shook his head. 'A potter, he tells me. Though why he's brought it already made, instead of making it here . . . I don't know. Perhaps he'll explain.'

For a moment Bruno's practised confidence had been

shaken. It must have been the first time something like this had happened, though his painting school had been going for fifteen months. We were in the middle of a glorious June and he'd opened it the previous spring.

'But come along in,' he went on, recovering well. 'Unload your car later. I'll show you to your room and have a tray of tea sent up.' He turned and looked at me with wide, innocent eyes. 'There should have been a Mrs Inskip. Veronica, if I remember correctly. Though perhaps not his wife, otherwise why would they have asked for separate rooms?'

He seemed to intend it as a genuine and not a rhetorical question. But I was no longer a Detective Inspector. Mysteries such as this were no longer a part of my life. I put the thought behind me.

'But before we go up, Bruno, I really must show Amelia the banqueting hall.'

'Oh yes,' she said eagerly, and Bruno took her arm with proprietorial interest.

We were in the narrow entrance hall. The walls were panelled with the original dark oak, gleaming with the lustre of time. From our right rose the narrow, turning staircase which I knew led up to the grand balcony. I paused to light my pipe. Somehow it seemed appropriate there, but perhaps that was an association with fumed oak. The general impression was of solidity. Nothing creaked. Sound seemed to be absorbed without echo.

'Aren't you coming, Richard?' called Amelia from the end of the passage. 'Oh!' she gasped, as Bruno threw open the doors. I strolled casually after them, having seen it before.

The long, lofty hall ran through to the rear of the house. On the back wall the diamond-paned windows were set high, admitting only a small amount of the afternoon light. Bruno depressed a switch. The three circular iron chandeliers, gently moving on their long chains from the high, vaulted ceiling, flicked into life, artificial candles now. Originally, no doubt, rush dips had been lit, then hauled far above the blare and confusion of a high banquet, with straw on hammered earth for the floor and lurchers crawling from the corners for the tossed bones. But now the floor was stone flags. Now the huge, wide fireplace along one side wall held banked electric log fires. But

9

still the vaulted beams were there. The balcony, originally a minstrels' gallery at the far end, was now extended round four sides of the hall.

'Your room,' Bruno was saying, 'is above our heads, along the front balcony. You can't see the door from here.'

Amelia was saying nothing. As I had been, she was overwhelmed. Slowly she wandered round, pausing at the suit of armour (not a family heirloom, Bruno had told me, but Chinese), staring at the crossed halberds over the fireplace (Persian, Bruno claimed) and finally transfixed by the Reynolds painting of a lady in a scarlet dress, which took up a lot of the panelled wall.

'You own a Reynolds?' she asked, standing back from it.

Bruno smiled. I said: 'Look at the lace, the hands, the fan.'

'It *is* a Reynolds,' she claimed. 'I've seen one like it in the National Gallery but with a blue dress.'

'Now look at the signature,' I said.

Bruno stood, head inclined modestly, as she peered at the signature. Then she turned, her eyes wide and startled. Her quick glance at me was for assistance.

'But it's a forgery,' she said faintly. 'Bruno Fillingley, 1962.'

'Not a forgery,' said Bruno gently, and you could just detect the pain in his voice, held firmly in place by his pride. 'Not even a fake. It's a painting in the style of Reynolds. A fitting decoration for the hall, I thought.'

Amelia looked to me to help her. She painted in the style of Amelia. It hurt her that any artist (and an RA at that) should adopt someone else's style. Bruno registered every nuance in her expression. He spread his hands, his shrug elegant.

'It's much more difficult than working in your own style. Believe me. And quite innocent.'

All right . . . innocent, if Bruno said so. But you could search the whole building and find no more than a dozen in his own style. Oh, I admit you'd find a number in galleries around the country, one in the Tate and two in the National Gallery, but . . .

'Wait till you see the balcony,' I told her.

'There are more?' she asked weakly.

'There are many more,' I agreed.

At that moment we heard tyres on the gravel outside and

Bruno murmured that he had to go out and do his welcoming act again, not using those exact words. 'You're in number three, Richard,' he said. 'Forgive me if I don't come up with you. Ring for tea, if you'd like it.'

We were in the room to the right of the head of the stairs, which opened on to the balcony. At that time, there being no outside windows at balcony level, the paintings there were no more than a line of blocked shadows so that Amelia didn't notice them. I showed her into our room.

It looked down on the stretch of recessed gravel that Bruno reserved for guests. This room, too, was part of the original building. The beams were there, the plaster, the four-poster bed without the posts (or the effect would have been too repressive) and the one door, with a simple latch inside. Amelia looked round.

'No bathroom, Richard?'

'Can't expect too much.' I'd crossed to the window. 'He's converted three rooms off the balcony into bathrooms. We'll just have to slum it for a bit.'

The car being parked below was not the red Fiesta Amelia had mentioned but a battered and ancient Mini. From it, his arms loaded with a bundle of canvases, was climbing a fierce-looking man with tousled red hair and a red beard, who might have been about thirty, in jeans to which he managed to add another tear on the jagged edge of the car door and a roll-top jumper too thick for the weather. Not having one free, he could not shake hands with Bruno, who inclined his head. I didn't hear what Bruno said but the newcomer said briskly: 'Lewis Hately.' Then he stood back to see what effect that might have, seeming relieved when Bruno did no more than place his hand on Hately's arm and lead him inside.

I heard them stump up the stairs, Hately's heavy boots thundering on each tread, and hoped he wasn't going to be stamping round in the night.

'Ask Bruno about the red Fiesta,' said Amelia.

'Does it matter?'

'Just interested.' In the woman who'd been driving it, she meant.

So I was out at the stairhead when Bruno walked back.

'Does everybody park there, Bruno?'

'Yes. I hope it's not going to disturb you. I could find you another room . . .'

'It's not that. There was a red Fiesta apparently on its way here. I mean, where else could it have been going? And it's not.'

'Mysteries, Richard? You're retired now, you know.'

'A small mystery, if you like. We came on her along the lane, with a flat tyre. I helped her change the wheel and she drove off ahead of us. So . . . where's she got to?'

I didn't go into detail about the other points that had aroused Amelia's interest: her anger, which seemed more a personal matter than at the tyre incident; her apparent helplessness when her general attitude was of competence; the fact that no artists' materials had been visible in the car.

I had felt, more than observed, that Bruno had stiffened. 'I must get down . . .'

'*Has* she arrived?'

'Not here, Richard, I assure you.'

'She was about five-ten, chestnut hair cut short, in a tweed skirt and a brown blouse. Roundish face, brown eyes, firm mouth. Hell, she didn't even smile at me once.'

'Marion,' he said softly, and I couldn't tell whether his voice was completely steady, nor whether he was upset or pleased.

'You know her?'

'Leave this to me, Richard. I know how to handle it.'

Then, very firmly, he pushed past me and down the stairs with a clatter. A moment later I heard the ting of a lifted phone in the entrance hall and the buzz of a dial. But he dialled only two numbers.

I returned to our room in time for the next car. 'She's not arrived here,' I said.

Amelia was at the window. 'Just look at that. Twins.'

The blue Escort now being parked beside the Mini was an exact duplicate of the one Bert Inskip, the potter, had arrived in, which was the other side of my Stag. In fact, looking more carefully, I could see that the two Escorts bore consecutive registration numbers.

'Not to worry,' I said, determined not to become involved with mysteries. 'Bruno mentioned a wife. Veronica, I think he said. They've simply arrived separately.'

Yet it did not seem possible that this slim, handsome woman, now standing beside her car and looking round with a commanding air of expectation, could be the wife of stumbling Bert. When Bruno appeared in a rush from the porch almost below us (a flustered Bruno, after his phone call) she seemed to expect him to carry her bags. Bruno was surprised at this but nevertheless relieved her of one as she took up the other.

'How strange,' said Amelia, frowning at the two Escorts.

'Come along, I'll show you round,' I offered, to take her mind, and mine, from the strangeness.

'If you'll just show me the nearest bathroom . . .'

'Oh . . . sorry. Of course.'

Which got us out on the balcony just as Bruno showed his new acquisition past us.

She was saying: '. . . a certain facility in oils and watercolour, but I intend to expand my abilities with pastels. You *have* worked in pastels, Mr . . . er . . . ?'

'Call me Bruno. Everyone else will.'

'Ah yes. And I'm Veronica.'

'I *have* worked in pastels. I studied under Herman Grauss in Vienna, and he worked with Degas in Paris from 1910 to 1917, when Degas died.'

'The poor man must be ancient now.'

'He's dead, Veronica. But even at eighty . . .'

'But Degas, my dear. *Un peu passé*, don't you think?' The lapse into French no doubt being inspired by the mention of Paris.

A door opened and closed, and their voices were cut off. Amelia glanced at me.

'Didn't Bruno say they had separate rooms, Bert and Veronica?'

I agreed he had.

'I wonder whose idea that was,' she said innocently, her eyes dancing.

I was pleased to see she'd recovered from the shock of Bruno's Reynolds, so that now I dared to introduce her to the balcony. At the stairhead I found the switches, and the lights sprang on.

They were those daylight strip lights, one above each painting, with little hoods so that they didn't dazzle. All round the balcony they shone out on their separate treasures, Manet and

Degas along one longer side, Berthe Morisot along the far end, Sisley and Renoir filling the opposite long side. Altogether there were forty, and all by Bruno Fillingley, RA. There were five versions of the *Absinthe Drinkers*, each in a slightly different arrangement of the essentials, the expressions of emptiness more or less profound, and a selection of pastels of plump women awkwardly bathing in tin baths. Manet was represented by versions of Berthe Morisot in seven different hats. (It was conceivable that Manet might have had the opportunity to paint her five times, she was after all a fellow artist and his sister-in-law). The *Vase of Peonies* was rendered over and over, in accordance with a progressing fall of petals. The Sisleys were village scenes, the Berthe Morisots all of her sister, Edma, in the garden, the Renoirs café scenes.

Bruno claimed that one painting for each artist was genuine. Maybe an expert could have told you which but I hadn't heard that any one had succeeded.

Amelia appeared not to have taken breath for two minutes. Then she stirred and, apparently having forgotten about the bathroom, began moving slowly round the balcony. Occasionally she paused, but only to say: 'But they're signed!' And finally, clutching my arm: 'Signed! Degas, Manet, Richard. Morisot, Renoir, Sisley.'

I said nothing.

When we had come the full circuit she almost stamped her foot in vexation. 'But he's a cheat, Richard. A crook. A thief.'

'But you've got to admit – a marvellous painter.'

'That's not the point.'

'I know, my dear. But wouldn't you like to own one of those, just for the sheer pleasure of hanging it on the wall and looking at it? They're better than photographic reproductions, and you'd have the only one in the world, because there's no two alike. They're not copies, you know, only . . .'

'You said. "In the style of".'

'Bruno said that.'

'But he's signed them as Degas and Manet, and whoever.'

'Not permanently. To be guilty of forgery he'd have to sell one as a genuine article. He doesn't do that. He tells you he did them all, except one of each artist. He's very proud of that and I don't blame him. You could rub out the signature with a bit of spit on your handkerchief.'

'It's misrepresentation,' she stated firmly.

'I don't see anything wrong with it. On the back of each painting he puts a label saying it's his own work. No, no.' I reached forward to restrain her eager hands. 'Touch one and the alarm goes off.'

'And that's what you came here for? To set this all up?'

Having taken her arm I began leading her along the balcony to the nearest bathroom. My voice was quite even, with not a hint of the amusement I felt. 'That wasn't why I came. Ah, here we are.'

It was plainly marked: Bathroom. 'I could have found it myself,' she told me.

'But I wanted to show you the paintings. And you haven't looked at these vases, yet.'

As there were eight guest rooms off the balcony and three bathrooms, that left ten expanses of wall between. In each of these, below the level of the paintings, there was inset a small alcove, two feet high and a foot across, obviously made to accept a graceful blue and white vase. There were ten vases. All the same. There was one of them almost beside the bathroom door.

'It's all right to touch this,' I told her. 'Go on. Pick it up.'

'I wouldn't dare. You're making me nervous, Richard. It looks valuable.'

'One of the ten is. It's a genuine Chinese Hsüan-tê vase of around 1450. The other nine are Bruno's copies.'

I lifted that one out. The base bore the underglaze marking of Hsüan-tê.

'I suppose this is the real one,' she said.

'Who knows?' I shrugged. 'Bruno's so damned good.'

'But this *is* forgery,' she cried, her tone rising a clear octave. 'You couldn't rub *that* out with a bit of spit.'

'But he doesn't intend to sell any of 'em. Do you realize, he owns one genuine Chinese blue and white vase, one genuine Degas, a Renoir, a Sisley, a Manet, and a Morisot, all collected by his grandfather, or *his* father. Any one of those would pay for the upkeep of this place for a few years, but he won't part with a single one. He'd prefer to make what he can from his artists' school and apply for grants. You see, he doesn't believe that

15

beautiful things should be locked away as an investment. He thinks they should be looked at and enjoyed. And so . . . that's what you can do. You can enjoy his genuine ones, if you can decide which *are* the genuine ones, or enjoy the whole over-whelming display as it is.'

She pouted. 'But all the same . . .'

'It's part of his security. Just think of the trouble a burglar would have, always assuming he could get in, when it came to deciding which was genuine and which not. Even an art expert would be baffled. The genuine ones aren't catalogued, you know.'

I'd won. She smiled. She approved of that, because it carried a logical justification. 'I can't stand here arguing,' she declared, and disappeared into the bathroom.

Placidly stuffing a pipe, I wandered back to our room wondering what I was going to do for the rest of the fortnight. As I turned to close the door I caught just a glimpse of a man standing on the balcony opposite. He didn't register until I had the door closed and when I whipped it open again he'd gone.

But he'd been too tall and staid to be the self-critical Bert Inskip and there'd been none of the ginger flash of Lewis Hately's beard. He was certainly not Bruno, not tall enough, and anyway Bruno was there beneath my window, welcoming a vigorous, busty woman, who was loudly jollying him along.

Bruno seemed distressed. 'Not again, Mrs Race!' I heard him plead.

She slapped his shoulder. 'I booked under my maiden name. You should've guessed, from the address.'

'I did ask you not to . . .'

But she'd walked past him into the hallway and I heard no more.

The man could have been a servant, I supposed. But why, then, had he been using a guest bedroom? And why was I left with the distinct impression that he'd had a pistol in his hand?

I stood at the window counting cars. The Mrs Race who'd just entered had left the tailgate up on a Cavalier, but that was the only fresh car in the row. So when had the man arrived and where was his car? All right, I told myself. Calm down. No great mystery there; he could have arrived earlier in a taxi. There, you see, logic wins through. I felt much better, and decided to go down and begin to fetch up our cases and Amelia's painting stuff. How many darned paintings did she expect to complete, anyway? There was a ream or so of twenty by sixteen Whatman paper.

When I reached the Stag, there he was, the man I must have glimpsed across the banqueting hall. He was standing beside my car and eyeing it with appreciation.

'Had one of these once,' he said. 'Have you got the hardtop, too?'

'We left it at home. The weather's more suitable for the hood.'

'It's in good nick.'

'I look after it.'

There were no suspicious bulges and not many places he could hide a gun in slacks and shirt, so I told myself it had been my imagination. He stuck out his hand suddenly as though he'd made up his mind to trust me with it.

'Roy Towers,' he said, and his rather craggy face split in a grin.

'I'm Richard Patton. I'm here with my wife.' Which wasn't quite true but it saved difficulties. We weren't married. 'She's the painter.'

'Not you?'

'I don't pretend to be.'

Then he gave a short bark of laughter, which didn't sound too pleasant. 'Most of 'em aren't, but it doesn't stop them pretending.'

'You've been here before, then?' I glanced up into his face, being busy bending over and lifting out cases. Roy Towers, I thought. Didn't the name mean something?

He teetered back on his heels. The grey eyes were expressionless, the heavy brows lowered. There was suspicion of my enquiry though it had been innocent enough. Was he a policeman? He didn't seem to have reached an age for retirement. Forty, perhaps.

'A few times,' he admitted at last. 'Seen 'em all. What d'you bet we'll get one with not the slightest ability and one who wants to work in secrecy. And the ones who keep coming and don't improve.'

'Like you?' I asked mildly.

'I get along.' But I'd made him uneasy. He switched the subject from himself. 'And there's sure to be one I've met before.'

'Pleasant to meet old friends.'

'That woman . . . I heard a voice. I'd swear I know it.'

'Bruno called her Mrs Race.'

I'd thought his lead-in had been rather awkward but we'd come to it at last. I'd confirmed a fear, judging by the momentary stiffening of his back. But he recovered well.

'Carla Race,' he said casually. 'Yes, she's been here.' Then he reached out a cigarette pack and fumbled with it.

The window above me opened and Amelia called out: 'Richard, do we dress for dinner?'

I raised my eyebrows to the one who'd know. He grunted, and said: 'Informal. Seven-thirty.'

'Informal,' I called up. 'Seven-thirty.' And when I turned back he was walking away.

'You'll never manage it all,' said Amelia. 'I'll come down.'

So I leaned against the Stag and drew on my pipe, feeling very relaxed and lazy and useless, and watched the two cars coming round the gravel oval. Two more painters. Surely they must be the last, I thought. Bruno could never accommodate any more.

The lead car was a TR7, driven by a handsome man of around thirty, using sufficient control to avoid a scrambling, gravel-thrown stop. It must have taken restraint, the urge surely being to show off to the young woman in the Metro behind him. As far as I could tell through the glass, she was a blonde with very attractive features, but she didn't seem to have the confidence that such a combination usually carries along with it. She climbed out and looked across her car to him.

'Thank you,' she called, and then she actually blushed and found something inside her car to attend to. Well now, I thought, a shy creature, in these days. How very rare. I could imagine her, as Roy Towers had predicted, working in deadly secret over the delicate detail of tiny flowers in watercolour.

The man got out of his car with casual elegance. He caught my eye and winked. 'She'd lost her way, so I led her here.' Did he need to excuse himself? Or was he quietly boasting of a personal charm that automatically attracted every pretty face?

But in fact, now that she'd found reason to hide it inside the car, her face had relaxed. The brief smile she'd given him had melted away and now her expression held the blank weariness of the habitually lonely with just a shade of annoyance with herself for the betrayal of the blush. In any event, it took her longer in the Metro than necessary, giving Bruno time to step forward.

'You'll be Rex Lightfoot?'

'The same.'

'Watercolours, I believe.'

'A mere beginner.' Only an expert would say that so proudly.

Bruno laughed. 'They all say that. Do you mind finding your own way up? You're in number six. I'll go and help your friend with her bags.'

I could see it on Lightfoot's lips: no friend of mine. But Bruno was already moving towards the Metro.

'Up the stairs on your right,' I called out, and Amelia passed Lightfoot in the doorway. 'Hello there,' she said to him, and I looked down at my pipe.

Two watercolourists; they'd surely gravitate together. I wasn't sure I liked that idea, and damned sure I didn't like his answering smile. My reaction even less. It surprised me. I'd always been well aware that Amelia was quite a number of years younger than myself, but it was only recently that I'd started to feel it, when the fact of my retirement had begun to work its way into my awareness. Amelia was vital and alive and intelligent – and there were fewer years between her and Lightfoot. He carried the confidence of his sexuality blatantly and he would not be interested in a meek and blushing blonde. I turned away.

She was struggling with her shyness. Twenty, was she? Not much more.

Bruno was a fraud, no getting round it. He was working hard to make her feel confident in her welcome; not being so effusive that she'd collapse into tongue-tied confusion, not too off-hand that she'd feel hurt. Good old Bruno.

'Number four, Miss Penney,' he was saying. 'But you'll have to get used to us all calling you Samantha. Or do you answer to Sam? Perhaps not. Never mind, then. These your paints? Ah, a lovely set. And so many canvases. You should have brought oil boards, they take up less space.' A hand to her elbow, so very gently. She flashed him a tentative smile. 'Time to freshen up. Dinner at seven-thirty. Quite informal, my dear.' That was the father-figure, in case she preferred it. The shy smile became more confident. She did.

The paint box was brand new, the canvases virgin and pristine. I could have bet she wouldn't be able to tell the difference between a sable and a hog's bristle. And that it didn't matter.

Amelia was at my elbow. 'She's very beautiful.'

'If she'd relax, yes.'

'Did you see her eyes?'

'She doesn't look directly at you.'

'Shame,' she said. 'Come on, I want to change.'

'Yes. Me too.'

Between us, we got it all up to our room in one go. Have you seen how much these painters need? I think it was Corot who had a gang of children to carry all his equipment. I was Amelia's gang.

'I suppose there's a studio,' she remarked, slipping out of her slacks.

'There certainly is. But you'll be working outdoors, surely.'

'Depends.' She was silent for a moment. 'Did you see that rather splendid young man with those gorgeous shoulders?'

'Rex Lightfoot?' My lightweight suit, I was deciding, wondering whether I needed another shave. 'He's water-colours, too.'

'How interesting.'

I decided to go for the shave.

We were using the dining room in the Victorian part of the

house, where Bruno had a large oval table and Sheraton chairs. In there he had just a few of his own genuine paintings, all industrial landscapes, with the sunlight playing tricks and bringing colour and beauty to smoking stacks and torpid canals. Bruno sat at the head of the table, me at the foot, which left four painters each side.

Now we met Bruno's team of servants, though I suppose that's the wrong word. As he ran the place like a five-star hotel, the women who served us were more correctly waitresses. The quiet man in the background was not a butler, he was a *maître d'hôtel*. This pleasant fantasy was partly confirmed when Bruno told me later that he did not have a cook, but a chef he'd bribed from Luchow's in New York.

The meal was wonderful. I know that, because Amelia told me so, later. The wines were from Bruno's excellent cellar. But I don't remember it in detail. I was far too involved with crosscurrents. Roy Towers (ex-policeman, I was now convinced) seemed not to notice anything subtle. He barely raised his eyes from his plate, for the moment he did so he'd find himself being surveyed with animosity by Carla Race. He was gripping his cutlery firmly, knuckles white. Nothing else betrayed the fact that he was disturbed.

Carla Race was beginning to display the reason Bruno had not wanted her there. The fact that she'd had to book under her maiden name confirmed that Bruno had encountered her before and wished not to do so again. But she was there, and he was working hard to keep her under control. He had her at his end of the table, on his right, but handsome Rex Lightfoot was between them, so that Bruno could not appeal quietly in her ear. Perhaps he'd hoped that Lightfoot would charm her but she barely noticed him.

She noticed no one but Roy Towers and I was rapidly coming to the conclusion that Towers was the reason she was there. Not the atmosphere, not the artistic expertise of Bruno; she was there for Roy Towers. Her hatred of him crackled across and down the table.

'They talk about justice,' she commented loudly over the soup. 'British justice. That's a laugh.'

'Justice,' said Bruno placidly, 'was not done to Van Gogh in his lifetime.'

She raised her voice. 'You've only got to look round this table to understand what I mean.'

'And as for Gauguin . . .' began Bruno resolutely.

'But Monet, dear Bruno,' called Veronica Inskip, at my left elbow, throwing her opinion along the table. 'Didn't he make money before he died?'

Bert clattered his spoon into the bowl and dabbed his lips, looking at her in appeal as though she'd challenged his opinion. I hadn't yet seen the two of them together, hadn't seen them exchange a word.

Bruno smiled at Veronica. He looked as though he deeply valued her opinion. 'I believe he did.'

'Money,' snorted Carla. 'Talking of making money, I wonder how much they pick up in bribes.'

Lewis Hately was sitting just beyond Veronica. He'd seemed not to be interested in conversation but now he lifted his beard, looking round the table in interest. 'Bribes?' he demanded. 'Are we talking about art critics?'

'No, we are not,' said Veronica crisply. 'We are trying to talk about artists but for some reason . . .'

'The police,' Carla cut in triumphantly. 'Bribery, corruption, distortion of evidence . . . and we've got a fine example at this very table.'

Amelia gave a yip of distress and sat, spoon poised, her eyes above it huge and appalled, concentrated on Carla. I felt that the rest of the table, knowing what I'd been, concentrated on me. But I knew Carla's objective was Towers and that cemented my awareness that he had to be an ex-policeman. It also went some way towards explaining why he'd retired early. I began to find the situation interesting.

Then Bruno laughed at something Amelia had not said, put his hand to her arm, and the moment was gone as the trim young woman cleared our soup plates and replaced them with hot ones.

And through it all, even during the transition period when there was no plate there, quiet Samantha Penney, the other side of Towers, sat with her eyes downcast, refusing to raise them in case someone spoke to her.

And that was just the first course.

Towers did not join us for coffee in the leather softness of the drawing room. It was there that we received Bruno's formal opening speech during which the rules of the game were laid out.

Meal times were explained. 'You'll find it all set out on a card in your rooms.' For a fortnight we were invited to treat the manor house and grounds as our own. All he asked was that each artist should let him know where they were working, so that he could keep in touch. Anywhere in the estate you could go and he'd find you, once a day at least, for advice as required. Anyone interested in still life work was permitted to borrow anything in the house. (I raised my eyebrows at that, thinking of his blue and white vases.) And acres of flowers were available in the sunken garden and the greenhouses. Then came the small snag.

'But you'll realize,' said Bruno, 'that with so many valuable articles in the house, I have to have special alarms. These work on a time clock. At seven-thirty in the morning they switch themselves off, so that you can get out before breakfast if you want to catch the early light, but they go on at eleven at night. This means that if you're late coming in from the pub in the village, for instance, you'll find the doors locked after eleven.'

There was a concerted grumble at this, mostly from those who had no intention of visiting the pub.

He smiled and raised his hand. 'But not to worry, there's a gatehouse down by the drive entrance.' (Was there? I hadn't spotted it.) 'The key hangs in the porch and there's an extension phone in the hall. Dial one, and you'll get me. I'm the only one who can key out the alarms. So all will not be lost. And if . . .' He paused for effect. 'And if I'm in bed, then I might decline to come down. In that event, there are bedclothes in a cupboard and an aired bed so you'll be quite comfortable there for a night.'

You had to hand it to Bruno. He had had to lay on that facility for those who insisted on staying out late but he'd made it clear that he didn't expect them to. In the nicest way. And now he oiled the hinges.

'And for those who prefer to stay at home, so to speak, let me assure them they'll not be deprived. There's a fully stocked bar in that far corner – you may not have noticed – and I expect you all have your own tastes. So you simply help yourselves. On the house.'

'Oh . . . h . . . h . . .' they all whispered, forgetting how much they were paying him. They'd have to spend their time trying to drink themselves silly to make a profit.

Amelia, sitting beside me, patted my hand as though this arrangement was mine but really, I suppose, the necessity for it had arisen because of my security suggestions. So I patted hers back and relaxed.

Rex Lightfoot uncurled himself with grace, looking so solemn that we had to assume he was carrying on the mood, throwing it back at Bruno. He glanced at Amelia but saw she was occupied, so he bent over Samantha, who just happened to be sitting next to him.

'Can I get you something, Sam?'

Her head darted up, her eyes wide at his use of the diminutive, her lip caught in her teeth. Then she shook her head vigorously, making a cascade show of her hair, and Bruno sprang in to save her.

'Later, for heaven's sake! You'll have me broke in a week.'

There was general laughter and Samantha was able to subside but I noticed that when Rex sat down again he leaned towards her and actually drew words from her. The swirl of her hair had caught his attention.

Bruno had slipped very cleverly round his basic difficulty, I realized. When he'd consulted me he'd been quite certain that his basic alarm system was sufficient security against attack from outside. It probably was. But his painting school produced a procession of strangers and whereas even an art expert might not spot Bruno's genuine treasures from his copies on just a stroll around, an expert posing as an amateur, with a clear run of fourteen days, might well find time for more critical tests, and alarm systems are vulnerable from inside. So I'd had to suggest a second system, designed against breaking out and not in. Which had left Bruno with the fact that he had to explain the restrictions without actually implying that one of his guests could be a thief.

He'd covered it neatly. No dissenting voice was raised.

'Later, for heaven's sake!' Bruno said. Everybody laughed

and when it died down he went on: 'I want to show you the studio, anyway.'

With the weather we were having, it seemed likely that they'd all be working outside, but no artist can resist a tour round a studio. We trooped after Bruno, Bert Inskip and his wife keeping well away from each other, Lewis Hately appearing bored.

Bruno had converted a barn at one end of a cobbled yard, but he had made sure that nobody had to stumble over cobbles in the rain by building a corridor off the rear end of the banqueting hall. At the far end of it, a wooden door opened into the barn.

It no longer had many aspects suggestive of a barn, the raftered roof now being pierced by windows on the north side. The floor was plastic tiles. Along the rear wall was a run of benches broken by a double sink unit and along the wall facing was a continuous run of soft-surfaced display board on which were pinned two or three watercolours from past courses. A third wall was pimpled with electric outlets and there were a dozen or so floodlights and spots on stands. Beside an electric potter's kiln in one corner there was a potter's wheel, beside that a door opening into the yard.

'Oh my!' said Veronica, making a dismayed gesture with fluttering fingers. 'A kiln. I haven't done pottery for ages.'

Bert at once hurried over to it, opening the door and peering in. I just heard his muttered comment: 'Not since the evening classes on car maintenance.'

'A good kiln,' Bruno told him. 'Special elements to take it up to two thousand or so. You'll be using it, Bert?'

Bert had brought a naked white vase for some purpose but all the same he was hesitant. 'I shall . . . yes . . . I suppose.'

'Hah!' said Veronica in contempt.

'You'll see . . .' Bruno raised his voice, '. . . that all the facilities are here for still life. And along that wall, at the end of the fortnight, we can have a display of the work you've all done. If you like . . .' He looked modest. '. . . I'll do a sort of criticism act.'

At my shoulder I heard a sharp hiss of indrawn breath, and glanced round to see Samantha with her hand to her mouth and her eyes wide with distress. I smiled at her.

'All except me,' I whispered. 'I'm excused.'

25

'Oh dear,' she murmured.

'I don't suppose it's compulsory.'

'I didn't realize . . .'

I could make a good guess that she'd never painted before. It could have taken all her courage to come there at all, the only spur being the infinitely worse prospect of not being there for this fortnight. She had come for the company, to be with people.

'Berthe Morisot began with sketches at a school,' I told her, Bruno having told me this.

'Who's she?'

'One of the famous Impressionists.'

'Was she good?'

'I'll have to show you round the balcony.'

She smiled. I'd offered her friendship and I was old enough not to present a sexual challenge. 'I'd like that.' Then she glanced away. I wondered what Amelia would say if she knew I'd now noticed Samantha's eyes, large, blue and intelligent.

At our backs the door opened, propelled by Roy Towers, behind first. He was carrying a plain walnut table, balanced on it a cluster of yellow daisies with brown eyes and a copper and brass hunting horn. He ignored us and marched across purposefully to the wall with the plug outlets.

'Here he is,' said Carla Race. 'You'd never believe that behind that innocent exterior there's . . .'

'Well at least, there's one of you going to use the studio,' cut in Bruno loudly. 'I've been explaining, Roy, that you've got the use of anything you like in the house.'

'He's heard all this before,' said Carla, looking round, making sure we were kept fully informed.

'You too, dear,' said Bruno. He couldn't quite keep the acid from his voice.

'Anything?' asked Roy.

'Within reason.'

'Well thanks.'

'It's like a second-rate play,' Carla commented, but we were all becoming tired of her interventions and there was a muttered hiss of disapproval.

Roy marched out. We waited to see what would happen. At

26

that point, I don't think anyone could have left. Amelia took my arm and looked up into my face mischievously.

'You managed to get Samantha talking, Richard.'

'She's lonely.'

'I'll obviously need to make sure you're not.'

Then Roy returned with a bare canvas under one arm, a battered black-japanned paint box in his hand, and under the other arm one of Bruno's blue and white Chinese vases.

Bruno stiffened. He moved forward and took the vase from beneath Roy's arm, then turned it over and stared at the base. He rotated it, studying the blue dragon design, then, I'll swear, he went pale. With a random choice from ten vases, Roy had dropped on the genuine one.

'You'll be careful . . .' Bruno whispered, and Towers grinned.

It was a small challenge. Would Bruno go back on his offer? He straightened his back, placed the vase carefully on the table, and stood back. Towers dropped his flowers into it and with a strangely feminine gesture fluffed at them until they fell into an arrangement that pleased him. He placed the copper and brass horn beside the vase, its bell facing forwards, and stood back.

He'd have to work fast if those flowers were not to go limp, I thought, and Amelia had the same idea. She filled a jug with water and emptied it into the vase. Towers raised his eyebrows, but said nothing. He was busy with a single spotlight, arranging it high to his right shoulder, from where he intended to sit.

There was still plenty of light in the sky so that the effect was not perfect. But you could see what he was aiming for. When all was dark except for the spot, there'd be a strong sidelight and heavy shadows. But the yellow of the petals was reflected in the glow of the brass, the brown of the flowers' eyes was reflected in the copper, and these colours contrasted with the blue, three-clawed design of the dragon on the vase. It was dramatic, but it lacked something. Even I, no artist, felt that.

Bruno voiced it. 'You need a third object to balance it. Something smaller than the horn. The other side of the vase.'

'You think so?'

'Oh . . . definitely,' said Veronica, tapping her teeth with her thumb nail. 'The triangle. Very strong.'

'Right,' said Towers, and he charged out of the door.

While we waited, Bruno set up one of the spare easels from the corner, clipped Roy's canvas to it, and found him a folding stool. Amelia said: 'He's not going to start now, surely,' thinking of that daylight trespassing through the high windows.

'When all the light's gone from the sky,' Bruno murmured.

His eyes were on me and he seemed nervous. I took out my pipe and concentrated on filling it. Samantha went to study the watercolours on the wall, Rex joining her. Wasn't he an expert on watercolours?

Then Towers returned. 'Just the thing,' he declared, his right hand buried in his pocket.

With a flourish he produced a short-barrelled thirty-eight Smith & Wesson revolver, all shiny and clean, and placed it beside the vase so that it leaned against it, barrel resting on the table surface and pointing in the general direction of his stool.

'There,' he said with satisfaction. '*Still Life with Pistol.*'

We were all to some extent shocked, me from the viewpoint of a not-so-long-ago policeman, the others artistically. The contrast Towers had introduced was not simply in colour and shape but in mood. The placid flowers and the vase lent an aura of love and care and creation. Even the hunting horn, with its overtones of past violence, was now retired into silent beauty. But the pistol represented stark, present, solid destruction.

'Oh no . . .' whispered Samantha, to whom violence was a television screen away.

'I think that'll do fine,' said Towers with pride. He sat on the stool, to get the effect from there.

'You're not starting now?' asked Amelia.

'Later,' he said pleasantly. 'I like to work at night, when I can control the light and shade. And when,' he added, looking round our ring of faces meaningly, 'I can work without eyes peering over my shoulder.'

Slowly we filtered out. Amelia tugged at my arm, sensing that I was disturbed. 'Richard?'

'Let's get clear,' I said softly.

Bruno led the way, shrugging, sliding responsibility from his shoulders.

Up in our room I stood and watched the sun declining. Amelia was completing the unpacking.

'It wasn't an imitation, you know,' I said. 'Not a toy. That thing's deadly.'

'It wasn't loaded, was it?'

'I couldn't see, from where I was.'

'Don't you think you ought to find out, Richard?'

I smiled at her carefully casual tone but she didn't notice. She was offering me something in which to take an interest. 'I'll just have a word with him, I think.' I pretended not to be in a hurry when I opened the door.

He was still there, alone now, arranging the precise position of his stool, adjusting the distance of the table from the back wall, so that no stray light from his spot would reach it, setting out his equipment. As I came up to him he turned and grimaced.

'Reckoned you wouldn't be able to keep your nose out,' he said sourly.

I jerked a thumb upwards. 'If you asked Bruno to fit blinds to that window, you could work during the day.'

'Maybe.'

'Then you wouldn't miss the social contact.'

'With that lot? You're joking.'

I reached past him and took up the pistol. The Smith & Wesson has a swing-out cylinder. I flipped it out. Unloaded. Flipped it back and tried the action. It was smooth, a barely-used pistol. The barrel was shiny with a fine film of oil. I replaced it beside the vase, trying for the exact position he'd had it.

'I suppose you've got a licence for it?'

'Right you are. All legal. I'm a member of a pistol club.'

'I wouldn't call it a target pistol.' Casual enough. Not making an issue of it.

'There's a sidearm group. We all use thirty-eights, most of them Smith & Wessons.' He was standing with his feet spread, head thrust forward and his prominent brows jutting.

'The cartridges are in your pocket, I suppose.' I don't know why I said that. I'd no authority to question him and felt I might be pushing him too far.

I was. 'Now who the hell d'you think you are?' he demanded. 'Coming here and throwing your weight around! I've got a licence for that pistol. I know how to handle it. So keep your comments to yourself.'

There was a lot in what he said, though I wasn't happy with the way he said it. I shrugged and turned away. 'Marksman, are you?'

'If you like.'

He'd relaxed, regretting the burst of aggression. His attention was back to his painting equipment. I moved towards the door, and paused.

'What's Carla Race got against you?'

'For Christ's sake . . . !'

'There's one advantage in working at night. It means you can wangle it so's you see less of her.'

'Yeah.' He tried a weak smile. 'There's that.'

I went straight from there to Bruno's office, knowing he'd be waiting for me. He was sitting behind his desk, hands flat on its surface, looking faintly apprehensive. I jumped right in. We both knew the subject of our conversation.

'He's been here before, Bruno. He told me that. Does he always do the same thing, work at night and produce a pistol?'

'Sit down, Richard. And *calm* down.'

'He's done it before, hasn't he? Him and you. Darn it, that little cross-talk act, you might have rehearsed it between you.'

He wasn't denying anything, wasn't upset. I felt deflated. Was it only me who was worried about a pistol being flashed around? I sat, spreading my legs.

'He's done it a dozen times,' said Bruno calmly. 'More than that. Now . . . now. Don't get heated. He's been here ever since I started the painting school. He's my night security guard.'

I thought about that. 'I didn't meet him when I was here before.'

'He wasn't actually in the building. I wasn't hiding him. I'm sorry. I should have told you. But I thought you'd be upset.'

'And so right you were.'

'You did suggest a guard, Richard. Yourself.'

'Not an armed one, damn it.'

'He's not armed. The gun isn't loaded.'

'I could load it in thirty seconds.'

He leaned back, sighing. 'You're being unreasonable, Richard. Just imagine . . . Suppose, for a moment, that we've got a potential thief here, with us. It does no harm for him to see there's a gun available, and imagine it could be loaded in thirty seconds. Now – ask yourself – does it?'

'D'you mean he *has* got cartridges . . .'

'Richard! He assures me he's left all his ammunition at home.'

'Home.' I drew on my pipe vigorously, and filled his small office with smoke. '*This* is his home, virtually.'

'Well . . . not really, you know. He lives in, but as an employee. Come on now. Think about it. I wanted a night guard but what would that have done to the image of a quiet, secluded country manor – an armed guard patrolling the corridors at night.'

'You said he wasn't . . .'

He held up his hand. 'An apparently armed guard, then. No, I couldn't have that. So I advertised for somebody with security experience and who could also paint. And believe me, Roy can paint. Damn it all, he's selling the things at a London gallery. Look, at every course he does the same painting and we go through the same act to persuade everybody he's a bit strange and likes to work at night. So . . . he works at night. And from time to time he has a look around. Quietly. What harm is there? Nobody suspects his real purpose and on top of that he earns money with his pictures.'

I sat and thought about it, uneasily aware that I'd made too much fuss. The trouble was that I couldn't shake off the feeling of consciousness for the public safety. I gave it one more try.

'And one night he'll load the thing, hearing strange noises, and shoot one of your guests on his way to the bathroom.'

Bruno sighed, linking his fingers on the desk in front of him, and forced a smile. 'He's got nothing to load it with.'

'Yes,' I said. 'Well.' I grinned at him. 'Reckon I'm a bit touchy. But . . . you said . . . security experience. What security was he in?'

'Oh – your lot. Detective Inspector in the police force.'

'Retired early, then.'

'There was some trouble. He didn't declare a personal interest in a case he was handling.'

'What sort of case?'

'A murder, actually.'

I stirred uneasily in my seat, not sure I wanted to hear any more. 'What sort of personal interest?'

'Why don't you ask him, Richard?'

'Hah. Yes. But I'm not a copper now, either. Can't go questioning people.'

'You're doing it to me.' Bruno sounded hurt.

'As a friend, Bruno. What was this special interest he failed to declare?'

He spread his palms, leaned his head. 'As I heard it, too much fuss was made of the whole thing. A man shot his wife's lover. Not unusual, I believe. Roy was in charge of the case and his work got the husband a life sentence. But afterwards Roy's wife went to his Chief Superintendent and told him of Roy's special interest. He was asked to take early retirement.'

'It must've been very special, then.'

He looked down at the desk surface. 'This husband who did the shooting . . . well, maybe he had a good reason. I mean, his wife was a bit warm, if you know what I mean. She was . . . sort of playing two lovers at the same time, not just the one who got shot. Roy happened to be the other.'

That *would* be a special interest, which Towers should have declared. Lucky they didn't scalp him. 'And that wife, Bruno?' I wanted him to confirm a suspicion that was developing.

He sighed again. 'It's Carla. Her husband, Walter Race, he's in Strangeways. She comes here . . .' His voice cracked with emotion. 'Comes, time after time, haunting Roy . . . haunting me, Richard . . . hoping to get him to admit he rigged the evidence against Walter. Hoping he'll break down if she keeps at him.'

The smoke drifted gently to the ceiling. I put my head back and watched it hang there, then puffed a bit more to join it.

'And do you think,' I asked quietly, 'that it's safe to have him here, with a pistol a yard from his hand . . . ?'

He didn't trouble to repeat that it was unloaded, just looked at me with mute appeal. I got up to go.

'Amelia will be wondering what's happened to me.'

Then I left him to think about it.

3

I told Amelia only sufficient to justify a minor concern and implied that I was satisfied with the explanation. Then I suggested a stroll in the grounds. The sun had nearly disappeared but the sky would be aglow for quite a while, and if there's anything she loved it was the soft, scented dusk, when it seemed the whole world was settling down to rest.

We explored the sunken garden, the flowers massed and their colours strangely thrown into contrast by the half light. We discovered the lake, silently shimmering in green shading to orange, with the crows still arguing about their roosts in the trees beyond it. Then we made a wide circle, until it was so dark we could barely see the boundary wall as we approached it.

Amelia later swore I'd picked our route deliberately, but this was not so. We came down a grassed slope, with a stand of pines at our shoulders and abruptly I was aware that we were approaching the drive at a point where the gatehouse must lie. You can say it was a subconscious urge to check that it really existed. It did. The shadows we saw against the trees had a hand-made symmetry to them. This was the gatehouse and there was a light in one of the windows.

As it was still short of eleven o'clock, this could not be one of Bruno's stranded students. But I took Amelia's elbow and without consultation we turned away, reluctant to pry.

The garden here was an appendage to the gatehouse and had received little attention in the past few years. But a natural thinning in the undergrowth guided us so that we couldn't help but pass close to the house. In the yard was standing the red Fiesta whose wheel I'd changed, so now we knew who was staying there, the woman Bruno had called Marion. We moved on quickly.

It was not surprising that I hadn't spotted the gatehouse earlier. The entrance from the drive was so overgrown that it was a wonder she'd got the car in. But, as Bruno seemed to know her, she'd probably done it before.

We walked quickly up the drive. It was close to eleven.

Bruno was sitting on the old oak chest in the hall, quietly enjoying a cigarette. He got to his feet.

'Ah, you're the last ones in. Amelia! You're looking stunning! Don't you think so, Richard?' I thought so, without having to check, so I said nothing. 'I can lock up now,' he said.

I touched his arm. 'Oh . . . Bruno. A point.' He seemed to flinch. 'You acted – in the studio, this is – you seemed to think Roy Towers had brought down your genuine vase. Was that so?'

He relaxed. 'Oh . . . that. Yes. Every course, we go through the same performance, and off he goes, and every time he comes back with the real thing. Blast him. It's his idea of humour. I switch 'em around when he's out of the way but he always gets the right one. He tells me he flicks 'em with his finger nail and he can tell by their ring. Perfect pitch, he's got. Or so he says. But whatever I do, he gets the genuine article. Mind you . . .' He smiled, a trace of embarrassment in it. 'It does mean he spends most of the night staring at it. What better protection could it have?'

Then he shut the front door, the plain wrought iron bolt modestly hiding the new electronic lock. Inside the chest was the setting equipment. He lifted its lid. There he had the keyboard, the switches, the indicator lights that told him if a door or ground-floor window was not properly fastened. To set the alarms he had to key in a code word. Bruno had another code word to deactivate the system in the night. Nobody knew either of the words.

We walked through into the drawing room for a nightcap. Only red-headed Hately and Samantha were in there, he with fists on his thighs staring with criticism at Bruno's works, she quietly flipping through a Phaidon on Renoir. We had our drinks, said goodnight, and left.

In the morning I was down early, leaving Amelia luxuriating in the bathroom just beyond room five, which was an empty room. I was interested to note that the missing blue and white vase, now in Roy's set-up in the studio, was from the alcove just before the bathroom. This meant that I'd been casually handling the genuine thing. The thought set the hair prickling on my neck.

Roy Towers was in the dining room, having an early break-fast before retiring to bed, I assumed. Trying to be friendly, I asked him how his painting was coming on. He looked up from his cornflakes.

'Satisfactory, thank you. And I didn't have to lose time shooting down any burglars.' He said this with a straight face but I detected more friendliness in his voice.

'You leave the gun there, do you?'

'It's quite safe. You can't imagine anybody touching it?'

'I was thinking in terms of somebody disturbing your group.'

He went to the long sideboard and began lifting covers, returning with bacon and eggs. 'It wouldn't matter. I shan't get to the gun till next week. You'll see how I work. Go and take a look.'

'Then why . . .'

'Why produce it this early?' He smiled. 'It's a bit of an act, that's all.'

I said nothing more about it. To me, it seemed more like a deliberate warning.

Afterwards I took him at his word and went to have a look while Amelia finished her breakfast. They were all at the table when I left.

Towers was one of those careful, detailed workers. If there'd been a greenfly on one of the flowers, he'd have painted it in, eyebrows and all. It was the flowers he'd started on, against a quickly dabbed-in, near-black background. Only four flower heads were completed. You felt that by bending to the canvas you could smell them. But at this speed he'd be at it the full fortnight.

I felt cooler air on my neck, and turned. The door to the yard was open, and the woman Bruno had called Marion was standing just inside it. As she caught my eye she stiffened, and I thought she was about to run away. But then she recognized me and her face softened.

'Hello,' I said, and stood aside, inviting her to join me in contemplation of the painting.

She approached slowly. I'd last seen her in clothes that hinted at a bulkiness in her figure but now I saw her in slacks and a blouse and I realized she was slim. Her hair was tidy and her face, early-morning shiny with a lack of make-up (she'd not expected to meet anyone), had a delicacy of features that made her quite beautiful. But her eyes were withdrawn, as though poised to flinch, and her lips had settled by habit into a line of tension. I wondered what it would take to provoke a laugh, but amusement was several layers down in her consciousness.

'Do you paint?' she asked, her voice strangely deep. So she knew this canvas wasn't mine.

I produced my pipe, always a useful refuge. 'The garden shed with a can of creosote, that's my level. And you?'

'I didn't thank you. The wheel . . .'

'You must get that tyre fixed as soon as possible.'

'Yes. Yes, I'll do that.'

She glanced towards the door leading to the house. She seemed nervous.

'Shall I see you around?' I asked. But she simply shook her head, lips compressed, and turned away. Before I could think of a follow-up she was gone into the yard.

I went to find Amelia and was in time to hear the end of Bruno's exposition of all the best paintable scenes on the estate. Amelia took my arm.

'The lake for me, Richard. There's supposed to be an old boathouse and a punt. Will you help me down . . .' Etc. Etc.

The painting fortnight had truly begun. I settled Amelia at a spot on the bank of the lake where the view gave a hint of the manor houses behind the trees, the punt, the boathouse, and a splash of colour along a rise. I didn't stay. I thought I might embarrass her.

I spent the rest of the day wandering the estate, hunting out the others. Well . . . it was something to do and good exercise. In my strong shoes and oldest slacks and my linen jacket, I plodded away, my new camera snugly in my pocket.

The camera had been Amelia's idea. 'An interest for you, Richard. A hobby.' So I'd come to that, a man in search of an interest. But it occurred to me that I had the ideal opportunity to make a set of studies: artist at work. One of everybody, possibly including the subject they were painting and the results of their efforts. The morning passed. We drifted in to lunch and their chatter was about the quality of the light. No tensions, no undercurrents. Only Bert Inskip and Roy Towers, who was in his room, were not out in the sun all day.

36

'Bert's in the studio,' said Bruno, when I asked him. 'Doesn't want any help. Doesn't ask for advice.'

Which was where I found Bert, utilizing the set-up Towers had created. I hadn't realized that the white vase that Bert had so carefully handled was the exact shape of Bruno's blue and white Chinese vases. He was using his own stool, not daring to sit on Roy's, moving round the table and making detailed sketches of the blue dragon design on the vase. Perhaps he didn't care to borrow one of the other vases. His objective was, he explained tentatively, to make a good copy of the vase. 'At least as good as Bruno's.' He blinked at me with nervous enthusiasm.

When I told Bruno, he said: 'Good luck to him.' But he was not optimistic. Bruno was hurt that Bert had not sought his advice.

When they came in to dinner, all mildly sunburnt and still with the first flush of enthusiasm firing them, Roy Towers joined us, freshly bathed and shaved. I commented on his expertise. He only shrugged. 'They sell,' he told me.

Samantha had the deepest blush but hers was not entirely sunburn. She'd spent the day on the terrace, her absolute lack of experience finally exposed, and Bruno had taken her in hand. 'You slap on the colour,' he'd told her. 'Not how it *is*, but how you see it.' This she had done, in an agony of despair, and something had emerged. Bruno whispered in my ear: 'She's a natural, Richard. Give me a month or two with her . . .'

'There's only a fortnight, and there are other students.'

But all the same, he too was excited.

That first day there was no containing their energy. There was a desire to catch the dying light. But, that being later, there was a general drift to the studio after dinner to comment on Roy's work. Roy wasn't happy about that. 'It's pure representation,' said Lewis Hately with disapproval, and Roy bunched his fists. There might have been violence between them if the door into the yard hadn't opened, letting in a shaft of evening sunlight.

Marion was wearing the same clothes but now had used a little make-up. She moved with jerky steps as though having to command one leg after the other and only Roy stood his ground. There was a scuffle of movement, provoked mainly by her expression. She had built herself to a point near breaking, her eyes wild, her movements stiff. Her fists were bunched together across her stomach.

'How long . . .' she whispered, licked her lips, tried again, though this time with her voice breaking. 'How long is this going on?'

The demand was aimed at Roy. To her, nobody else was present. He lifted a hand. 'Now Marion . . .'

'I can't go on like this,' she cried, her head jerking. 'I come . . . plead and apologize . . . and what more can I do, for God's sake!'

Roy sagged as though he'd been struck in the stomach. 'I can't leave this. You know . . .'

She cried out incoherently and opened her fists, revealing that her right hand was clasping a short kitchen knife. 'Damn you!' She was choking when she lunged forward.

'Marion!' shouted Bruno, and I saw him moving forward on my right. My arm was already reaching across Roy's body but she wasn't heading for him.

'Your stupid, stupid painting!' she whimpered, and she made a wild double swipe at it with the knife. The canvas and easel went flying as Veronica screamed piercingly and from behind me there was a high-pitched howl as though the knife had struck home. Carla sprang into my field of vision, hands flying, clawing for Marion's face. Bruno kept moving. But now it was Carla he was aiming for. He got her arm, halted her, and snapped her name so furiously that it was like a slap in the face. Carla was suddenly still, her features distorted.

My fingers had closed round Marion's wrist. She made no effort to resist. If Carla had reached her, she'd still not have resisted. But all the same I was glad when the knife clattered to the floor.

Roy stood transfixed, his eyes on her as Marion buried her face in her hands. Then Carla turned to face Roy. 'Your poor painting!' she said hoarsely, with a gesture of pitiful explanation. It broke some restraint that had held him. He turned, and spat the words at Carla, carefully spacing them at vicious intervals.

'Keep . . . away . . . from . . . me!'

She flinched, lifted her chin, and turned from him.

It was Bruno who hurried forward and put his arm round Marion's shoulders and bent his head to whisper to her. Then he led her away, back into the yard, leaving a heaving silence behind them.

'How wicked!' said Veronica, on an intake of breath. 'She's ruined it.'

Roy bent and rescued his canvas. 'It's nothing,' he said gruffly. 'Acrylic, so it's dry.' But his hands were shaking.

When I picked up the knife I saw it was so blunt it wouldn't have split a custard, and Roy confirmed this, turning his canvas to the light. There was an insignificant indentation on a bare portion of canvas. Samantha suggested a damp cloth on the back. Then everybody hurried to the sink and I drew Amelia aside.

'Good job she didn't knock the table over, eh?'

'Who *is* she, Richard?'

'Perhaps I'll find out.'

Roy didn't come into the drawing room later and the house was quiet. I left Amelia with a gin and tonic and found Roy smoking on the terrace, sitting in one of Bruno's tubular steel chairs. I drew one up beside him. The sky was rose and green beyond his shoulder.

'Not coming in for a drink, Roy?'

'You're being nosy again.'

'Certainly I am. There's sure to be talk. A strange woman attacks you with a knife . . .'

'She went at the canvas. It's symbolic.'

'Of what?'

'Our separation. Marion's my wife.'

I had thought this must be so. Bruno had told me Roy's wife had reported his special interest in the murder case and he'd been forced to retire. It would not improve their relationship. This job would satisfy two requirements in his life; to get away from her, and to find work that involved both painting and security. I filled my pipe, waiting to see whether he wanted to tell me more. I waited a long while, then he spoke.

'They called it special interest because of my own affair with Carla Race. You've seen her, so you'll say I was crazy. But you should've known her then. Nearly three years ago, that was, and Lord, she was all life and woman. You know what I mean,

Richard. The way she moved, the way she looked at you. I was crazy for her and that's the only word. And she was playing God knows how many men at the same time. I just knew of the one. Griff Pierce. That was the dead man, when the murder turned up. Griff Pierce, a traveller for electrical appliances. Humourless. You know. You wouldn't have thought he'd got any life in him. But Carla told me . . .'

'*She* told you?'

He laughed, a harsh little bark of derision. 'She discussed that particular affair. There were others, she didn't mind me knowing that. No names, but she loved telling me – probably saw how it annoyed me. She told poor Walter . . .'

'Her husband?'

He nodded impatiently. 'Walter got the lot. She never kept anything secret from him. Said she was trying to put some life into him. She meant jealousy, of course.'

'A stupid woman.'

'If you like. She was certainly stupid to try it with Griff Pierce. It worked with him. Possessive, that was Pierce. He wanted her all for himself. I met him once, in a pub. He didn't know me. He was dry as a stick, knew what he wanted, and knew how to get it.'

'But he died.'

'They found him in a lay-by, sitting in his car with a bullet hole in his head.'

'And you found yourself in charge of the case?'

'I was a good copper, Richard. Good. I prided myself on my impartiality.' He was gesturing earnestly.

'It must have taken a beating, then.'

'I leaned over backwards . . .'

'I'm sure you did. But there'd been other things, not usually attributed to good coppers,' I observed.

He leaned back and cocked his head, eyeing me with consideration. 'Oh, she's got at you all right. That Carla! Poison in every word. What'd she say? Bribery? Rigging evidence? Oh come on, Richard, you know how it is. You're offered a bribe and it's not always a good idea to refuse it. It gets you in on the inside. But they were all declared and handed in, properly covered.'

'All?'

'Every bloody penny. Don't raise your eyebrows at me.'

'All right, Roy. But what about the evidence rigging?'

'Hell!' he said violently. 'You've come across it a hundred times. You know who's done the job, but the evidence you've got would never get him sent down. Probably never even get him into court. You emphasize a few things, hold back a few others . . .'

'Can't say I did.'

'Mr Goody-two-shoes.'

'I always preferred a solid, unshakeable case. But in this one – Griff Pierce's death – you had a special interest. You can't deny it.'

He was leaning forward again in agitated emphasis. 'I don't deny it. I admit it. Proud of it. Walter was my friend.' It was clear he thought I'd meant Walter. I hadn't known about the friendship.

'You were in love with his wife,' I corrected.

'I know, I know. If you can call it that, I was. But don't you see, that was the reason I worked like hell to clear him. The evidence was unbreakable, though. He didn't have any alibi – in fact he'd driven past that lay-by that night. And the bullet matched his gun . . .'

'Everybody's got guns,' I complained.

'We were in the same pistol club, he the treasurer, me the secretary. Of course he had pistols, one of them a thirty-eight.'

'Like yours?'

'Like mine.'

I pointed the pipe stem at him. 'So now she hates you, this Carla. Haunts you and jeers at you.'

He sighed. 'I don't think she's sane. She thinks I'm going to break down and admit I rigged the evidence. But it didn't need any rigging. Hell . . . I'll tell you, Richard . . . if I could've rigged it *for* him, I'd have done that.'

'And your wife? Marion.'

'Don't you see! Working like that, to do everything possible for Walter, all I could do in the end was to show his justification, and there was plenty of that, the way Carla had been carrying on. So Marion got to know about me and Carla and what did she have to do but go prancing off to the Chief Super . . .'

'Who didn't already know?' I asked quietly.

'What?'

'If you were digging out evidence of Walter's motive, how come your own affair with Carla didn't come out *then*?'

He licked his lips. 'Come on, now.'

'Wasn't that suppressed evidence?'

'Not quite like that.'

'No,' I said. 'Perhaps not.' I unscrewed the pipe stem and blew through it. 'Am I keeping you from your painting?'

He wanted to pursue the question of self-justification, but now he realized that it would be no more than pleading. I got to my feet.

'The canvas is drying,' he said. 'We soaked the back.'

'Won't take long in this weather,' I assured him, then I went to find out whether Amelia wanted to catch the last of the light.

But she said she was tired. She'd been working hard to capture just one decent picture. I hadn't known watercolours were like that. You didn't set up your easel and keep working on the same picture. Oh no. This was fast work, and the washes had to be perfect. If it didn't come right first time, you threw it away and tried again. Hence that ream of paper.

During the following week she worked steadily through it and became increasingly quiet. What should have been relaxation became a challenge. She wanted one good painting, one item of perfection.

So it went with all of them, though it affected them differently. Veronica Inskip produced good results with remarkable ease – and she knew it. She confided in me that she was ashamed to find herself so successful in everything she attempted. But, in so far as the shame went, she was lying, though this too she did well. Bert plugged on stubbornly, secretly now in his room, painting the dragon design on his vase with a dirty grey solution of cobalt salts. (I saw him mixing them at the studio sink.) This, he said, would turn blue on firing. This firing was due to take place towards the end of the second week. Bruno shook his head over the chances of success but didn't discourage him. Unfortunately, we never did get the firing.

Rex Lightfoot produced a dozen watercolours in that week. He seemed quite pleased with them though to me they fell short of Amelia's discarded ones. But I'm prejudiced. Lewis Hately threw colour at canvas and produced nothing recognizable, then challenged Bruno to comment. Bruno came to me, worried about that. 'How can I tell him it's all powerful and dynamic, when he'll assume I'm condescending?' he complained. 'Ask for his advice about your own,' I suggested. But he rejected this with horror.

Carla made no pretence that she'd come there to paint, though she'd brought a couple of canvases, just for show, which remained tied together face to face in her room. Her business there was to harass Roy Towers, who gave her less and less time to do it in.

Unfortunately, this gave her too much spare time so that she attached herself to the only other person with spare time: me. After all, she could hardly exercise her sexuality on men who're staring at canvas all day and Bruno was on an eternal dash from one artist to the other. So she had to make do with me and I soon realized what Roy had meant about the fascination she could inspire. I had my work cut out to remain indifferent to it without actually avoiding her. That I didn't want to do, because she seemed determined to tell me her version of the murder of Griffith Pierce.

Roy had been correct about one thing; she made no secret of her love affairs. 'Can I help it if they find me exciting, Richard?' she asked. 'You could try to fight it,' I suggested. And she laughed. But Roy, it seemed, had been quite as possessive as Griff Pierce, quite as jealous of her other conquests. 'Silly man.' The only difference was that Pierce had been too intense. He actually wanted to confront Walter and demand that he should release her. 'He must've been mad. I ask you! In this day and age.' And how could she live without Walter? How *was* she living without Walter? How could she go on living without Walter, for possibly another ten years? (Some hysteria there. I calmed her, patted her hand. She clung to me for comfort. *That* was how she'd manage.)

But Roy hadn't told me about Walter's pistol. It had never been found. So how had they proved that the bullet that killed Pierce had come from his pistol? Ah, that had been Roy's cleverness. He'd remembered the previous night. (Pierce had died on the Tuesday.) That Monday evening Roy and Walter, bosom friends, treasurer and secretary, had gone down to the pistol clubhouse together to perform a once-a-month duty. This was to empty the sandbags from behind the targets in the indoor range and sieve them. In this way they rescued the old bullets, which the club members shared between them. They all liked to reuse shell cases, measuring their own weight of charge because there was no point in firing commercial high-power rounds over such a short distance. So they melted down the old bullets in order to cast new ones for the old shell cases.

This sifting job they'd done and replaced the sandbags with new ones, then Walter, who was still wearing in his new thirty-eight, had fired off a couple of dozen shots in stall number one. The murder occurred the following night, the immediate suspect being Carla's husband, Walter, the motive being that Pierce might have approached him about Carla, without telling her.

'He could have done, Richard, because I'd forbidden it.'

When Walter couldn't produce his pistol, the suspicion grew. Then it was that Roy remembered Walter's bit of practice with brand new sandbags behind the target area. No one had used the range since then, so he'd taken along a sergeant and they'd recovered Walter's spent bullets and it was these that'd been matched to the bullet that killed Pierce.

I found this all very interesting but it didn't conform with Roy's statement that he'd worked hard to clear his friend Walter. He could easily have 'forgotten' that short session of practice. Or was it that Roy *had*, as he claimed, conducted the whole thing impartially and as a good copper? But I couldn't take Carla's word for anything, as she now hated Roy for putting Walter away.

I was not bored in this first week, as you'll understand, in fact it took some ingenuity to persuade Amelia that I was merely involved in a throw-back to my old job as a policeman and simply extracting information.

During this time Samantha, from varying points on the terrace, was producing flaming oil colours that progressed from competent to marvellous. By Friday she'd come to believe it herself and blossomed before our eyes. No longer the shy, reserved girl. Now we had to share her excitement, Rex first, because she ran to him with each completed canvas before the paint was dry for him to confirm that the magic had not deserted her. Poor Rex, to whom conquests must have come so easily, was confused. She threw herself at him and if there was sexuality there, she gave no hint of it.

We all watched progress with amusement.

By the second Tuesday Roy was reaching the end of his painting. This was quick for him but he'd been spending longer hours of darkness on it, justifying longer sleep, if only to dodge Carla.

The pistol came last. All the rest was done and he could overpaint the gun in, as though he was physically planting it in the picture. Tuesday morning saw half of the pistol there on the canvas. It looked menacingly real, in spite of the fact that he was painting it exactly as it was, with the chambers clearly empty of cartridges. I looked forward to seeing what Tuesday night would produce. We all did.

But Bruno told me it wouldn't, even then, be finished. Previous ones had all featured dropped petals, fallen on the pistol, the symbolism in this way emphasized.

That Tuesday I'd been stolidly photographing, going from painter to painter. This was partly to avoid Carla. The little Ricoh that Amelia had bought me almost did the job for itself, self-focus, self-exposure calculation, built-in flash if needed. I carried it in the pocket of my lightweight zipped jacket.

That night I didn't sleep well. This was partly because Amelia had been ribbing me about Samantha, who'd taken to bringing her paintings to me when she found it increasingly difficult to find Rex. Amelia's attitude worried me because I wasn't completely certain she was joking. At one o'clock I was still awake. At two I got out of bed quietly, wondering whether I could make a cup of tea with the equipment Bruno had thoughtfully provided and by the light of the moon, so avoiding waking Amelia. I stood at the open window while I waited for the kettle to boil, tea bag in the mug, and it was from there that I noticed a sudden change in the shadows outside.

It was a hot, sultry night but a slight breeze had sprung up. Not enough, I thought, to move trees and shrubbery about. And there it was again, now closer to the house, as though somebody was approaching cautiously, using available shadows.

I reached over and switched off the kettle, then went to the door, opening it as quietly as possible. No sound, but I did think I detected a slight movement of air, as though an outside door had been opened and shut. Which seemed to be an impossibility.

It was as I closed the door behind me that I realized I was naked. That was how I'd been lying on the bed but not how I could prowl about someone else's house. Just imagine if I met Samantha, who was in the room next door, she on her way to the bathroom.

Quickly I slipped back and fumbled into slacks and the zipped jacket. I went out on the balcony again and closed the door behind me. The house was absolutely silent.

Clearly, if anyone had been moving around outside in the night, it was most likely Roy Towers, but I didn't think he knew the code word to deactivate Bruno's alarm system. All the same, the obvious first place to investigate was the studio.

I eased open the studio door and quietly called out: 'Roy.' I didn't want to startle him. No reply, so I moved inside.

The only light was from his spot. He was lying on his back behind the stool, which was on its side. The palette was still on his left thumb, a fine sable brush lying beside his outflung right hand. There could be no question that he was dead, because one of the two shots had got him through the heart, the other through the shoulder as the impact of the first flung him back.

The painting had progressed. There were four petals perched on his pistol, along the barrel and on the top of the frame, and three lying beside it on the table surface. He'd painted in the four on the pistol, but he hadn't recorded the snub noses of the bullets now revealed in the cylinder, one missing beside the breech. This fitted with the fact of two shots having been fired from a full load of six.

I registered the fact that the barrel, which had been shiny inside (this gleam being faithfully recorded by Roy in his painting), was now dull.

I pounced for the phone on the bench.

4

For the following few minutes my actions were entirely automatic. I was first on the scene of a crime, a major crime, something that had never happened to me before, and I was taking advantage of a unique opportunity. Time erodes. With evidence there was no telling what the immediate impressions would reveal. Without realizing it, I had fallen back into my old official image.

You'll say that it was hardly professional, handling that phone, but I had to make an instant decision. To reach an outside line would require a trip right through the banqueting hall to the entrance hall and I didn't think I should leave the scene for one moment. It was hardly likely that critical fingerprints would be on that phone. I risked it and dialled Bruno's extension. One.

He answered irritably, at the third ring. I cut him short.

'It's Richard, Bruno. Listen carefully. I'm in the studio – never mind why – and Roy's dead. He's been shot, apparently with his own pistol. I'll stay here and keep an eye on things . . . you hearing this, Bruno?'

He was breathing deeply, panting. 'When? When did this happen?'

'As though I know that! Don't be ridiculous, Bruno. You'll have to phone the police, and . . . now get this right, will you . . . come down and cut out the alarms so that they can get in and tell them to come in by the side door from the yard. Get it? We don't want too much disturbance. And this is important. Are you listening, Bruno?'

'Of course I'm bloody listening. Trying to climb into my pants, but listening.'

'Right. Then tell them to enter quietly and gently. There's evidence here that they won't want disturbed and one draught could destroy it.'

'Richard, you're making mysteries again.'

'But do it,' I snapped, and then I hung up.

I stood looking round. The door to the passage, close it. I did that. I hadn't been fooling when I'd spoken about the delicacy of the evidence. I'd been referring to the seven petals.

Now I approached the circle of illumination again. The spot was confining the visible area so precisely that Roy's face, just outside its rim, was barely discernible. The same thing applied to the rear space behind the table. Here also the light cut off sharply, so that the yard or so of gap between table and wall was in heavy shadow.

It would have been possible for anyone to stand behind that table and not be seen by Roy, on his stool. If he'd been conducting his duties correctly, Roy would have been absent from the studio for the time he took on one of his formal patrols. He wouldn't have taken the pistol with him (what, and disturb the set-up!) so that it would have been possible for anybody to load it and wait for his return. Take it a step further, and Roy might have failed to notice that the pistol was no longer in his group set-up until he'd taken his seat again, put the palette on his thumb, and taken up his brush. And the gun would have flashed its destruction at him from the shadows.

It was there that my mental reconstruction went crazy. Because not only had the fired pistol been returned to its exact placing in the set-up, but the petals scattered on it (not one but four) were still perched on the pistol in the exact positions that Roy had recorded them on canvas.

It took a great mental effort for me to drag my mind from consideration of this problem. Time, I told myself, would no doubt produce sense but I was still working on instinct and hadn't realized that time, and very little of it, would remove me from the action.

But first, the body. I bent over Roy, careful not to touch, not to put a foot where a foot should not be. Bruno had asked when Roy had died. Very relevant. To start with, it could not have been Roy I'd seen (or thought I'd seen) moving in the grounds. The time scale was too tight. I'd have heard the shots. Looking closer confirmed this. There had not been much blood. There usually isn't from heart shots. But what there was suggested his death had not been recent. The coagulation was what I'd have expected from death an hour or more before. The autopsy would be more accurate . . .

It was at this thought that I realized I would not be seeing an autopsy report. This was not going to be my case. I was no more than the civilian who'd discovered the body. I was, even, a possible suspect.

I stood back. The thought was like a physical shock. Suddenly I had very little time. Minutes perhaps. But . . . time for what? All I was required to do was stand there and wait. Touch nothing – wait: the standard instruction to anyone reporting a serious crime. But now I was the wrong end of the phone. Now (and this hit me) I was in no position to control the way the evidence was handled. In spite of my instructions to Bruno, they might come rushing in and destroy what could be the most vital evidence there: the petals and their disposition.

It was then that I remembered I was carrying a camera, and I'd shot only three from a full spool. I glanced at my watch. It was 2.17. I'd been there for four minutes I realized, and then I was struck by the fact that instinct had even led me to check the time of my arrival. I had perhaps another five minutes.

I ran off the rest of the spool, using the flash, taking several of the body and its relationship to the stool and to the easel, a dozen or more of the set-up and the painting together, then the rest as close as I could get to the canvas alone, and similarly close to the set-up from what would have been Roy's viewpoint. All this I did quickly, but moving so stealthily that no breath of air would disturb the petals.

I ran out of film. It was 2.19. Nothing more to do but wait. I filled the time by dialling our extension upstairs, in case Amelia woke up and wondered where I was. She answered sleepily and I told her the situation crisply. Beyond one gasp of distress, she did not interrupt. I told her to throw something on and quietly wait on the balcony. We wanted no panic, no rushings around. Quietly, she said she'd do that, but her voice was shaking. I think she'd liked Roy.

Then I waited, guarding the hall door with my back to it and watching the yard door for the expected police arrival.

There was no warning from sirens. Three cars must have drifted round the drive but I hadn't heard the crunch of gravel. My instructions (requests) had been completely ignored because they came through the door behind me like a pack of rugby forwards.

49

The three petals slid from the table to the floor.

Pushed by the door, I took two steps forward, and turned.

'I did ask . . .'

'Who're you?' their leader demanded.

Two men in hastily thrown-on clothes, the speaker wearing jeans and a sweater, were leading in two uniformed patrol car men, then four others in a disarray of clothes. My opponent (why did I think of him in this way and after only five words between us?) was a stocky man with a red face and a head of crisp grey curls, though he wouldn't have been more than thirty-five. He wore gold-rimmed spectacles that kept sliding down his nose. Being brought out in the middle of the night should not have been unusual for him but perhaps a murder case was. Whatever the reason, he was rattled and uncertain.

He stood aside for the others to move past him. I answered neutrally.

'The name's Richard Patton. I'm staying here, and I found this . . . business . . .'

'You know that man?'

'He's Roy Towers, also staying here. But you'd better talk to Bruno Fillingley about that.' I took a breath. 'When I got here, there were three petals . . .'

'Petals?' The glasses skidded down his nose. 'Do I want to hear about petals?'

'I don't know what you want to hear. That was just what I thought you should know.'

He looked beyond me, shrugging slightly. You could see it in his eyes: this is one of those crazy painters.

'Geoff,' he said, 'get Terry going on the photographs. The doc'll be here in about ten minutes.' He turned away from me casually, almost insolently. I wondered whether I had seemed like that to members of the public.

'May I ask who I'm speaking to?' I said.

He turned, raising his eyebrows. 'You may. I'm Inspector Poynton, if that matters to you. And you . . . Mr Patton, was it? . . . you can make yourself useful. Round up the people in this place and get 'em all together. There should be somewhere . . .'

'We usually gather in the drawing room.'

'There, then. Constable.' He raised a finger. 'Go with him.

See they stay together.' He returned his attention to me. 'Can I trust you to do that?'

'I'll do my best,' I said placidly, smiling because I didn't like him. 'Come on, Constable.'

'Mr Venables,' said Poynton heavily, not having finished with me, 'will no doubt want to see all of you later. Probably . . .' He lifted his chin, because I topped him by two inches. '. . . much later.'

I left, the constable at my elbow. He was a beefy, open-faced young man, not long in the force I guessed. He'd said nothing. I marched along the corridor determined not to be disturbed at being so lightly dismissed. He marched stolidly at my shoulder. It was not an unusual situation to me but he was not to know it.

'You worked with Inspector Poynton, Constable?'

'Not previously, sir.'

'Bit crisp, isn't he?'

'A stickler for procedure, I heard.'

'Really? I wouldn't have guessed.'

He said nothing. When we walked into the banqueting hall, Bruno was there and he had all the lights on. Already there were several of the guests downstairs, the rest peering tentatively over the balcony rail. Amelia ran to me.

'Richard, what's happened? Is he really dead?'

I nodded. 'Really dead.' I looked round. Lewis Hately in pyjama top and grey slacks, strangely skulking in the farthest shadows, Rex Lightfoot in a silk dressing gown and bare legs sticking into slippers with his arm round the shoulders of Veronica Inskip, Samantha Penney sitting on the brick surround of the huge fireplace, knuckles tight to her lips and in a nightdress almost transparent, even in that light. Those were the ones downstairs. And Bruno, looking distraught and completely confused, but neatly dressed in fawn slacks and a shirt, even with his silk scarf knotted at his neck. Bruno, I could see, was going to be useless.

Peering down at us was Bert Inskip, white face staring, his fists clenched on the rail, in a sloppy towelling bathrobe, and Carla Race in a jumpsuit, her face as grey as its material.

'Amelia,' I said, 'we've all got to wait in the drawing room. At least we'll be able to get a drink. Will you go and get Bert and Carla from upstairs. They look like they're stuck there. I'll watch this lot. Bruno . . .' He was staring through me. 'Bruno!' I said more sharply, and his eyes focused. 'Bruno, your staff. How many are living in?'

'Only the chef, Henri, and Charles, my major-domo.' So that was what he called them. 'The rest come in daily from the village. Richard . . .' He reached forward a hand. 'What're we going to do?'

'We wait, Bruno. A Mr Venables will take charge. Do you know him?'

'He's the . . . I've met him . . . Chief Constable, I think.'

'Chief Superintendent, sir,' put in the constable, who was eyeing me with speculation.

'Right,' I said. 'The Chief Superintendent. So you go and dig out Henri and Charles, Bruno, and bring them along to the drawing room, where the constable, here, will keep an eye on all of us to see we don't escape by way of a secret passage.'

I cocked an eye at the constable, who smiled weakly. I raised my voice. 'And Samantha. Do go and put on something heavier, will you. There's a dear. Will you look after her, Amelia?'

Amelia leaned on my arm for a second. I think there was a hint of reproach for my official voice but there was a reason for it. A brisk, practical approach would help most of them through the shock. Oh, it would come, in various ways, and would be unpleasant all round considering we'd be confined together. But death is always shocking; sudden death in a violent manner can unnerve anyone. I felt that Amelia's fingers were shaking.

'Right,' I said. 'If you'll all follow me into the drawing room. Come on, Sam, you don't want to unsettle the constable. Go with Amelia. That's the way. We'll all have a good strong drink.'

We trooped into the drawing room, where I snapped on the lights. The others trickled in, awkward, stumbling, hesitant. The constable stood in the open doorway. When we were all there, I turned to him.

'Now what you do, Constable, is to go outside and shut the door, and lean on it.'

'If you don't mind sir . . . you seem to have some experience.'

'Yes. Ex-CID.'

'I guessed. Then you'll know, sir, that I'd be better placed inside the door. I'm sure Mr Venables would agree.'

I grinned at him. 'I'm sure. What was your name . . .'

'Flack, sir.'

I got him a chair and placed it by the door. He relaxed and sat down, crossing his legs, even reaching for his cigarettes.

'Bruno,' I called. 'Where's that brandy bottle? We could all do with something. Except the constable. Mr Venables wouldn't approve.'

Flack smiled. He was the only one. I wasn't going to get very far with a jocular tone. It was out of place, even indecent. So I went and sat beside Amelia while we all had drinks, then I put them in the picture with an explanation of what had happened. Even distasteful truth is better than the unknown. I said nothing about my activities in the studio.

They were all still shocked, but most were working out of it. Only Veronica (so practical and so efficient Veronica) had completely gone to pieces and it was still Rex who was doing the comforting, Bert staring across the room in disorganized terror, that she might call on him for practical assistance, perhaps. Samantha, who seemed to have shrunk into herself, was watching Rex pathetically, calling silently to him. Lewis Hately was in a morose, withdrawn state. Carla was restless, pacing up and down, waving her arms.

'Oh . . . damn him!' she suddenly burst out. 'Whoever did this, damn him to hell.'

'Carla!' said Bruno, shocked by her fury.

'How'll I ever prove it now, with Roy dead?' she cried, leaving us in no doubt about her completely self-interested view of it.

The constable stirred in his chair.

I nodded to Amelia, gestured to Bruno, and took the two of them into a far corner. Here, due to the jut of the fireplace and the placing of the grand piano, we were out of sight of the constable. I didn't want to have him see us in urgent conference. And I did feel it was urgent, if only to put my mind at rest.

'I wanted your views,' I said. 'An exercise in pure logic.'

Amelia's expression was a mixture of distress and interest. She voiced the interest. 'You sound concerned, Richard.'

'Something I noticed and can't understand. I'd like to be contradicted, if possible.'

Bruno grunted. He'd recovered sufficiently to realize what distress had fallen on him, and wanted to slip into a quiet corner and brood about it. I forced his attention.

'It could matter, Bruno, and it's your home. Are you listening?'

He sighed. 'I suppose . . . if I must.'

'Right. Now . . . when I got to the studio I had time for a good look at how it was. Already there's been part of the evidence disturbed. Three petals lying on the table surface. They blew off in the draught, but fortunately . . .'

'Do they matter?' asked Amelia quietly.

'Frankly, I don't know. But there were also four on the pistol itself, on the barrel and on the frame above the cylinder, and for all I know those have been blown off too, the way those idiots . . .' I shrugged. 'If they have, then the police are going to be working on an entirely distorted view of it.'

'That's their worry, surely,' said Bruno wearily.

'But let me explain. Four petals, resting on the pistol. I don't suppose they drifted down and conveniently settled there. Roy probably placed 'em there, very carefully, to make it look as though they'd landed like that. For effect. But that gun had been fired. The inside of the barrel looked dull so I'm sure it was.'

'Considering Roy's been shot,' said Bruno sourly, 'I'm not surprised to hear it.'

'Listen will you! Roy had been painting those petals. He'd just finished, I'd say, because on the canvas they looked perfect. Not just perfect but exactly the same as they were on the pistol. So . . . will somebody please tell me how that gun could've been lifted from the set-up, fired at Roy, and then put down again – and with the petals not disturbed one iota.'

'They were put back.' Bruno was impatient.

'Come on!' I said. 'You're not thinking. How could they have been put back? It'd be a tweezers job. Can you imagine it, crouching there in front of the set-up and trying to perch four petals on a slippy metal surface and making them match the painting exactly! These are the hands of a murderer, Bruno. They wouldn't be all that steady, not after *that*. And there'd be urgency. No . . . it just couldn't be done.'

Bruno stared round for an excuse to escape. 'Nobody's saying it was, except you, Richard.'

'I'm saying it wasn't,' I told him patiently. 'I'm saying that the petals Roy placed on the gun, and then painted on canvas, couldn't have been disturbed and then replaced. They must've been placed just that once, then Roy painted them. After that, the gun couldn't have been touched.'

They were silent for a long while. I thought I'd lost Bruno, but Amelia was making an effort and eventually shook her head. 'You must have made a mistake in observation, Richard,' she decided. But her eyes were bright.

I reached forward and touched her arm. Bruno said: 'I'll just get another drink.' But I held him by saying:

'It has to mean that Roy was shot with another gun.'

Then I sat back, filled my pipe, and watched them work on it, Bruno now uneasy, Amelia frowning, her interest fully involved.

'But Roy's gun *had* been fired?' she said at last. 'You didn't make a mistake about that, Richard?'

'I didn't make a mistake.'

'But that's silly!' she cried. 'It would have to mean that he fired it earlier on – at something – then put it back and started painting petals.'

'Exactly.'

Bruno's eyes, when I looked at him, were now veiled. An uneasiness was stirring inside him.

'He fired his gun,' he asked, leaning forward, 'and then calmly put it back . . .'

'Then placed his petals and carried on with his painting.'

'But why in heaven's name would he do such a thing?'

'Now *that* I hoped was what we might discover. By discussing it.'

'I don't see why we need to discover anything,' he complained.

I could hardly tell him that it was to calm my mind. My trouble is that I can't prevent myself from trying to make logic out of everything. This was a purely academic point and thinking about it saved me, and the other two, from considering too closely the fact that we had a murderer in that room. I smiled at Bruno.

'I mean . . . it seems such an illogical thing for Roy to have done, unless he was trying to rig himself some sort of an alibi, say.'

'For what?' demanded Bruno, his eyes looking a little wild.

'For having fired it, of course.' I said it lightly, not wanting him to take me too seriously.

'Of course,' agreed Amelia, capturing the mood. 'Richard's so good at this,' she explained.

But Bruno reached for her arm, silencing her. Suddenly it meant something to him. 'He's got something in mind. I don't like the sound of this.'

I shrugged, taking it on another step. 'But you see, even that's not logical. If some sort of an alibi was intended . . . something like Roy being able to say, later: "what – me! But I've been working on this painting all night . . ." Well, if that was the idea, why didn't he take time out and do a good job of it – unload it and clean it?' I shook my head. It was a theatrical gesture; I now wanted an end to it.

'Alibi?' Bruno croaked, leaning forward aggressively. 'You're saying he fired his gun and might have needed an alibi?'

Amelia patted his arm. 'It's only words, Bruno. You mustn't take Richard seriously. I never do.'

'I'll get you that drink,' I said quickly, not liking Bruno's intensity.

'But if he fired two shots . . .'

'How could he have done that?' Amelia asked. 'We'd all have heard. Now Bruno . . . it was only talk. Where could he have fired two shots, and not have been heard?'

'Outside the house,' said Bruno hoarsely, ignoring the fact that two had been fired in the studio, and they had not been heard.

'But Roy didn't know how to get out,' I said, trying to put an end to it. 'He didn't know the code words.'

'But Richard . . . he did, you know.'

I stared at him. 'Oh Lord!' I said.

'We're sitting here,' said Bruno, nearly choking, 'discussing this . . .'

'What're you thinking, Bruno?'

'The gatehouse,' he gasped. 'Marion.'

Amelia gripped my arm. The very fact that I was sitting there and calmly discussing my futile logic should have warned me. My mind raced. I should have realized that Roy would have had to know the computer code words.

Bruno was half on his feet. I could see the word 'Constable' on his lips. The logical course, that, to let the authorities know and leave them to deal with it. But now my logic only plunged me into embarrassment. How could I explain? How long would it take?

'We're probably too late,' I said, and Bruno's head rocked with the panic my words provoked. 'How can we get out of here?' I asked. Now I was carrying the logic forward into action, which I didn't want, but Amelia saw it only as a natural progression.

'Richard, you must hurry.'

'There's a door right behind you,' said Bruno desperately.

'We only want to check,' I told Amelia, but assuring myself. 'Where does it lead to, Bruno?'

'Out through the kitchens.'

Now he was poised so close to movement that I thought I wouldn't be able to control him. But I still had hopes of reaching the gatehouse and hopefully returning, reassured, before the Chief Superintendent arrived.

'We can't go clattering out,' I hissed. 'Amelia, do you think you could create a diversion?'

'I'm an expert at diversions.'

'There's probably nothing in it.'

'Don't stand there arguing.'

Then she made up my mind for me by stumbling into the centre of the room, moaning, and fainting. I didn't stop to see the effect this had. 'Let's get moving,' I said softly, but Bruno was already at the green baize door in the corner. We slipped through silently and it closed behind us with a sigh.

Bruno ran ahead down the long corridor, then round a corner into the kitchen. He'd certainly set up his chef in regal quarters, I thought, pounding through. Then we were out in the yard, the studio looming to our left. Here we had to be cautious as there could be a constable at the studio's yard door, but the shadows were heavy there and we moved round successfully, under an arch in an ivied wall and so out to the oval of gravel.

'Keep to the grass,' I said, panting, but Bruno knew what to do and loped ahead. He led me on, outpaced me, down the drive and to the restricted entrance to the gatehouse. As we reached it a car turned into the drive, a large car whose headlights swept round like a searchlight. I dived forward into darkness, feeling certain that the beam had impaled my trailing foot.

The building was silent and dark, a mullioned old mini-castle with an entrance on one corner, a beam supporting the overhang. Bruno reached up behind the beam and produced the key. (So Marion had her own, I thought.) As he swung open the door he called out her name, but softly I noticed, already on him the dread of what we might find. I was making efforts to keep on his heels up the wooden staircase, in case it became necessary to prevent him from disturbing another scene of crime. Praying that it wouldn't be.

The door at the head of the stairs was vaguely illuminated by a shaft of moonlight through a window. Bruno plunged at the door, stabbed a hand for the light switch, and stumbled in. And stopped.

'Marion!' he said hoarsely.

She was lying, naked, face down, limbs spread to display the maximum area of flesh to any cool air that might drift through the tiny open window. Sweat was dripping from my chin. I blinked my eyes to clear my vision as she lifted her head, stared over her shoulder, and screamed.

In one rapid movement she swung from the bed, her eyes hunting for something, anything, to cover herself. One hand reached back for the bedspread, but that would take time – you could see the thought behind the panic in her eyes – as much as a second. She chose a quicker cover. She flung herself into Bruno's arms from where she peered at me round his shoulder, her eyes wild, chestnut hair flying.

'What the hell're you doing here?' she shouted at me.

'Marion!' croaked Bruno, almost limp in his relief. 'You're all right . . .'

'I *was* all right,' she said furiously, 'until you woke me up. Blast it, what's going on?'

Bruno, had he been the gentleman he presented himself to be, could well have edged her sideways to a chair, over which I could see a dressing gown, could even have reached it for her. But he held her tightly, calming her.

'There, there . . .'

I waved a hand, fumbling with my other for my pipe. 'We were worried about your safety,' I said.

'Your damned theories!' Bruno snarled over his shoulder.

'But I'm glad to see everything's all right.'

She brought a hand up and threw back her hair. 'I don't see why you should worry about me.'

'There's been a serious crime up at the house,' I explained. 'A murder.'

Then Bruno realized that he was clasping the naked widow. His arms fell to his sides. She dived for the dressing gown, modesty no longer the point at issue.

'Who?' she asked, moistening her lips.

'It's Roy, Marion,' Bruno told her, his tone apologetic.

I didn't see her reaction to that. The door opened behind me, catching my shoulder, and a voice demanded:

'What the devil's going on here?'

In this way I came face to face with Chief Superintendent Venables.

5

He insisted on driving us back to the house. 'I'm not letting you out of my sight.' We waited on the small landing, the three of us, while Marion scrambled into something decent. He seemed not to be impatient. This was a man who had a murder waiting for him but he calmly selected a cigarette, calmly lit it (refusing the offer of my lighter) and seemed prepared to wait for ever.

Marion, when she came out in jeans and a shirt, was twittering with nerves and shock, demanding to know what had happened, but he wouldn't allow us to exchange words.

'But he's my husband,' she protested.

'We'll see,' he commented, as though even that could be in doubt.

Venables, I decided, would keep an open mind until every smallest fact was placed before him. No inspirations, no plunges into the unknown. Unswerving patience was his pattern.

He was young for his grade, in the early forties I guessed, his mass of untidy black hair showing no hint of grey. His eyes were brown, soft as a spaniel's, equally unrevealing. His jaw was strong and relentless. There was going to be no messing about with this chap, who'd found time, at two in the morning and in an emergency, to run a razor over his square chin and search out a clean shirt and a pressed suit. Perhaps there was a deliberate attempt to present a confident image. If so, he'd succeeded.

We drove up to the house in his car, in which his driver had been waiting placidly but without daring to take the opportunity for a quick smoke. There we led Venables through to the drawing room as though he marched us to execution. Marion had not said another word but was now stiff and hostile. She hugged her distress to herself. Bruno, I could feel, was smouldering with resentment at the situation I'd provoked. I was feeling wretched with self-condemnation, ashamed of the upset my logic had brought about.

What I'd expected to find was a ring of expressionless faces. What we walked into was continuing chaos. Amelia, it seemed, had overdone the act, prolonging her recovery. Rex had proposed mouth-to-mouth and Lewis had suddenly gone wild and attacked him. Constable Flack had called for assistance, and for a few minutes the centre of action had moved from the studio to the drawing room. The doctor had left the body to attend to Amelia, and two scene-of-crime men had rushed to subdue Lewis. I realized that Rex must have observed Bruno and me retreating rapidly and had played up as usual, realizing Amelia's faint to be faked. Lewis had clearly been cherishing an interest in her.

It all became sorted out in ten seconds flat when Venables walked in. We were instructed to sit still and behave. Constable Flack, ruffled, was told by Venables to keep his eyes open in future, in a kind and gentle tone that left Flack's face drained.

I went over to where Amelia was sitting, a glass, nearly empty, in the fingers on her lap. I grimaced at her.

'So much for logic,' I said.

'I can't see where we went wrong.'

'Jumping the gun.'

She showed her teeth. 'Your observation was at fault.'

I shrugged, and we were silent. The logic still seemed valid to me. The gun in the still life *had* been fired, yet nobody was running round looking for two spare holes in something, or somebody. I was reluctant to admit that my observation had been at fault. It's part of a copper's equipment. Had I to admit that it had atrophied with retirement?

As we sat, one or two dozing, I worried about it. After a while Venables began to call us in, Bruno first to lay the background. Venables was using Bruno's office for this purpose. By that time, the scene-of-crime men would have left, the doctor departed, and the body would have been despatched to the lab for autopsy. The studio would now be sealed away, unavailable to any of us as long as Venables decreed.

It went on for hours. Venables wasn't in any hurry, and none of us had to rush off home. We were already there. He was in a unique situation in that Bruno's alarm system almost certainly guaranteed that the murderer was resident under that roof.

They left me till last, Amelia just ahead of me. It gave me plenty of time to sit and think and wonder why I should believe that thinking was necessary. Amelia left. I waited. Why was I last? You'd think the first interviewed would be the one who'd discovered the body. During my time, that was how it'd been.

Flack returned from taking Amelia to the office and resumed his seat. He didn't look at me. I said:

'You don't have to guard me now, you know.'

'Orders.'

'Ah yes.' I nodded. 'Never trust a copper, eh?'

'You made a run for it. All hell broke out here.'

'Sorry about that.' He was making me feel worse.

'I was up for promotion.'

Oh hell, I thought. 'You can still make it.'

But all he did was give a sarcastic snort.

The sky was lightening when he walked me along to the office, opened the door, said: 'Mr Patton, sir,' and shut it behind me.

'A bright lad,' I said, hoping to do a bit of rescue work.

Venables pointed a pencil at the chair facing him. 'He wants to work with dogs, so that's what he'll be doing. He doesn't seem much good with people.'

I sat. Like that, was it? He was an unrelenting man. Inspector

Poynton sat at one side, his face expressionless. A tape deck was busily recording on the desk.

'Now,' said Venables, sitting back. 'From the beginning. You found the body. How and why?'

I told him about the movement I thought I'd seen in the grounds, how I'd gone down and found Roy. I did not say that I'd run off a spool of photographs; he'd have his own in the morning, or whenever he managed to get to his own desk. I did not mention petals.

He waited until I came to the end. I reeled it out in the way I'd have dictated a report. He nodded, glanced at Poynton, and leant forward to shuffle papers on the desk.

'Now,' he said. 'Mr Patton, that was a very professional statement, but only what I'd expect. You'll be wondering why I left you till last. Well, after speaking to Mr Fillingley I sent off an urgent request and I've got your pedigree here.' He bent forward and peered. 'Hmm!' he said. 'You finished up with the grade of Inspector. Any reason you got no further?'

'You'd have to ask my superiors.'

'Only if it becomes necessary. But the experience is there. No black marks. So, will you please explain why an experienced officer should've gone running from the scene of the crime, tricking my constable, for the apparent purpose of embarrassing a naked lady.'

I opened my mouth but he ploughed on, his eyes cold, his head thrust forward. 'A woman who turns out to be the wife of the dead man. I'd have thought the best thing would've been to phone her – she's on an extension from here. Why the rush? Why the panic?'

All this had been delivered with perfect politeness but it was an effort to reply evenly. His voice had been icy.

'I'd put two and two together and it seemed to come up with evidence that Marion Towers could have been . . .' Damn it all, the thing was beginning to sound farcical. I stopped, searching for a better way to put it, reaching for my pipe. A dead giveaway, that.

'Yes?' he encouraged. 'Which two did you put with which two?'

'The petals,' I said.

'Petals . . .'

'The four on the pistol. He'd just finished painting them on canvas, and the gun had clearly been fired.'

'So?'

'Provided you didn't disturb the petals,' I said enquiringly.

'We did not. What about them?'

'You must surely see – it's quite obvious – that the gun couldn't have been fired *at* him. Or at least, it's obvious if your people didn't disturb the four petals.' No response. His face was set, giving nothing away. 'As you claim,' I added. 'Considering they'd already disturbed the three on the table.'

He raised his eyebrows fractionally. 'So, having decided, arbitrarily, that the pistol on the table had not killed Towers, you decided, what?'

'That he must have fired it elsewhere.'

'And your thoughts went immediately to Marion Towers, the wife of the deceased. Why should that be?'

'It was the only place.'

'She's been living at the gatehouse, not here. And there's an empty room upstairs. Number five. Strange, don't you think?'

'They were sort of separated.'

'Some enmity, would you say? There was a knife attack.'

'His canvas, that was all.'

'But all the same, an attack.'

'You're thinking in terms of motive,' I suggested in the same tone I'd have used to my superior in my active days, chatty interest, inviting comment.

'Never mind what I'm thinking,' he snapped. 'What did *you* think, that's the point?'

I shrugged. It seemed to be taking a long while to fill my pipe. 'I thought it should be investigated.'

'By you?'

'Your team was busy.'

'But all the same you thought there was a possibility that Towers could have shot his wife?'

I lit my lighter and deliberately took time getting the pipe going properly. 'I didn't rationalize it to that end,' I told him, puffing out smoke.

'That's the trouble – you didn't rationalize. But . . . from four bloody petals you played around with theories that've only complicated matters.'

63

'But surely you can see . . .'

'I see nothing, Mr Patton. I don't fiddle around with ideas before I've got all the facts. You had none.'

'The petals . . .'

'None!' he said angrily, an anger even more impressive because he didn't raise his voice. 'You deduced,' he said with scorn, 'and I'm sure you'd use that word, you deduced that the gun you saw had not been the one to kill Towers.'

'If you'd let me explain . . .' When explanation should not have been needed by a man of his seniority.

'I don't need explanation. I don't need fancy logic. I need a lab team and forensic evidence. And this I've got.' He slapped the papers in front of him. 'We move fast in this district, Patton. We got an undistorted bullet from that notice board the other side of the studio. There was blood on it and the position was directly behind the stool. I sent it, with the pistol, to our lab by motorcycle messenger with orders for it to be attended to at once.' Now his eyes betrayed him; the self-satisfaction in the power of his authority. 'And it was. Do you know how long it usually takes to fire a test shot and put the two bullets under a comparison microscope?'

'I used to expect a report in two days.'

'But I've got mine now. Only a phone call, but report to follow. And d'you know what? The bullets match. That gun was the one that killed him.'

Silence. My pipe went out, but I didn't relight it. Poynton cleared his throat. I felt that he considered his chief had gone too far and required a warning. Venables didn't glance at him but his face smoothed as though wiped with a chamois.

'Fingerprints,' I murmured.

'We'd checked it. There were none.' A flicker of a smile. 'But there would have been if Towers had fired it.'

I nodded. 'It's good of you to tell me this.'

'Don't fool yourself. It's for me. I find myself with an ex-Detective Inspector on my hands. I don't think I like that, not one who lets his mind run away with him. And I can't send you away. I want you here. You're a suspect. So I thought I'd just tell you that small fact. All your logic . . . and it was false. So take that as a lesson, and don't wave your theories under my nose again. All right? Do we understand each other?'

'Perhaps a draught disturbed the petals.'

'There was no draught.' He lowered his head. 'Thank you.'

'That's all?'

'You can go.'

'No slapped knuckles?'

'You can write out a hundred times: I must not interfere.'

I got to my feet and moved to the door and turned. I did not surprise any trace of humour in his expression.

'I had my camera with me,' I offered.

'I had mine. Good night, Mr Patton.'

'Morning, actually.' I closed the door behind me. Poynton, I realized, had not said a word. Had not dared?

The fact that I'd seen Venables only in a very smart silk and mohair suit didn't mean that he was a CID officer. He probably had overall responsibility at a station, or for a district, as a uniformed Chief Super. The case would probably be Poynton's. I wondered whether he'd be able to keep control of it.

Amelia was sitting at the window, watching the sun rising. She turned as I entered.

'I tried to explain,' she said, 'but he wouldn't listen.'

'To me neither. But he had good reason.'

'The man's a fool.'

'No. He happened to have forensic evidence. That gun killed Roy, and there's no disputing it.'

'Then how do you explain the petals?' she asked.

'I don't explain them. I don't try. That gun killed him and that's it.'

'And you're letting it go at that?'

I stared at her, sitting there all bristling with indignation that my logic had fallen flat on its face. I laughed. Walked to her and kissed her on the forehead. 'Nothing else I can do. It's not my case, love.'

For a few moments she was silent. I hunted out my pyjamas, as it was becoming cool with the dawn. Then she spoke quite gently and seriously.

'I've watched you, Richard. These last few months, you've been edgy.'

'Me? Edgy?'

'Yes.' She nodded. 'You've been bored.'

'I've been happy. Just being with you.'

She shrugged that aside. 'But it's not enough, is it? Not for a man. There's been nothing to occupy your mind. Now tell me, seriously, Richard . . . didn't you feel just something, some interest, when you found Roy dead?'

'It was instinct.' I couldn't deny it.

'But all the same, you *wanted* to be involved. Admit it.'

'Oh . . . wanted. Of course. But I'm *not* involved. I'm outside it all.'

'But that doesn't stop you from thinking, does it?'

'Nothing to think about, my dear. There's no evidence landing on my desk. No reports coming in. Nothing.'

She smiled at me sadly. 'You should have heard how you said that.'

'With relief?'

'With nostalgia. Sadness.'

'Now, Amelia. There's nothing here for me.'

'Then what was that you said about photographs?'

'Oh, those.'

'You're surely not going to bed. At this hour?'

'We've had no sleep.'

'And those photos could help you.'

I lay on the bed and stared at her. She didn't ever let go. 'To do what?'

'To check your observation.'

'But now we know it must have been wrong.'

'And how often has that happened?' she demanded.

I looked away. 'We can still get an hour or two of sleep.'

'How often?'

'I'm just getting older.'

She was furious. 'Now don't you dare say that, ever again.'

'Come to bed, there's a love.'

'You just said you're too old.'

'For observation, my love.'

'I'm not sleepy.'

'You usually are, afterwards.'

She plonked herself beside me, looking serious. 'Now promise me something, Richard.'

I was suspicious, never liking to make promises unless I know I can keep them. But her eyes were so full of compassion . . . 'If it's to keep you quiet – anything.'

'You'll get that film developed.'

'All right. And then you'll see. I simply made a mistake.'

'You *want* to be out of it!' she cried.

'Yes,' I lied.

'Then you *are* getting old.'

'Come to bed,' I pleaded.

'What, with an old man!'

I reached for her and dragged her down beside me and kissed her.

'You're only making excuses,' I told her, 'in case you decide to leave me.'

'You'll never shake me loose.'

'Lewis Hately fancies you.'

'Never!' She cocked her head. 'He *is* rather interesting.'

And so it went on. We often engaged in these cross-talk acts, and they always ended the same way. And then we slept.

Almost everybody was down by lunchtime. All except Samantha. Bruno made a little speech, as he'd obviously been instructed by Venables. We were required to make ourselves available, which, as it was only Wednesday of the second week, meant carrying on with the course. That last bit was Bruno's inspiration, I was sure.

They all looked as jaded as I felt and there was no enthusiasm for artistic endeavour. But Venables wouldn't want us scattered.

'We'll carry on as best we can,' said Bruno listlessly.

But there seemed no likelihood that Bert would be able to bake his vase. He accepted it with resigned despair. Life was like that for Bert. And Carla's one purpose for being there was dead.

'Well, I think it's an imposition,' she declared.

'You must tell Venables that,' said Bruno. 'Perhaps he'll let you go.'

'I'll certainly have words with him.'

'We'll be sorry to see you leave.' Bruno was so waspish that I looked at him in surprise. His veneer was becoming deeply scratched.

Lewis was impervious to atmosphere. 'I suppose we can still have our show?'

'Well, I hardly think . . .'

The beard was cocked. 'At the end of the fortnight. You said that. It doesn't have to be in the studio.'

'Oh Lord, I hadn't thought about it.'

'I wouldn't want to miss your criticism act,' Lewis said smoothly.

'For God's sake!' Bruno snapped, and he almost ran from the room.

'Not tactful,' said Veronica briskly. 'I do believe that the man was his friend.'

'All the same . . .' Lewis looked round for support, then subsided.

That was the general mood at the time. We dispersed, nobody wishing to talk to anybody in case they were chatting to a murderer.

I found Samantha on the terrace, which she seemed to have made her own. But she wasn't painting. She couldn't have been more detached from it.

'You didn't come in for lunch,' I said reprovingly, taking a seat beside her.

'I wasn't hungry.'

'Got to keep your strength up.'

'What for?' she demanded. 'It's all spoilt. What's there left?'

'A few days. And your painting . . .'

'My painting!' Her voice was bitter. 'Oh, I admit Bruno's been very kind, but you know and I know it's hopeless.'

She was deep in a despair that had nothing to do with what had happened. 'I don't know that.'

'And just when I was beginning to believe it . . . this has to happen.'

'Things will cool down. You'll see. There'll be time.'

'There never is. Or too much. I'll drive away from here and that'll be the end of it.'

'You can go on with your painting at home.'

She looked at me with despair. 'On my own?'

It would always be like this for Samantha. Brief periods of wild excitement and then, without that stimulus of praise, a fall back into emptiness. Brief glimpses of romance – and then the sight of Rex comforting Veronica, who had no need of it.

'You're not on your own now,' I pointed out.

'Until Saturday.' She made a pathetic gesture. 'Then what?'

68

'If you sit here like this, I wouldn't be surprised if Bruno doesn't come and tell you off for not working.'

Then I went to find Bruno, and tell him he'd bloody-well better, and, 'smile, Bruno, for heaven's sake.'

'At you, Richard?' he asked, lifting a corner of his lip.

'At Sam.'

Then I went to ask Amelia whether she'd like a run into town. She was lying stretched out on the bed.

'I was going to rest. Where did you think of going?'

'I want to find one of those rapid processing places, and get that film developed and printed.'

She sat up. 'You're going to do it, then?'

'Of course. I'm going to check my point about the petals.'

'Then we'll see,' she told me placidly, nodding. 'But I don't think I want to come, Richard. If you don't mind.'

'I don't mind.'

Leaving her dozing, I climbed into my Stag and drove down the drive. Just before I reached the gatehouse Marion dived out from the greenery almost under my wheels, waving. I stopped.

'Oh, it's you,' she said, not too pleased that it was.

'Trouble?' I asked, because she seemed mildly agitated.

'That wheel you put on for me – the tyre's nearly flat.'

'And you need to go somewhere?'

'I *can't* go anywhere. Bruno says I've got to stay here. But I don't want to be stuck.'

'Of course not.' I climbed out of the car. 'It's Venables who says that. It's to keep everybody here while he decides what questions he should have asked in the first place.'

She stood with her head cocked, more relaxed than I remembered her. There was no visible evidence of mourning but she was a woman who would consider her sorrow, if any, as private. She even managed a small smile for me.

'For an ex-policeman, you're very sarcastic about them.'

'Self-defence,' I assured her. 'Who told you I was in the police?'

'I can tell 'em a mile off. Besides, Roy said you were.'

'Let's have a look at this tyre. I haven't got a pump, but . . .'

She led the way. I stared at the front tyre. Too low to drive with. 'I'll need the jack,' I said.

'But I thought . . .' She fluttered for a moment. The mention of her husband had not affected her at all; my offer of concrete assistance did. 'You know, if you'd just stop at the nearest garage and ask them, they'd send somebody.' She tilted her head at me.

I straightened. 'That's expensive. I've got a better idea. We take both wheels in and get them seen to.'

'We?'

'All right, I'll do it myself, and pick 'em up on the way back. No hurry, is there, with you not going anywhere?'

'Well . . . I suppose . . . no.'

'The jack?'

She got it for me. I crouched, chocking the back wheels, clattering away with the jack. 'When did Roy tell you that?'

'What?'

I glanced up. A slight blush on her cheeks, I noticed. 'About me being ex-police.'

'Oh . . .' She waved a hand, put it to her hair, pouted. 'We talked, you know. Man and wife.'

I lifted the wheel off and rolled it clear. 'You talked?' I looked sideways at her. 'But you always went at him with a knife.'

'Not always,' she said very quietly.

'Only when you're angry?' I carried it to the Stag's boot, she hugging my heels.

'And it was the painting I hated,' she told me.

I turned to fetch the other wheel. We were very close, face to face, she stumbling, trying not to land in my arms.

'But he was a very good painter,' I said.

She stood aside and I walked past her, collected the other wheel, and marched back. She was in exactly the same position, backed into the bushes and frowning morosely. Decision coming up, I decided, whether or not to confide in me. But after all, we'd met in intimate circumstances and the corner of an emotional barrier had already been lifted.

I dumped the second wheel in the boot and slammed the lid. Indecision still clouded her eyes. I said: 'I've got a better idea. You come with me, we dump the wheels at a tyre place, then you have a look round the shops. I'll be a couple of hours. It'd be a break for you.'

Her face cleared. 'Oh yes!' To get away from there for only a short while! 'I'll have to get my bag.'

'I'll wait.'

She bounded away like a startled hare and was back in a minute with a shoulder bag, and over the door without opening it.

'Nothing for your hair?' I asked.

'Let it blow.'

So I drove away. She wriggled down into the seat and flashed me a look of pleasure. Her face was serene, empty of strain and distress. I turned out into the lane, still taking it slowly, then, once we hit the main road, I let it rip. Her hair streamed, her face flushed. Years flowed away from her.

'Where are we going?' she shouted.

'Hereford, I thought.'

Then I eased back on the throttle until we bubbled along, the V8 engine smooth as silk. I was hoping for conversation.

'I'm a great fool, Mr Patton,' she said at last. 'A perfect ninny. You know what they say: heart controlling the mind.'

'They call me Richard.'

'Do you ever do stupid things . . .'

'All the time.'

'. . . simply because you're furious and knowing they're stupid. Sheer spite, it is, but it's yourself you're hurting. And you can't stop yourself.'

She was silent. I said nothing. Hereford – twenty miles, the signpost said. The day was now so hot that the breeze was welcome. She was staring at the dashboard with concentration.

'I knew Walter Race, you know,' she went on. 'Well, I would, Walter being one of Roy's friends. And Carla, of course. We invited each other to our homes. Social evenings, that sort of thing. But Walter . . . well, you could never get close to him, if you know what I mean. Oh . . . not that he was distant. Friendly enough, ready with a joke. Rather witty, really. But you never saw inside him, kind of couldn't tell what he thought. Whether he was happy or sad – you never knew. His eyes were always neutral. That was *her* fault. Carla's.'

'His eyes? Her fault?'

She turned to face me, her whole body twisting. 'What she was, what she is. That was how she'd made him. Neutral. You've seen her. What d'you make of her?'

I shrugged. 'Can't say I've thought about it.'

71

'Of course you have. All men – you're all the same. Five minutes with Carla, and you don't think of anything else.'

'A bit sweeping, don't you think.'

'It worked with Roy, anyway. Damn it, right under my nose, under Walter's. Under our own roof she flirted with him so openly that if he'd said yes she'd have had him upstairs in two minutes, leaving me and Walter to watch the telly.'

'You exaggerate.'

'Only a little.' She pouted her mischief at me. 'And Walter – you know he was an accountant, I suppose, and you know what *they* are!'

'No,' I admitted.

'Everything's got to be right. Their whole life's like a balance sheet, not one penny up, not one penny down. Regular and correct, Walter. You married, you loved your wife, and that was it. A balance sheet. No one existed but Carla. You could see it in those eyes of his, registering and recording, but warning you off because they were neutral. So it had to be the same, the other way round. Carla was his wife, and Carla belonged. There she was, on the debit side, an asset, and one that nobody else was going to realize. Heh! Did you get that? It was good.'

'I get the picture.'

'So Walter wouldn't accept it. Like . . . well, like a computer that'd thrown up a wrong total. It just couldn't happen. He watched her do it, but it did not happen.'

She was silent. Hereford – ten miles. I wondered whether she'd finished with Walter.

'But, the way I heard it,' I said tentatively, 'she *told* him it was happening. All over the place, it was happening. And she told him about every single lover.'

An Alfa 33 came rasping past and pipped his horn in challenge. I resisted it.

'And so she did. She told me and told me she'd told Walter.'

'She told you about Roy?'

'Oh, now . . . don't be silly, Richard. Of course not. I had to be left to worry about Roy. But she told Walter because she didn't like being an item on a statement. It was fine for him. He loved being taken for granted. It was what he'd built his life on – the good old dependable Walter. Anything he said – just once – was sacred. Love, honour and cherish! Well of course. Hadn't he said that at the wedding ceremony? From that moment on, Carla was supposed to take it for granted that she was honoured and cherished and loved. How splendid for her!'

'You sound as though you despised him.'

'Oh no, no, no. But how marvellous to be able to relax, knowing he was there . . .' She allowed it to drift away on the breeze. I thought I heard her sigh but it could have been tyres on tarmac.

'But I expect,' I said, 'you'd need little reminders from time to time. The cherishing and loving bit.'

She laughed. 'Well, yes. But Carla didn't know how to handle it. She'd never be able to imagine there could be love without jealousy. I mean . . . jealousy's a reminder, isn't it?'

'Of a sort.'

'So she tried to make him jealous by letting him imagine things, and when he wouldn't react to that she tried harder, and I reckon she found she enjoyed her men, and still Walter refused to believe it. So she told him right out and to Walter that had to be a lie.'

Marion was a warm and loving woman who could understand Walter. Not his reticence, perhaps, not his strange, choked embarrassment with loving words and deeds, when his life was built on frigid figures. She wouldn't fully understand that. She understood his loyalty, though, but found it impossible to understand that Walter had no weapon against Carla's scorn. He'd have to retreat to his stubborn belief that the computer couldn't lie. Whatever Carla said it was not true, because she was his wife and *that* was truth. He might not have understood why she was torturing him with her lies but lies they had to be.

There had been a long silence. Then she burst out:

'And that fool Griffith Pierce had to go to Walter and explain to him that Carla was in love with him!'

'Do you know that, or is it a guess?'

'It must have been something like that. Walter was so . . . so gentle. Wouldn't harm a fly. But on that Monday – Roy told me – he was acting crazy. Down at the clubhouse . . . did you hear about it?'

'The couple of dozen rounds Walter fired? Yes, I've heard.'

'But did you know . . . Walter was silent all that evening. No laughing like he usually did with Roy. And when he set up the

73

target, Roy said his face was . . . well, kind of vicious. And the way he fired them off . . .'

Roy said, 'It doesn't sound like Walter.'

'It's Carla he should have killed,' she burst out.

'So there's no doubt he shot Pierce?'

'Doubt?' she demanded. 'What doubt could there be?'

I changed down for the first island, coming into Hereford. 'It's in the past. He was found guilty. Why are we talking about it, if there's nothing but certainty?'

She bit her lip and shook her head. Another island came up. I saw a tyre specialist's premises up ahead. 'We'll pull in here. There's only Carla seems to think he's innocent.'

'Carla!' she said with scorn. 'That's just her guilty con-science. Walter might've pulled the trigger, but *she* killed Griff Pierce, as certain as if she'd fired it herself.'

I let her sit in the car while I gave instructions about the two tyres. They were her tyres but she'd upset herself so I allowed her to sit there and look miserable. When I got back behind the wheel she jerked her head at me and said: 'Now what?'

'Now I'm going to hunt out a car park, then find somewhere they do rapid developing and printing. After that I'll hang around for a couple of hours or so until the prints are ready.'

You can see where all this was leading. I wasn't going to be able to shake her free and we'd spend those two hours together. But she'd intended to tell me something and I felt she hadn't got round to it. It was I who wasn't going to be shaken free.

'We'd better stay together, don't you think?' I asked, as we walked down the stairs from the multi-storey car park.

Then she smiled at me, linked her arm in mine, and as we came out on the street she did a little skip and fell into step, making ridiculous long strides to match my pace.

As I said: she was a warm and loving woman, this widow of something like sixteen hours.

6

I found what I wanted by asking a policeman. I have always had great faith in the police.

At the film processing place I gave explicit instructions. Large prints, eight by six. One of each, even though they might appear to duplicate. I was promised two and a quarter hours.

Then we searched out a café and had scones with strawberry jam and cream on them, which I hadn't eaten for years, and two pots of tea, we were talking there so long.

Halfway through the second pot she suddenly realized that Roy was dead. She snuffled, patted her nose with a screwed-up morsel of wet handkerchief, and peered across the table at me with red-rimmed eyes.

'He's dead, Mr Patton,' she whispered.

We were in a secluded corner. 'Richard,' I reminded, offering her my clean handkerchief.

She gulped and took a deep breath. 'I hated him, you know. Hated. It was not just the affair with Carla – there'd been others. But with the others, you know, he hadn't left me. I'm not talking about physically but emotionally. I don't know. Can't explain. But with Carla I knew it was the end of our marriage.'

If she could only see it she was so like Walter, I thought. His marriage was a sacred edifice he'd constructed around him; hers was a solid pedestal they'd smugly rested on. I nodded.

'Not just *that*,' she said intensely, chomping the last of the scones in half and managing to leave a blob of cream on the end of her nose. 'It was the careful and detailed way he worked to get Walter put away. His friend. His *best* friend. Like a spider carefully picking a fly to pieces. And the damned hypocrisy of it! He said to me: "I don't *want* it to be Walter, but it is." Even before he'd really got started. And then, when Walter couldn't produce his pistol . . . well, it was only what Roy had expected. But the motive was there, the opportunity. Walter drove right past that lay-by, you know, on that Tuesday evening.'

'I know.' I glanced at my watch. We had another hour. 'Shall we stretch our legs?'

She continued talking along the sun-baked streets of Hereford, no longer touching me, her feet dragging.

'But there were those shots Walter had fired, at the club-house. Oh, don't fool yourself, Roy hadn't forgotten. He'd put up a notice on the clubhouse door: CLOSED DURING TEMPORARY REORGANIZATION. I remember the exact words. He'd got it in his mind right from the start, but it wasn't *safe* enough. You'll know what I mean, Richard.'

'Rocky,' I agreed. 'He'd want something tighter.'

'And he dug for it, and dug, and dug. Searches here and there to find Walter's pistol, when it was probably at the bottom of the river long before.'

'Routine.'

'Dig, dig, dig,' she said passionately. 'Just like his painting. Don't imagine that's new. He used to do it at home, only it was fruit then. Niggle, niggle,' she said through her teeth. 'Detail and more detail. Have you ever thought how you'd paint the ribbles on an orange? Have you?'

'Not really.'

'Or the bloom on a grape, for heaven's sake! He'd go at it for hours. Niggle, niggle. It got my teeth on edge, till I felt I could scream. And that's how he finally got Walter arrested and tried. In the end, he used bullets from that sandbag and then there was all the worry and impatience while the Director of something . . .'

'Public Prosecutions.'

'. . . decided it was fit to go to trial.' In her agitation she was now clattering away at full pace, me sweating beside her. Why don't women sweat?

'And all the while,' she said breathlessly, 'I knew, and he knew, that all he wanted was to put his friend out of circulation and then he could leave me and go to Carla. The trouble was that he didn't understand Carla. Oh, the idiot! He couldn't see . . . she'd only been using him to work on Walter's jealousy. But with Walter locked away – and even she could see it'd been all her fault – then Walter became everything to her. Every-thing. And Roy couldn't *see* that. It nearly drove him crazy. So, d'you know what I did?'

She'd caught my arm and brought us to an abrupt halt, her face turned up to me, all crimped with suffering.

'I know what you did,' I said softly. 'You went along and told his Chief that he'd had a personal interest in the case.'

She almost stamped her anger into the pavement. 'Because I assumed they already knew,' she declared. 'So I thought it wouldn't do any harm but it'd give him an excuse to go to Carla, him being so furious with me. But they didn't already know it so that all I managed to do was get him suspended. And it didn't even drive him to Carla, so that he could be *told* she didn't want him, which was what I'd intended. She came to him, at our house, and there was a right old fight, she accusing him of trickery over Walter, and me there in the middle. Lord, but didn't I make a right botch of it! That very night he marched out and later he got the job with Bruno and there he was, at it again, painting. Niggle, niggle with his detail. Do you see why I hated his painting, Richard?'

'I can understand that.' I steered her from obstructing the pavement. 'But all the same, you came along to the manor just to see Roy, and you managed to find time to talk. You and Roy. Sort of civilized.'

She crimped her mouth into an apology for a smile. 'Oh, we talked. I still loved him, you see.'

I provoked her into walking again. 'You said you hated him.'

'Both,' she declared.

There were two meanings to the word 'love' in Marion's philosophy, one of them being the loyalty you owed a husband. My pipe had been cold between my teeth for half an hour. I said: 'So he came to you last night, at the gatehouse . . .'

'Oh no!' she cried.

But of course, the shadow I'd seen from my window could not have been Roy. He'd been dead over an hour by then.

'That was Bruno,' she said.

By the time we'd reached the next corner I'd come to accept it. 'Did you tell that to Venables?' I asked.

She tugged at my elbow. 'Now who's being silly!' One of her favourite words.

There could not be any doubt that it was me. Here I was, extracting information that might or might not be relevant to Roy's death, in circumstances that could have no appeal to

Amelia, and I was receiving confidences in such a way that I would feel guilty in betraying them. Yet I had a clear duty to take my findings directly to Venables when at the same time I knew he would not accept anything from me without suspicion, even annoyance.

'It's just along here, I think,' I said.

'What is?'

'That photographic place.'

Her eyes went blank. We were no longer talking about her.

They'd done a good job. It was expensive, but well worth it, if only for the look in the salesman's eyes. He'd obviously seen the ones of Roy's dead body.

We sat in the car. 'Aren't we going to drive back?' she said. But I was giving them a first, quick look through. Damn and blast them, the prints confirmed that there'd been nothing wrong with my ageing observation. The petals on the pistol exactly matched the petals on the canvas.

Feeling now distinctly less perky, even uneasy in my stomach (though that could have been the scones and cream), I drove out of the multi-storey and we went to fetch Marion's two wheels. A faulty valve in one, a nail in the other. She paid, I got them in the boot, and we drove back.

'You're not saying much,' she shouted over the wind roar.

No need to reply and anyway I was driving at the peak of my ability. Concentrating. Not wanting to think about petals.

I dropped all three of them off at the gatehouse, Marion somewhat deflated, the wheels otherwise. She said rather stiffly that she could put them on, thank you very much. I think I managed a smile. Up at the manor the cars still squatted there as I'd last seen them but there was no activity indoors. I walked through to the terrace, where Samantha was working again. The enthusiasm had been revived.

'Bruno says I should use purer colours,' she said, lashing on with the chrome yellow.

'Where is he?'

'Around,' she told me happily.

As I set off for the lake, Bert Inskip pounced on me from the shrubbery and caught my arm. No more lurking in his room for Bert. There was no objective in it, with the kiln sealed away.

'Mr Patton, couldn't you ask them?'

His hand was clamped on my arm. 'Ask who what?' I asked.

'You're a policeman. They'll listen to you. What'll I do without the kiln? I'm all ready to fire my vase, and they won't let me in.' So he wasn't reconciled to it, after all.

'I'm sorry, Bert, but I'm retired you know. They won't listen to me.'

Poor Bert! Bruno had told me that he had grand ideas about re-creating the methods of the Chinese porcelain makers of six hundred years ago. The carcase in pure kaolin, the design in cobalt salts on the still-green carcase. (By 'green' he meant unfired.) And the glaze over the design in feldspar. That was simplifying it, said Bruno, because Bert was tackling something that wasn't going to work. That single firing at a high temperature, which was one of the reasons Bert had brought his vase to Bruno's kiln, was critical. Experts had failed.

'But *you* did it, Bruno,' I had said. 'Nine times.'

He'd grinned at me. 'But not like that. I used modern methods and even then I had to do thirty-seven to get nine. He doesn't stand a chance. Heavens, the original materials the Chinese used aren't available any more.'

Which, I thought, gazing down at the hand clasped on my arm, was as good a reason as any for keeping Bert away from the kiln. Perhaps dreaming that it would've worked was better than staring at failure.

But his eyes were moist and his hair dishevelled. 'It's going to work, you know. It's really going to work.'

'I bet it will.' I was trying to sound cheerful on his behalf, and managed to get free without upset.

An hour or two to dinner. It wouldn't wait that long, I decided.

'Have you seen Amelia?' I shouted to Lewis, on my way through the spinney. He was stamping on a canvas that hadn't come up to his strange standards. To me – before his foot went through it – it seemed quite good.

'She's seen me,' he cried, distraught, 'and walked the other way.'

'Towards the lake?'

'With that Lightfoot character,' he said, his beard muffling his distaste.

I walked on. Veronica, covered with pastel dust, was sitting with her back to a tree rubbing something vigorously into the paper with her forefinger.

'Fog,' she explained. 'Fog drifting over the meadow.'

There was no fog, and no meadow in sight. I left her to it.

Amelia was seated by the lake, her easel open at that peculiarly shallow angle they use. Six rejected attempts lay at her feet and at her shoulder, on another foldable stool, sat Rex. He had, I gathered, lent her his shaving brush. I could have lent her mine but she hadn't asked.

I waited for one of those breath-held pauses while the basic wash dried and decisions were taken. All the painters, apparently, were back at work, shock and mourning dispersed. No doubt they'd recalled what this fortnight was costing them.

'I wanted to speak to you, Amelia,' I said.

'But Richard, you can see . . .' She gestured, smiled at Rex, apologizing for me.

'It *is* rather important.'

'I'll be finished soon. I've got a feeling. This time I'm going to get it.'

'The light on the water,' Rex explained. 'The reeds. Very tricky.'

Against my thigh I slapped the brown envelope containing the prints. 'You're having a break, are you?' I asked him.

He lifted his shoulders. 'She's using my shaving brush. She'd never tried one before.'

'One brushful,' she told me, 'and you can cover the whole sheet.'

'Lovely,' I agreed. 'We'll dash into Hereford tomorrow and buy you a brand-new one.'

But her mind was far away. 'Is that where you've been?' she asked, mixing a container of brown wash. 'Now Richard, please . . . I have to concentrate.' With a fine sable she tried the wash on a spare piece of Whatman. 'You think that's right, Rex?'

'Exactly right.'

'Then,' I said, 'I'll see you up at the house.'

'Right,' she agreed, but absently, that lost look in her eyes.

As I turned away I saw Samantha running from the house, waving a canvas in her hand. I'd been shielding her view of

Amelia so that she might have expected that Rex was alone. She saw he was not and stopped. The canvas fell to her side, then she turned back.

Blast Rex, I thought. I'll kill him, I decided. Stuff that badger brush right up his set. I lengthened my stride and overtook her.

'Nearly time for dinner,' I said.

'I might not be there.' She was averting her face. 'I'll be working on this.'

I seized her wrist and turned the picture towards me. She'd caught the heat of the day, the blaze of the flowers, the hot stone of the terrace. 'I'd leave it alone, if I were you. It's perfect as it is.'

'But you're not a painter.'

'These watercolourists, they don't understand the brilliance of oils,' I told her. 'Don't touch it. Ask Bruno what he thinks.'

We walked on a few paces. She was deciding whether to confide in me. At last she did.

'But Bruno's being very strange. Have you noticed? Has he said anything to you?'

'Said? What's he been saying?'

'Well . . . nothing.' When I glanced down, she was blushing. 'It's more the way he's been.'

Women are sensitive to mood and inflexion. They call it intuition. Ask them to put it into words and they're hopeless. So I didn't try.

'Where is he? Do you know?'

'In his office, I think.'

I raised my eyebrows at that. Bruno had worked so hard at spreading his advice and consolation amongst his painters. Now he was slacking.

'I'll dig him out.'

I left her on the terrace, looking forlorn, and went to find Bruno.

Normally I would have knocked but Bruno hadn't been honest with me. No reason why he should have been, of course, but I'd thought we were friends. So I simply walked in and there he was on the phone, looking up startled and guilty.

'He's here now,' he said, and hung up quickly. He put his hands flat on the desk surface. 'Richard?'

I used the chair I'd sat in when Venables held his inquisition, but this time I was the interrogator, Bruno the victim.

'Was that Marion?' I asked.

He did his best, the Bruno face smoothing, a smile blooming. 'She tells me you took her to Hereford.'

'Two flat tyres,' I explained. 'Did she tell you what she let slip in conversation?'

He grimaced. 'She can be very foolish.'

'You too, Bruno. I bet you didn't tell Venables about it.'

'Damn it Richard, I'd been out of the house a couple of hours. I was with Marion. It's got nothing to do with Roy's death.'

'How do you know that?'

'Well . . . obviously.'

For the first time that afternoon I was able to sit quietly and refill my pipe. The action is soothing. 'Bruno,' I said, 'I saw you sneaking back.'

'I was not sneaking,' he said with dignity.

'Returning, then. I had to tell Venables I'd seen something, because it explained why I went down and found Roy. Now he'll be thinking about that shadow – which happened to be you. He'll be wasting his time speculating . . .'

Bruno raised his eyebrows. He was quite sincere when he answered. 'What should I care about that? Why should you?'

I gave that some consideration. I was a civilian; Venables had made that clear. My concern should not have been for his difficulties. As a normal civilian, I recalled with bitter experience, I would no doubt have suppressed the facts. Was I any different? Did my official sense of duty carry over? I compromised.

'I think you ought to tell him, Bruno.'

'Well, I don't,' he said flatly. 'What there is between Marion and myself is personal.'

I looked up from my pipe, surprising his stupid expression of pride and protectiveness. 'Between you?'

He gave a snort of scorn. 'Do you really think she came here, time after time, just to have rows with Roy? Do you think she really wanted him back? That was all show, my friend, the dutiful wife remaining faithful to her promises. What she actually came for – comes for – is to see me. Lord, she's got stuff she leaves in the gatehouse for the next visit.'

By heaven, he'd been sticking his neck out!

'Two points,' I said gently, when dozens were pounding away in my brain. 'Two points occur to me. One: haven't you ever worried what would happen if one of your painting circus *did* get locked out, and went looking for a bed in the gatehouse – and found a woman already in it?' I watched his face. 'Probably naked,' I added.

'Well . . .' He gave a sickly grin.

'Or worse still,' I prodded, seeing that he wasn't really comprehending, 'found you there, in similar attire, with her.'

'It *is* funny,' he said, 'when you put it like that.'

'It's *not*.'

'Then why did you make a joke of it?'

'Because I'm trying to control my temper, Bruno. Better a joke than thumping you on the nose.'

He half rose to his feet. 'There's no need to take that attitude, Richard.'

'Isn't there? This is murder. It matters that Roy is dead.'

He was very pale. 'I didn't wish to imply . . .'

'But you don't seem to realize *how* it matters.' You have to be patient with people who live in a closed world, into which violence does not intrude. They can't handle it when it does. 'Point two: Venables has gone away from here with the impression that this house was a sealed box last night. Nobody could get in, nobody out. He's sitting there at his desk with the absolute conviction that the only suspects he's got to consider are you and me, your chef and your fancy butler, and your set of painters. Guests, Bruno. But now, it appears, the house was wide open for two solid hours. *Anybody* could have got in and shot Roy. Anybody.'

'You can't really believe that, Richard.'

'What the hell does it matter what I believe?' I shouted, the patience exhausted. 'It's Venables who matters.' I stopped there, wondering whether I'd really said that. I went on. 'He's thinking about one tight group of people as suspects when maybe he ought to be widening his investigation.' He was looking at me with a dead face. I was beginning to realize he wasn't as bright as I'd thought him. 'If he did, that'd lift the pressure from your guests, Bruno. For God's sake, don't you think you owe them that?'

I'd got through to him. Appeal to his sense of duty as a host and he knew what you were talking about.

'I hadn't thought of it like that,' he admitted. 'What d'you think I should do, Richard?'

I sighed. 'Tell him.'

'It's not really the sort of thing . . .'

'Tell him, for pity's sake.'

Looking worried now, he reached for his phone. I grabbed his hand. 'Not over the phone. Personally. Face to face.'

'I was only intending to make an appointment,' he said with dignity.

'Lord help us!'

Timing it beautifully, Detective Inspector Poynton tapped on the door and put his head in.

'Ah, there you are,' he said, meaning Bruno, I assumed. Hoped.

It was a measure of the personality of Venables that I'd somewhat discounted Poynton. But it was Poynton's case. Wasn't it?

Poynton came in. He seemed hesitant, crushed. He was like a lion tamer whose boss allowed him only a short whip. Crack it too loudly and the lions might notice its size. I glanced at Bruno, an instantly welcoming Bruno, affable, hand outstretched.

'How pleasant to see you, Inspector. You'll stay to dinner, of course.'

I headed for the door. 'Tell him, Bruno. Now.'

When Amelia came up to the room, I had the photographs spread out on the bed. The door flew open.

'Ta-ra!' she cried, and she stood there with the drawing board in her hands, the painting proudly displayed.

Now I could see what she'd meant by achieving one perfect result. I know nothing about balance and composition and all those technical things but what I saw I knew to be right. She'd captured the light on the water, the dazzle brilliant through the reeds, which seemed to shimmer with it.

'It's bloody marvellous,' I said, and she stood there grinning with her cheeks warm and all plumped up like ripe apples while I searched for more superlatives. At last she laid it aside, still

84

glowing, but now with the steady warmth of solid achievement.

Then she caught sight of the prints on the bed. 'Oh . . . you've got them! Let's have a look.'

She came and stood beside me, suddenly silent, and eventually selected the best two, full frame shots, one of the group and one of the canvas, and held them together.

'Nothing wrong with your observation,' she decided.

'I wish there had been.'

'They're exactly the same, the group he was painting and the canvas.'

'That's what's worrying me.'

She looked sideways at me through her hair. 'Apart from the three petals on the table surface.'

'It's the ones on the gun that matter.'

She tossed them down. 'There has to be an explanation.'

'The point is . . .' I looked out of the window, back again. 'The point is that there's evidence here that Venables might not have. The three petals blew off the table the moment his men arrived, and from what he said I wouldn't be surprised if the other four got blown off the gun. And it could matter. In fact, it's so damned impossible that it has to matter.'

My voice had been rising, exasperation growing inside me.

She looked me up and down, frowning, deliberately changing the subject. 'You're surely not coming down to dinner dressed like that.'

'I hadn't thought . . .' I crossed to the tall mirror inside the wardrobe door. 'What's the matter with me?'

'You look wild, that's what. Hair standing on end, your shirt half out of your trousers. I can go on . . .'

'I'll change.'

I'd handled those two wheels too freely, I admit. There was silence while I dug out clean slacks and another shirt. Behind me, she said softly: 'You mustn't let it worry you, Richard.'

So we were back to the photos. 'And not just that,' I said heavily, 'it turns out that Bruno had been down to the gatehouse for two hours with Marion.' I met her eyes and nodded meaningly. She bit her lip. 'Aren't you going to change?' I asked. 'There's paint on that blouse.'

'It's a shirt.'

'It's still paint.'

Annoyed, she tore it off. Buttoning up the fresh one, she said: 'We'll talk about those photos later, Richard . . . oh, damn! Now look what you've made me do. I was intending to go and freshen up . . .' She tore that one off, too, then threw a housecoat round her and marched off to the bathroom with her diddy-bag.

It was clear we were both rattled. It was the photos that had done it so I looked at them again. There was no getting round it.

When she returned, Amelia was clearly excited. 'I've had an idea.'

'Can it keep?'

'Will you do me a favour?' she asked.

I shrugged. 'Of course.' Amused at her enthusiasm.

'Go through it again and I'll pull you up where you go wrong.'

Where I'd gone wrong, she meant. I sat her on the edge of the bed, the same two prints in her hands.

'Right,' I said. 'Roy was painting. He'd about finished and it was all there except the four petals on the gun. It'd be natural to leave those till last because they'd be apt to move. Hell, he would've had to hold his breath all the time he was painting them, and the way *he* worked that could be an hour or two hours. He'd hardly dare to shift in his seat in case he caused a draught. So, he's got seven petals, four on the gun and three on the table surface. He completes the four and maybe decides he needs a break. So he . . .'

'That's *it* . . .' she burst in.

'What's what?'

'You said: he completed painting the four petals. But what if he didn't, didn't even start on them?'

She was exploring a mental path I'd already ventured along tentatively but shied from. But I nodded. 'Go on.'

She reached out and touched the back of my hand with her finger. 'If his gun was fired . . .'

'It most certainly was.'

'And if that gun killed Roy.'

'Venables says so.'

'Then there's only one answer. Roy couldn't have painted the petals, not so that they would look like the ones on the gun, because he was dead. So they had to be painted after he was dead.'

It was the conclusion I'd reached and rejected. Too fanciful, too complex. I took the prints from her fingers and tossed them down. 'But just try taking it the next step,' I told her. 'Hadn't we better get down? They'll be waiting.'

'You can't leave it like that,' she protested.

I grimaced at her. 'I've got to. It's just not acceptable.'

She shook my arm. 'You're so infuriating. Somebody else must have painted them. It *must* be important, for anybody to do such a thing – sit there for an hour or more, carefully painting petals, and with Roy lying there dead. And why? What would be the point?'

I steered her to the door. 'Yes,' I agreed. 'What would be gained? And imitating Roy's style, too. Don't forget that. I'd have sworn Roy'd done them. His own style. Niggle, niggle, as Marion called it. I don't like to think about it.'

She considered me carefully for a moment, possibly wondering when Marion had said that, then she jutted her lip. 'Not liking didn't stop you, when you were in the force.'

'Things weren't so close to home then,' I told her. 'And in this business you've got to think . . . if it was done, by whom? That's where the not liking comes in. Because the only person round here who could do that happens to be Bruno. We'll tackle him after dinner, if you like. Maybe he can tell us the why part of it.'

We went down. The soup was being served. Detective Inspector Poynton had joined us and naturally had taken Roy's chair, which was at my right elbow. I smiled at him.

'Worked out the answer to the petals yet?'

'I'd like to know the technique he used to paint them,' he admitted. 'Are you a painter? I do a bit myself.'

7

There he sat, Arnold Poynton (call me Arnie), wading into what would have been Roy's dinner, his gaze darting round the table, anxious to pounce in whenever the conversation touched on the subject of painting. Which it naturally did. We had another eager amateur artist and how he lapped it up! Venables had been clever. Poynton had been planted on us because the murderer was probably sitting at that table. Poynton was there to listen and observe, which he seemed good at. He'd absorb impressions, build up character studies. Whether he was really interested in painting I never discovered.

The question now haunting me was whether I should unload my photographs on him and hand the whole problem over to the police. But I hesitated. For one thing, I'd mentioned Bruno as being the only one, apart from Roy, who could have painted the petals. I hadn't thought further than that, but to hand the idea to Poynton as it stood would land Bruno right in it. I would prefer to give it more thought. Certainly I had to consult Bruno about it before taking drastic action.

You'll say I was only trying to justify myself and that I'd already decided to go on with it in my own way. But there was no decision. Simply, I wanted to keep the whole thing between myself and Amelia until I was able to destroy the theory. So I looked towards her for support and she offered me nothing. All through the meal I tried to catch her eye, intercept a smile, but she was in her usual seat on Bruno's left and Bruno was back on form. She was chattering happily to him and he was responding faithfully. And there was Rex, directly facing her, and devoting all *his* attention to her, too.

The whole table was very nearly back to normal, Roy's absence being covered by Poynton. In practice, everything was more relaxed, but this was due to Carla's silence. Without Roy there she had nothing to say. There was now no hope of the confession (to what? I wondered) she'd been aiming for. It was peaceful, that silence of hers.

I tackled Amelia as soon as we returned to our room. 'It's no good trying to slide over it,' I said. 'The idea's so fantastic that there must be something we don't know.'

She laughed. 'Well certainly, Bruno didn't paint those petals.'

I raised my eyebrows. 'You've spoken to him about them?'

She patted my arm and smiled. 'Poor Richard! A mention, that was all. He didn't even know what I was talking about.'

'Over dinner!'

'Why not?'

'I'd have thought . . . it's too important to use as table talk.'

'Lord, but you can be so pompous,' she said, then she softened it by reaching up and patting my cheek. 'In so far as a big, grumpy old bear can be pompous.'

Isn't it strange to hear what other people really think of you? Big I was. A grumpy old bear? Well, sometimes, I suppose. But pompous? I felt hurt.

'It is rather serious.'

'Words,' she claimed. 'Only words. You said that yourself.'

'I was about to say that it's a serious matter to interfere in a police investigation. I've got nothing to work on except ten minutes in that studio and about 'thirty photos. Venables's in-tray will be piled with reports and forensic information. And now . . . all we can come up with is some farcical idea of a murderer crouching over Roy's body and meticulously painting petals on a pistol. Does it *sound* logical?'

I stopped. I *was* being pompous.

'I promised Bruno you'd tell him about it.'

'Promised?'

'He's a dear. He won't be insulted, you know.'

'Oh Lord!' I said, then, nothing else coming to mind, I gave her a poor smile, eased out of the door and tramped down the stairs, warm with the shame of my pomposity, and went to find Bruno where I knew he'd be waiting: in his office.

He smiled. 'Richard! Amelia said you wanted to see me.'

I sat opposite to him again. He seemed always to need the desk between us. I did not at once show him the photographs.

'I see Poynton stayed to dinner,' I led in.

Bruno was at his ease now. He laughed. Amelia had done a good job on him. 'You'll never guess what he'd come for.'

I didn't react.

'He wanted to know what the fees were for a course here. He nearly passed out when I told him. He seemed to have no interest in Roy's death.'

'You weren't taken in by that, surely?'

'I'm not *that* stupid, Richard, whatever you may think. No. I called his bluff. I suggested he should give it a trial run – on the house – until the end of the week. After all, number five's empty.'

'You never cease to surprise me, Bruno.'

'And I couldn't offer him Roy's room. He's gone home now to collect a bag. Just his clothes. No painting stuff. I asked him what medium he used but he stalled. Said he'd just hang around and watch.'

'I bet he will. And you told him about you and Marion?'

Bruno spread his hands. 'It was an ideal time. Yes. But, of course, he already knew.'

'Of course?' I asked casually.

'Well . . . Venables saw us together. Marion and me. He put two and two together, and had a go at Marion. She told him.'

'Ah,' I said. 'I see.' She'd given me a different impression altogether.

There were things Venables knew and things I knew. The only difference was that I knew less, and later. I almost threw in my hand there and then with the simplest way out of leaving all the photos on the dressing table in room number five. I rather wish I had.

'He didn't,' said Bruno, straightfaced, 'think it was relevant.'

'Right,' I declared flatly, 'so I'll just show you the pictures and explain what they seem to mean then we'll hand 'em over to Venables and see if *they're* relevant or not.'

'Where's your sense of humour, Richard?' he complained. 'You're grumpy as hell.'

Just a great big, pompous, grumpy bear. I tossed the photos on his desk. 'Take a look at those.'

I waited, filling my pipe, then puffing impatient smoke across at him.

'Well?' he said, looking up.

I went carefully through it again, simply taking it more ponderously for Bruno, until I got to the point:

'So the gun that killed Roy had to have the petals placed on it after the shot and as the painting exactly matches the petals then they had to be painted afterwards. You get what I'm saying?'

But his thoughts were not with me. Perhaps he'd been ahead of me. 'You know, Roy never used seven petals before.'

'This time he did. Or intended to.'

'He always left the petals till last. Balanced 'em on the gun, and did them. The same painting over and over.'

'So that they wouldn't be disturbed,' I said. 'Leaving the petals till last.' There was logic in it.

'Yes, I suppose. But that was what he did. You see, Richard, it usually took him a full fortnight to finish one of these but this time it went quicker. He was spending more time on it and more time in his room. Dodging Carla, I'd guess. So he was early.'

'All right, so he was early. Tuesday night saw it finished.'

'Except for those three petals,' he reminded me.

He seemed to be deliberately trying to provoke me. I smiled at him. 'Why should they worry you?'

'They would have ruined the composition, that's why. If he'd got round to painting them in, the balance would have gone. And Roy had a good sense of balance.'

'But all the same, there they were, on the table, just as I got them with the camera.'

'So I see.' He looked up at me, smiling placidly. 'Isn't it as well he didn't get round to painting them in! It would've ruined his picture. Quite destroyed the balance. There's an idea for you, Richard. All you've got to do is look for somebody with a fine sense of composition, somebody who shot him rather than let him ruin his painting.'

I shifted in my seat. 'I haven't found it yet, Bruno, that sense of humour of mine. And you're not helping.'

He put his fingers together. 'He sold them, you know.' I nodded. 'There's probably half a dozen like this at the gallery right now. His fruit, too. He was marvellous at the bloom on . . .'

'I know – grapes.'

'I was going to say plums,' he told me severely. 'But not one, I think, of his vase and flower groups had seven petals.'

'Bruno, you're trying to be clever, and I appreciate it. But I'm not worried about the three extra petals. What I'm worried about is the fact that somebody possibly painted the four petals *for* him, after he was dead. Can you tell me who might be capable of doing that and who's an expert in copying other painters' styles?'

'You're as subtle as that door. You mean me. Oh, I knew what you were getting round to. I just hoped you wouldn't say it. I had the idea we were friends.' He raised his eyebrows, but I didn't comment. 'But haven't you asked yourself: why would I have done such a peculiar and outlandish thing?'

I stood, in order to lean over and tap out my pipe in his

ashtray. It brought our faces close together so I left it like that for what I had to say.

'Yes, I've asked myself, and I got nowhere. But now you've given me an idea, Bruno. Let's say you were on your way to see your other friend, Marion, and just thought you'd pop in and see how Roy was doing. This would seem amusing, seeing you were on your way to have it off with his wife. But it wasn't amusing when you found him dead and his painting nearly finished, but without the four petals. So you picked up the gun from where it had been left . . .'

'Heh! Hold on. What *is* this?'

'And put it back into his group, because the painting wasn't finished. The balance was wrong without those four petals and balance is so important, so you perched 'em on the gun, then did a smart job of painting them in, and *then* you went and had it off with Marion.'

'For God's sake!' he shouted.

I sat down again, grinning. 'Funny, Bruno, my sense of humour's come back. Just like that.' I snapped my fingers.

'You're mad. Crazy.'

'But you'll notice I gave you the benefit of the doubt,' I soothed him.

He dabbed his brow with a silk handkerchief. 'You didn't give me the benefit of anything.'

'I said you *found* him dead. I didn't say you killed him yourself.'

'But why should I kill poor Roy?' He stopped. I'd incorporated the classic murder motive in my exposition. 'You're surely not accusing *me*,' he appealed.

'Actually, no. I just wanted you to hear how ridiculous it is to think that *anybody* would paint petals on that canvas after killing Roy.'

'But Amelia said . . .'

'She's full of enthusiasms. But there's certainly something strange about that still life group and the painting, if I could only see it. And I *don't* see it, and I'm worried. For you, my friend.'

'Is this still your sense of humour, Richard?'

'No.'

He eyed me shrewdly. Bruno had these shrewd attacks when

his brain ticked over nicely. Abruptly he got up and produced a bottle and glasses from a cupboard.

'I need a drink,' he said. 'You?'

'I'm not a spirits man, Bruno. But I'll join you.'

We raised glasses to each other. He drank. He said: 'Tell me, then.'

I looked at him over the rim of my glass. 'Petals apart, Bruno, guns apart if you like, I don't think you could've killed Roy, because of the cartridges. Somebody loaded Roy's pistol, and I don't think you'd have the cartridges.'

'Certainly not.'

'And I don't think you'd have access to any. Even if Roy did have some in his room, I'm sure you didn't know that. From the way you spoke about them, I know it. You're quite transparent, you know.'

He laughed uneasily. 'Is that supposed to be a compliment?'

'In this context, yes. But the point is, you see, that Venables didn't hear how you spoke when I mentioned cartridges to you. *He* doesn't know you had no access to cartridges. But he does know you've got the only good motive around here for killing Roy.'

'Richard!'

'Think about it, Bruno.' I set down the empty glass. 'Now, I'll go and find Amelia and tell her how innocent you are.' I laughed. 'Innocent of painting those petals on the gun, that is.'

He was silent, watching me leave. I went in search of Amelia, and found her outside, painting again. They were all outside, working hard and making up for the time lost in feeling miserable and shocked. The light was still good, and if they timed it right, and worked fast enough, they'd catch the haunting dying-day effect without the sickly convention of the sunset in all its glory.

She was alone with her cherished lake. Rex had taken back his shaving brush. She was toying with gentle shades of green but nothing so serious that it couldn't be abandoned.

'Well, *that's* out of the way,' I said cheerfully. 'Bruno didn't paint those petals.'

'Of course he didn't. But somebody must have done.'

I took a seat on the grass and hunched up my knees, causing

myself some discomfort. 'I don't think so. It was a nice exercise in logic, but the end result is unacceptable.'

'Well, there could be another end result.'

'My dear, in all these questions of who did what, the basic idea is to discover why it was done. What was gained. And if you're going to believe that somebody went to all that trouble . . . then they'd have to have a damn good reason. Agreed?'

'Well yes. If you remember . . .'

'And nothing was achieved. The gun could simply have been left lying on the table, with the petals scattered, and the result would've been the same.'

She stared at me for a moment, tapping her teeth with the end of her paintbrush. 'You know your trouble, Richard,' she said. 'You give in too easily. If somebody did that, they'd have to have a reason . . . yes. But that could be so obscure that we can forget it for now. What we've got to find out is who *could* have done it. Technically, I mean.'

'We haven't got to do anything.'

'You're not going to leave it there!'

'I am.' At times, I'm very good at lying. 'It's Venables's pigeon.'

She gave me one of those smiles that meant she saw right through me. And waited.

'And there's only Bruno, anyway,' I said, 'who could've done it.'

'But we don't know that,' she pounced in with triumph. 'And that's what you ought to be doing. Finding out.'

I levered myself to my feet, dusting down my seat. 'None of this lot, surely.'

'You're not even going to try?'

'It's not my line. I'm not a painter.'

'Then I will,' she declared as I turned away. 'Because I am.'

I paused. 'I don't think you should.'

'Do you realize you're standing in my light, Richard?' she asked. 'And anyway, I could've painted them myself.'

I removed my shadow and plodded back to the house, pondering the phenomenon of female enthusiasm. All right, so Amelia could think about it. No harm in that, surely.

On the terrace I discovered two people whom Amelia could surely remove from her list, Samantha, a beginner, and Carla, no artist at all. Sam was hard at work on a new canvas and Carla was reading a magazine. Safe in such company, Sam absorbed and with no time for me, and Carla too morose for conversation, I settled in a terrace seat and watched the sunset that nobody had the nerve to compete with on canvas.

There is a way that pages can be turned that conveys annoyance and at the same time begs for comment. I ignored the signal, forcing Carla to speak. At last she did.

'I do think you could do something,' she told me severely. 'You must have *some* influence.'

Her tone indicated a general antipathy for ex-policemen. 'I suppose you're talking about being stuck here,' I said.

'What else would I be talking about?'

'The beauty of the sunset. The sheer pleasure of being able to sit quietly in these surroundings.'

'Sit here, doing nothing, when I could be . . .' She stopped, banging the magazine into her lap with anger.

I knew what she meant. Walter. 'Is there anything you can do, here or anywhere else? I'm sure you've exhausted all the appeal procedures.'

She looked away. With Roy dead, her last chance, if there had been any chance at all, had gone. I considered her profile. There was a hardness in the precise line of it, when perhaps, three years before, it would have been considered to embody classical perfection. There were lines at the corners of her mouth, shadows beneath her eyes. Marion had said that Walter was now everything to Carla. Perhaps that was because her sensuality was deserting her and few men would now give her that special, speculative glance. Suddenly I felt sorry for her.

'You weren't going to get anywhere with Roy, you know,' I told her. 'What could you have expected to force him into admitting? He built up his case against Walter. That was his job and he did it, personal involvement or not. I can admire him for that.'

She turned to face me only when I stopped. 'Admire him? You never really knew him.'

I had been forgetting he'd been one of her lovers. 'I saw very little of him. But *what* did you expect?'

She stretched her head back, then drew her hands over her face with a small sigh. 'Oh, I suppose I was just hoping. For anything. I don't know. I saw Walter again, a week or two ago. Can you imagine how I hate going there! I really have to force myself to go and I spend the previous day working myself into a mood when I can smile. I've got to do it. He lives for my visits. If I don't go – if I missed once – I think he'd just give up. As it is . . . his face! Oh dear Lord, you can see the flesh dropping off him. His eyes! They stare. It was Walter who said . . . kept saying . . . see Roy. The poor idiot. He still thought Roy could help him when the bastard ripped the whole thing. Walter's innocent, Mr Patton.'

She'd slipped, unrealizing, into the formality of my surname. She was appealing to me as a policeman, an officer of the law.

'I'm sure Roy would have helped him if he could.'

'There had to be something,' she whispered.

Sam painted on. The weight of the deepening shadows pressed down on her visual consciousness. No other senses were operating.

'Such as what?' I asked. 'Did you have one single fact in mind? Did Walter?'

Carla was silent. Somewhere, an owl stretched its wings and cried out for the dusk. She gathered her magazine in her hand and lifted herself from the seat, then paused. One side of her face was blood red from the sun as she stood at Sam's elbow.

'Walter signed a statement, you know.'

'Statements are usually taken.'

'In it he freely admitted firing the shots in the clubhouse the evening before. Now you tell me – you're the big brain round here – you tell me why he'd admit that, on paper, if he'd gone to the trouble of throwing his gun away. As they said he had. Just tell me . . . where's the logic in that?'

Then she walked away. She still had the ability to disturb a man, to distract him from the thoughts he knew he should be pursuing. I watched her move away into the shadows of the house. No amount of distress could do anything about the way her hips swung.

'Isn't it awful,' said Samantha softly. I turned to face her. Her eyes shone redly. 'Oh, she must love him so much.'

The two women had seemed to be unaware of each other and yet Sam had taken in every word, as no doubt Carla had observed the painting.

I was more than twice Sam's age. So far, she had not explored many of the facets of life, and knew more about what it had failed to offer than what it could snatch away. Carla had possessed, and probably still had, a large capacity for love. It was just a pity she'd spread it around so recklessly. What could Sam know of Carla's love?

'It's a complicated thing, love,' I offered mildly, I thought in a tone of wry amusement, but she took me seriously, as people are apt to do when I don't want them to.

'Oh yes,' she said, sighing, 'isn't it.'

'Are you coming in?' I asked. 'You won't be able to see the canvas, soon.'

'Perhaps it'd help,' she said, staring in disillusionment at her latest effort.

I levered myself to my feet, intending to go over and give it my expert opinion, but she saw my intention. 'Oh no!' she cried, grabbing for it.

The easel went flying. I was pleased with the speed of my reactions. My hand didn't reach to catch the easel, it plucked the canvas out of the air before it could fall face down on the mossy flags. The light was now very poor but I got one brief look at it. Then she snatched it away from me.

She'd worked from memory. As Bruno had thought, she was a natural artist and perhaps a burning intention had guided her hand. It was a portrait of Rex, a wild burst of colour that captured his carefree smile, his dancing eyes, and, though she hadn't intended it, I was sure, his fleeting arrogance.

'You weren't intended to see that,' she said fiercely.

'I didn't see anything.'

'It's a secret.'

'What's a secret?' I asked blandly, and she pouted at me.

Amelia was in the drawing room when I got there. Most of the others were, too. Strangely, considering it was all free and lavishly offered, the drink, during these late evening sessions, was not wildly distributed and eagerly consumed. Bruno told me later that this was always so. Offer an abundance, and delicacy forbids taking advantage of it.

Amelia had a dry sherry. I mixed a lager and lime and went to sit with her. She did not mention the petal painting theory but chatted quietly about the day and how it had been with her. No mention was made of Rex and his intentions. He did not glance in our direction. He was not, I noticed, glancing in anyone's direction, no doubt feeling Samantha's burning, imploring eyes on him.

Bruno came in around the time we usually broke it up. He beamed around. 'Everybody got a drink? Good. Good.'

His voice was stiff with the effort towards geniality. Behind him, hesitant, came Inspector Poynton.

'On the house, is it?'

'Help yourself, by all means.'

It was clear that Bruno had not been able to shake free from Poynton. I went to his rescue, after a murmur in Amelia's ear.

'Bruno. Can I have a word.'

'Of course. Certainly. You'll excuse me . . . er . . . Arnie?'

Arnie Poynton raised his glass and grinned. I steered Bruno to the curved settee in the corner.

'Amelia said she could do it,' I said.

'What . . .'

'Paint those petals.'

'You're not still thinking about that?' he asked, startled.

'I'm not, but Amelia is. Don't be surprised if she has words with you on technique and things like that.'

'Oh Lord! What am I to say?'

'Answer her questions. You don't have to be too abrupt.'

'As though I would. This business is driving me crazy, Richard.'

'Yes,' I said. 'It's upsetting.'

Then I sat silent. If only I could see it, there had been something strange about Roy's painting and the still life group. However I looked at it, there had been a special effort in some way to make the canvas match the group, and after the shooting. But why? What had been achieved?

I looked round the room. Poynton was now sitting beside Lewis Hately, who was gesturing and talking rapidly, absorbed in his own words. Hately seemed, at that moment, to be radiating more confidence and authority than I'd seen in him. Bert Inskip had joined Sam and they were chatting together intimately. In Bert there was none of his usual nervous energy. He was absorbed in Sam, who was flickering little smiles at him as though he was well into a stream of risqué stories. Veronica wasn't pleased but she made no move to break it up, busy using every posture in the book to attract Rex's attention. But Rex was morose. Perhaps he'd lost his shaving brush. Carla, making an abrupt decision, went to sit beside him but he seemed unresponsive. I thought that Carla must have mentioned Sam because Rex's eyes flicked momentarily towards her. But in response, he simply shook his head.

Bruno, beside me, suddenly broke into my thoughts.

'Spotted any murderers, Richard?'

'One thing's certain,' I told him. 'The murderer's in this room.'

He looked startled and distressed.

At that point Amelia got to her feet and made retiring motions. I said goodnight to Bruno, goodnight generally, and caught her at the door.

'Early to bed?' I asked.

'I'm very tired.'

'We'll get a good night's rest.'

But we did not. For one thing, the air was sultry and the night hot. It seemed impossible to lie still, the sheets clammy against our skins. My skin, anyway. After an hour or so of tossing around I rolled off the bed, put on my dressing gown, and went to sit at the open window, smoking quietly, listening to the night rustle of sound, and thinking.

I might even have dozed there, the pipe laid on the window-sill. As it was, I had no idea as to the time when I jerked awake. The screams seemed to come at my elbow, but I realized later that Samantha, too, had her window wide open and she was in the next room.

They pierced through me, on and on, repeated like the siren of an urgent ambulance, until I wondered when breath would be taken. They cut the placid night apart as I plunged for the door, Amelia struggling awake on the bed and crying: 'What is it? What is it?'

'It's Sam,' I shouted, tearing the door open.

8

The balcony was dark, a little darker, even, than the room had been. For both there was no illumination other than the moon, as full and as bright as it was going to be, but the windows in the banqueting hall were below the level of the balcony. Dark out there, but all the same there was a deeper movement of shadow at its far end. The light switches were no more than six feet from my left hand, at the stairhead, but Sam's room was to my right and round the corner of the balcony. The decision took only a small part of a second and as she was still screaming Sam had to come first. All I knew, when I lifted the latch on her door and pounded in, was that there *had* been a shape so that Sam was not the victim of a nightmare.

The moon offered more light here. She was sitting up in bed, again in that flimsy nightdress, on the top of the bedclothes as Amelia and I had been. Her window was open, but no slightest movement of sultry air dispelled the heat. Sitting up, with her hands pressed against her face, fingers spread to allow the continuing, piercing progress of those terrible screams.

'It's Richard!' I shouted. 'Me, Sam. It's all right. Sam . . .'

I went to her with steady, quiet confidence, which I thought would reassure her and not startle. I stood beside her, then crouched, reaching forward just to touch her arm. The nightdress was up around her hips. By heaven, surely she hadn't been raped! I was glad I hadn't snapped on the light.

'It's Richard, Sam,' I whispered.

Then the screams died, leaving a roaring silence, which at once seemed to be crowded with shouts and the hollow thump of feet. She removed her hands from her face and flung them round me and threw herself against my chest, her arms enclosing me, and sobbing frantically.

Perhaps her father had been large and shaggy. Maybe he, too, had smelt of tobacco. I reached forward with a free hand and gently drew down the hem of her nightdress. This was the moment Amelia chose to put on the lights and stand in the doorway.

I gave her no more than a glance. First things first. 'What's happened, Sam?'

'I thought . . .' she whispered, 'I thought it was him.'

She offered this as an even more important intimacy than her wet cheek on my bare chest. We both knew whom she meant.

'But what . . . ?'

'I . . .' A gulp. 'I was lying here, trying to sleep. So . . . hot! I could smell your tobacco smoke, Richard. It seemed – you know – peaceful.' I grunted. At her own pace, I decided. She'd be reluctant to put it into words. I glanced round. The doorway was crowded with faces. No one seemed inclined to speak. 'Perhaps . . .' Sam shifted her head to peer up at me. 'Perhaps I did go to sleep. When I opened my eyes he . . . it . . . was there.'

I patted her shoulder. The hysteria was rising in her voice. Where the hell was Poynton? His room was only the other side of Samantha's.

'There?' I murmured. 'Doing what?'

'A pillow,' she whimpered. 'Had a pillow. Above my face. And put it down . . . on me . . . down on me . . .'

'And what did you do, Sam?'

'Fought and scratched and kicked and wriggled . . . and they went away.'

Fierce little tigress, Sam, fighting for her life. You never know what you're capable of, till the time comes. It'd been sheer luck that she'd not been encumbered with bedclothes.

'Did you see a face, Sam? A face.'

She shook her head numbly. I looked round. 'Brandy?' But Amelia had thought of that, and was pushing her way through with bottle and glass. Amelia, who'd seen me with Sam clasped around me, and yet had rushed to the drawing room for brandy. I smiled when she reached my side, not simply in thanks for the brandy.

'What's going on here?' demanded Poynton from the door-way.

I surrendered Sam to Amelia, who knew the correct, feminine things to say, and got to my feet. 'And where the hell have *you* been?' I demanded. It came out close to a snarl. I needed somebody to hit, and hard.

He ignored me, marched up to the bed, stared down at Sam, then turned to glare at me. Why had I decided he was insignificant? His eyes were cold and his jaw was firm. 'Tell me,' he demanded.

I relaxed. I told him and incidentally everybody else. When I'd finished, he said: 'All of you, back to bed. You can't do anything around here.'

They turned away slowly, whispering to each other, leaving Bruno there looking shattered but summoning up a little spirit.

'I will not be ordered about in my own house,' he said.

'Please, sir. You can't help.'

The 'sir' did it. Bruno left. Poynton turned to me again.

'Did you see anything?'

'I thought I saw a shadow on the balcony. I didn't have time to reach a light switch.'

'No. I suppose you wouldn't.'

'She fought, you know. Scratched and struggled. There could be something, a bruise, an abrasion.'

He rubbed his chin. 'It's late, but it's worth a try. I'll get a policewoman here.' He met my eye. 'It *could* have been a woman.'

'Then don't forget to ask Bruno to switch off his alarm system.'

He was moving away. 'It's already off,' he threw over his shoulder. 'Where d'you think I've been? I was patrolling the grounds.' Then he left, heading for a phone with an outside line.

I stood for a few minutes with my hands in my dressing gown pockets watching Samantha and Amelia. Sam's eyes were less wild. She was talking so quietly that I couldn't catch her words.

It was decided that Amelia would remain with Sam the rest of the night. The bed was a double one, as in all the rooms. That gave me the chance to stretch on our bed, but with the lights on, and to examine the scratches Sam had inflicted on my chest. I could only hope that Poynton wouldn't want to examine me.

I lay a long while thinking. Nothing came of it except that eventually I slept.

In the morning, over breakfast, it was generally decided

that the painting fortnight had ceased to be feasible. It was Thursday, so only two days would be lost. Nobody consulted Sam, who'd had a tray sent up to her room, but it was assumed that she, too, would want to leave. But Bruno considered the group decision to be a personal slight on his position as host and tried to rally interest.

'When everything is coming along so nicely,' he appealed.

Veronica gave a flat, sardonic laugh.

'I'm sure you all feel you've gained something,' Bruno tried.

'Hear, hear,' put in Rex.

'And we haven't had our exhibition, and there's still time to complete that special picture I know you've all got in mind.'

'Yes.' We all stared at Lewis, who ducked his head in embarrassment, but wasn't to be stopped. 'What *about* that show? We must have that.'

And: 'When am I going to get at the kiln,' Bert bleated. 'I tell you, I'm not leaving till I've baked my vase.'

'And I'm not staying,' said Veronica flatly, her tone including Bert without any argument.

Bert almost jumped to his feet in agitation and marmalade flew from his toast. 'And suppose I don't want to go?' he demanded. Then a look of happiness came to his eye as he thought of the ideal clincher. 'And how're we going to know what wonderful things you've been doing, if we don't have the exhibition, Veronica?'

She raised her chin. Her knuckles were white but she was silent.

'We might hold it in the banqueting hall,' suggested Bruno. 'It doesn't have to be in the studio.'

'But . . . the kiln . . .' Bert protested.

During all this, Poynton had not said a word. The search for scratches and bruises had yielded nothing and he looked jaded. Now he raised his voice.

'Nobody's asked me about this.' His eyes went coldly round the table. 'Mr Venables wants you all to stay around.'

Legally, he couldn't hold them. He could only request. But clearly it was an advantage to have them there, if future questioning became necessary. Once they had scattered, interviews would have to be farmed out to local forces. By this time, most of the forensic evidence would be in, but there'd still be a vast amount of work on personal backgrounds. Venables was not yet ready to form theories. Even two more days with his suspects there could be important.

There was a concerted outbreak of near-revolt and it was then that Samantha chose to come down. She was pale and withdrawn but she was firm in her movements.

'Well I for one,' she announced, 'don't intend to go home till Saturday.'

'Good girl,' I murmured, but to myself. It made it easier to keep an eye on her.

Everybody gathered round Sam, completely flustering her, but the massed concern for her welfare did wonders and colour came to her lips. Bruno put his arm round her shoulders.

'I couldn't let you leave,' he told her. 'You're progressing so well . . .' And so on.

Then into the clatter of dispersal with, as far as I could see, no group decision taken, Bert raised his voice. 'Then what about the studio?' he wanted to know. He was still exalted by his show of defiance to Veronica and didn't want to abandon that feeling of power.

Poynton squashed him easily. 'But *that* isn't a request,' he said firmly. 'It's officially sealed, until we're sure we've finished with it.'

Veronica laughed flatly.

I followed Amelia up to our room. 'What do you want to do?' I asked, wondering how much I'd be asked to carry and how far.

'What I *want* to do,' she said heavily, 'is to get away from here. It doesn't seem to affect you, Richard. I suppose you're used to it. But I can tell you, for the rest of us it's becoming too much. Personal attacks, now! To think that anybody in this place could be capable of such violence.' She shook her head in disbelief.

'Not necessarily in the house,' I said quietly. 'Didn't you hear what Poynton said: he was outside last night, patrolling the grounds. That means the alarms were off again for God knows how long. Off on Tuesday night, when Roy was killed. And it means – by implication – that the police are at least thinking seriously about an outsider.'

'You've been thinking about it!' She seemed pleased. 'I knew you'd come up with some new ideas.'

I went to look out of the window. 'Nothing new,' I told her, staring towards the gatehouse.

She came to stand at my shoulder. 'You're thinking about Marion?'

'Presumably she's still at the gatehouse.'

'She was Roy's wife!'

I laughed. 'Wives are always shooting their husbands. It's an occupational hazard.'

'It isn't amusing, you know.'

'I'm sorry.' I grimaced at her. 'Were you going down to the lake again?'

'I don't know. I suppose.' She darted a look at me. 'Why do you want to know?'

'Simply – where to find you. If I get a sudden attack of theories, who else do I run to?'

'I might not be there. I think I'll just stroll here and there. Talk to some people.'

I sighed, gripped her by the shoulders, kissed her firmly, and said: 'I'll see you around.'

Then I wandered away downstairs.

It was going to be even more oppressive. The sky was taking on a metallic sheen, though there was not a sign of cloud and you could feel the pressure in the air. Thunder before the week-end, I thought. I walked out on to the terrace.

I'd hoped to find Samantha in her usual spot, with luck painting, a natural therapy. She was there but not painting, sitting in one of the wooden chairs and staring sightlessly at the sunken gardens she loved so much. The timid take longer to acclimatize to the concept of violence. Beside her, in another of the chairs, sat Lewis, not looking at her, just talking. Maybe he thought it would help her if he held forth on the subject of violence. His voice droned on as I found another chair. Neither of them seemed to notice me.

'. . . don't know what the world's coming to – violence everywhere you look. Me, I try to ignore it. One lot of loonies bashing another lot of loonies. But you can't ignore it all the time and sometimes it comes too close.' He thought about this, glancing at her as though he thought he'd been offensive. 'But when you've done nothing . . . that's what gets my goat. You haven't *done* anything to anybody, Sam. Nobody could imagine you . . .' He cleared his throat. 'Only maybe you have, Sam. Thought of that, have you? All ignorant, sort of. There's such a thing as jealousy, you see.'

She jerked her head at that, then lowered it again quickly. Lewis hadn't noticed. He didn't seem to be able to look directly at her. He went on placidly.

'Of your painting, Sam. You know. Couldn't bear to see how well you're doing. Had to do you in, to stop you at it.' Then he gave a little whinny of laughter just to show he wasn't being too serious. 'But you don't have to let it stop you – that's what I mean. You're all upset. Well, who'd blame you for that. But you've got to keep going, Sam. Not sit here. Get the old paints out and get going on the next. Always, it's the next. That's the secret. You get me? You get me, Sam?'

She made no reply. He shambled to his feet, jutted his beard, and produced an embarrassed 'hrmph' from inside it, reached over and touched her hand, and stumbled away. I wondered whether Sam had detected that behind it all he'd been a very angry man.

She lifted her head then and gave him a tiny smile, but too late because he didn't see it. A pity. Lewis could have used that smile to good purpose if he'd been good enough to capture it on canvas.

I gave it a minute or two, smoked my pipe, knocked it out, filled it again, lit it, then went over and took the seat Lewis had used. I turned it to face her. I wasn't afraid to watch her responses.

'Feeling better now?'

She fluttered a smile at me. 'Lewis has been talking to me.'

'I know.'

'He's a very . . . very *angry* man.' So she'd realized.

I nodded. The meek, when roused, can be awesome. 'I don't think he wants you to be frightened away.'

'I wasn't intending to leave.'

'You said that. It took a bit of nerve, I'd think.'

She looked very serious. 'I'm not a brave person, you know. But Lewis said it. I haven't done anything to anybody. It's not fair to try to frighten me away.'

She'd forgotten it'd been more serious than a frightening.

'What did you see, Sam?' I asked.

'I told you – only a shadow leaning over me. A shape.'

'I don't mean last night. I mean the night before, the night Roy was shot. You must have seen or heard something. It follows.'

'When could I . . .' She looked away from me. Her words had been angry.

'You can tell me, you know.'

She gnawed at her lip. 'It was nothing. And anyway, how could they have known it was me?'

I waited. She shook her head and worried the thought into shape, then she came at it from a tangent.

'I go to a lot of these things, Richard. Residential courses. Oh, any old thing. Picture framing, French for holiday makers, classical composers, oh . . . anything. I've got a trust fund, you see. Daddy looked after me. The money just arrives. Oh, they say, how yummy, you can just please yourself and not go to work. But it's not yummy.' She grimaced at the word. 'You don't get to *be* with people. You don't learn a job and you don't make friends. So, I go where there are people, only sometimes that's worse. I mean, you make friends, and they say they'll keep in touch, but they never do. And there was never anybody *special*. You know what I mean.'

I knew. The person you meet and you know at once. But the people she'd meet at these courses would be equally uncertain and hesitant and nothing would solidify into a relationship.

'So you came here.'

'A whole fortnight! Usually it's only a week. Too short. It takes days . . .' She stared out over the garden. 'But here, well, there was Rex. He looked at me – sort of interested. He's been kind and friendly and he laughs a lot. But casual and not . . . well, serious. You know. Oh, I'd recognize the smallest sign. You get to recognize any sign. And he didn't give me one. I suppose . . . supposed he hadn't got patience with me . . .' She took a deep breath. 'I . . . well, I have to go to the bathroom in the night. It's very annoying. And here, you don't want to wake people by putting on a lot of lights. But I found I could manage without them. Those vases in their little recesses – they stand out – and there's been quite a bit of moonlight.'

She stopped. I was recalling that there was one of those recesses immediately before she would reach the bathroom from her own room. One bedroom, number five, then a recess, then the bathroom. That was the recess from which Roy had borrowed Bruno's genuine blue and white vase.

'Go on.'

'You couldn't see room numbers, you know. Nor the bathroom sign. The doors are set right back.'

'It's the thick walls.'

'So I went by the fact that there was no vase in the recess my side of the bathroom.'

'Just made for you.'

'But I . . . I used to go all the way round the balcony, in the opposite direction.'

'In the dark?'

'I don't mind the dark.'

'You weren't frightened?'

She shook her head.

'But why should you do that, Sam?'

'All it meant was that I kept my hand on the baluster rail and looked for the door just before the empty recess. No different, really. Just as easy.'

'But why *do* that, Sam? The simplest way was past only one door to the bathroom. Easy.'

'He's in number six.'

It burst out in a gasp of embarrassment. Rex was in number six.

'I see,' I murmured. 'Going all the way round, you'd pass his door.'

'Just *pass* it, yes.'

'There was always the chance.' I let it rest there, smiling as though I did that sort of thing myself. But it had been . . . how many years? It seemed that, after all, daddy hadn't done her much of a favour with his yummy trust fund.

'Why is it,' she demanded furiously, 'that there're never words to explain your stupidities? Like a silly schoolgirl with a thing about the sportsmistress! I'm disgusted with myself.'

The passion died. Her cheeks were flaming. I said gently: 'But that was what you did. Every night?'

'Sometimes,' she said, 'twice. Depending.'

'And on Tuesday night?'

'It was – oh, I can't be sure. I didn't look at my watch. Maybe

12.30. Or later. I *did* see something moving on the balcony. That frightened me a bit, but of course . . .'

'It could have been him?' I nodded.

'Yes. Right the other end of the balcony, so it could have been. But you see . . . and I've thought about this, Richard . . . I was on my way in the wrong direction, as I always was. And if that somebody saw me, then I'd only be a shadow to them, so how could they have known it was me? How? Certain enough to . . . to try to kill me?'

'They waited and watched. There would be that second when the bathroom light went on and before you shut the door. Then they'd see you.'

'But I didn't go into the bathroom,' she said breathlessly. 'Not till *ages* later.'

'You didn't?' I looked down at my feet.

'It was the vase, you see. The vase not in the recess. I got confused . . . with the shadow. Sort of felt my way round and found the empty recess and went back and opened the door just this side of it. The same as I'd done before. Lots of times. But there wasn't any cord to pull and I stood there, and the moon was streaming through the window, and there was Rex, sitting with his back to the headboard, in nothing more than his pyjama trousers, sitting like he'd been waiting, and Richard . . . I . . . I didn't turn and run. Like I should've done. Don't be angry with me for not running.'

'I'm not angry with you, Sam.'

'And d'you know what I thought,' she hurried on. 'In that second . . . or however long it was . . . I thought: the vase. It hadn't been there, in its recess. And I thought . . . Rex did that. I thought he'd watched me, after all, and noticed me, on those trips all round the balcony. I thought he'd taken the vase out of its recess just so that I'd get the wrong door . . . his door. I thought he'd given me a sign. That he w-w-wanted me. So . . . I went to him.'

She was silent. One wrong word and she'd have gone to pieces.

'And on your way back to your room,' I said casually, 'you didn't, by any chance, see another shadow?'

'I didn't see anything.'

'Not even whether the vase was back in its recess?'

'Oh . . . it *was*. But he'd been out to the bathroom, himself. He must have put it back.'

Oh Sam, Sam! I thought. Sometimes in the dark you see what you want to see. Or fear to.

'Well, I hope you found the right bathroom eventually.'

'Yes. Yes, thank you. But why . . . Richard, tell me *why* he wouldn't speak to me all the next day.'

She hadn't imagined *him*, had she? Or perhaps dreamed the whole thing? I smiled and said something quite ridiculous.

'Perhaps he didn't want to fracture a very delicate and tender image, Sam.'

Or perhaps he was keeping an alibi in reserve but wasn't certain it would stand up. 'The weather's breaking up,' I said.

'Oh dear. Then I'd better rush and fetch my painting things, while there's still time.'

I went in search of Rex Lightfoot.

My way took me through the banqueting hall and there was Bruno, with paintings spread face up all round him on the floor.

'You weren't serious about the exhibition, Bruno?'

'Why not? They like encouragement from a professional. But how I'm expected to encourage Lewis when he turns out this sort of stuff, I don't know.'

I looked down at Lewis's work. The results, even to me, seemed childish and immature.

'I see what you mean. Have you seen Rex?'

'Not for a while. I think he's with Bert.'

I knocked at both their doors but neither Rex nor Bert was there. I went outside, circled the house, staring into the distance for scattered painters. Nothing shaped like Bert or Rex. My ears did it, in the end. There was a clattering sound coming from the direction of the yard. I made my way towards it.

Bert and Rex were struggling with a large extension ladder, cursing and laughing, in that order, and making a botch of it. There's a knack in handling ladders. Neither of them knew it. They were trying to erect it against the side of the old barn, now the studio.

'And what the hell do you two think you're doing?' I demanded.

Bert turned. The ladder crashed to the cobbles. Rex, grinning, cleaned his hands on the seat of his pants.

'Don't be so stuffy, Richard,' he said amiably. 'All Bert wants to do is see if he can get in through the roof. Why else did he come to this place? It's not right to lock him out.'

'Right or not, that's how it is. D'you want him to break his stupid neck?' I turned to Bert. 'You ought to have more sense. There must be other kilns.'

'I wanted to use this one,' he panted, waving his arms, tripping over the ladder.

'And get yourself arrested? D'you want that? They'd assume you'd got in to muck about with the evidence. Oh my God, how could you be so stupid!'

Bert looked from one to the other of us. 'It's not fair!' he bleated. Then he stumbled out of the yard.

Rex moved to follow him, still smiling. 'Spoil-sport,' he said.

'I wanted a word.'

'Any time.'

'Now will do. It's about Sam.'

He held the smile but his eyes became wary. Rex was the gifted type for whom life presented a gilded path. Flex that smile and his way was all joy. So he moved with events, accepted them, smiled, and moved on. But with the change of expression in his eyes there came a tightening of the jaw and suddenly the handsome face was hard. But the smile held. The teeth were white and strong.

'You've been talking to her,' he observed, and now he relaxed.

'You were playing tricks with a vase, I hear.'

'What vase? What tricks?'

I had completely confused him. He'd been expecting me to say: tricks with Sam. 'Took it out of its recess,' I said. 'The one by your door.'

'Now I know you're crazy. Look, I've got things to do.'

I placed my palm on his chest. He stared down at it, then looked up at me. 'Things to do right now,' he said quietly.

'They can wait. A minute.'

He tensed, then laughed, standing back. 'You're so damned serious. Okay, I'll tell you how it was. I came here and right from the start there she was, with that look in her eyes. You can tell, a mile off.'

'Across a crowded room? That sort of thing?'

'Don't be so bloody corny, Richard. We're talking about the basics. Sex. But you've got to be careful and she wasn't the type. Too intense. Oh, I've met 'em. You can never shake 'em off. Want to own you. You'll know.'

'I don't know. Try telling me.'

'There's no future in it. You want to be able to move on, not get hung around with weights like that round your neck. Too romantic. I told you. So I passed it up. That Veronica! Now . . . there's a different proposition.'

'And that Amelia?'

He laughed. 'You're not going to catch me out like that, my friend. I lent her my shaving brush.'

'Your idea of a romantic gesture?'

'I don't make . . .' He stopped himself. I was grinning, showing him my confidence in Amelia. 'There's nothing else,' he said shortly. 'Nothing I'm telling you.'

'Sam came to your room.'

'So it's that! What the hell's it to you?'

'Did you send her away?'

'Don't be stupid. Would I pass up a chance like that? She wanted it and she was warm. Man was she warm!'

'How long was she there?'

'As long as it takes . . .'

'How long?'

'An hour. More. Hah!' His anger had faded. He poked at my arm but I did not react. 'You won't believe this . . . but she was a virgin. At *her* age, by God. I wouldn't have believed it, these days.'

I said quietly: 'And you didn't remove a vase?'

'Of course not.'

'Or put one back?'

'What the hell's this about vases? If she told you that . . .' He stood back, eyeing me up and down. 'Look at you. Like an outraged poppa. She's been having you on, whatever she said. She wanted it and I was able to oblige. It's over and done with.'

'Two more days,' I said.

'What?'

'Two more days you'll be here. I'd watch my step, Rex, if I were you. You might not make it to Saturday.'

He snorted at that, flicked his lapels, and turned away. I watched him go. My fingers itched, but I watched him go. Wasn't I retired? Which meant from action, too.

9

I was sitting at the open window, puffing smoke at the leaden night. I was in slacks and shirt. The room was dark. It was fifteen minutes to midnight.

Amelia stirred. 'Aren't you coming to bed, Richard?'

'I love to watch thunderstorms at night.'

'That's not true and you know it.' She sat up.

One of my character faults is that I cherish accuracy but fail to keep that fact to myself. 'It's true that I like thunderstorms,' I assured her. 'It's not true that it's the only reason I'm sitting here.'

'You've got something in mind,' she said eagerly, coming wide awake. 'I'll slip something on.'

'It'll be better if I'm alone.'

'With your thoughts?' she asked. 'I can help there.'

'Mmm!' I said on an intake of smoke. 'In a few minutes' time I'm going for a quiet walk round the balcony. Just to see if anything's moving.'

'You'll be at it all night?' she asked. 'This prowling of yours.'

It's nice to know you're wanted. I could barely see her face but she'd pouted. 'I don't know. But it's not finished, is it? Somebody's got to keep an eye open because there's been one attempt on Sam's life and you know what the latches are like on the doors. She can't lock herself in, you know. I'd just like to be around, and ready, if there's another go at her.'

She wasn't pleased. 'There's a genuine full-time police Inspector on the premises,' she reminded me. 'It's his responsibility and his room's right the other side of Sam's.'

On the horizon I could see the first flickers of lightning, like torches raking the clouds, but I could hear nothing.

'He's not in his room,' I told her. 'Probably out wandering the grounds again.' This time the sky was lit up and I could hear the distant rumble. 'Though maybe the rain'll drive him in.' A breeze was rustling the trees.

'Let's hope it will. Then we can get some sleep.'

'No reason you shouldn't, my dear.'

'As though I can rest with you wandering around,' she said, sounding drowsy already.

I levered my bulk out of the chair. 'I'll be a few minutes.'

I closed the door very carefully behind me, not even disturbing the air, and for a minute or two stood silently outside. There was no sound other than the sighs and grumbles of an old house cooling down. The lightning, now, was filling the whole bank of windows below me in the banqueting hall, casting sudden, stabbing shadows into the rafters. I began to move quietly to my right.

Past Samantha's door, with a pause to listen, but there was no sound from inside. I hoped she'd closed her window against any sudden downpour, remembered I'd left ours open, wondered whether Amelia would realize. I moved on, past room five, which should have contained Inspector Poynton and didn't. (I'd checked earlier.) Then the bathroom that Sam had been heading for on Tuesday, but in the opposite direction, then room six, Rex Lightfoot.

Was he sitting with his back against the headboard, clad only in pyjama trousers, as Sam had described him, waiting patiently for Veronica to come to him panting with passion? It hardly seemed likely that this would be his normal procedure. In my day, the male had pursued the female. Nowadays, I appreciate, the balance of pursuit and surrender is a little changed but all the same Veronica would surely expect, or rather demand, that her lover should come to her. If this was on the menu, Rex wouldn't have far to go; there was only one room, another bathroom, between his room and hers, number seven.

I moved on. I'd now reached a corner diagonally across from our own room. I paused. The play of white light on the windows below the balcony facing me was spectacular. The distant shake of thunder was like a shiver of anticipation throughout the building.

The next room was empty but locked. It had belonged to Roy. I wondered idly whether it would be worth while to force an entry, but decided that Poynton's men would have stripped it of any clues. In any event, I was in no mood for breaking and entering.

Carla's room was quiet. I wondered whether she'd perhaps decided to defy the police and had slipped off home. But what was there for her at home? Her protests had been mainly rhetorical, I thought.

Another bathroom, then Bert Inskip. This was followed by Bruno's own room, taking by far the largest slice out of the balcony run. Beyond that was the corner, then Lewis Hately's room, and so back to my own.

In front of the stairhead I leaned over the balcony rail. Perhaps that might be the best place to wait and watch. It offered an open view of the whole balcony but had the disadvantage of presenting my back to the open stairway. I didn't anticipate personal violence but at that time anything seemed possible.

It was a coincidence that the first definite rumble of thunder to rattle the windows should have occurred just as I was trying to dismiss that thought. The thunder was like the pounding of feet up the stairs. I tensed and a finger tapped my shoulder.

'Richard!'

I whipped round, fist poised. The lightning flickered over Bruno's strained face.

'For heaven's sake, Bruno.'

'I wanted a word.'

'Then why couldn't you just have opened your door.' I looked beyond him. The door was open on a dark room. 'What're you doing, sitting in the dark?'

A ridiculous question. He might well have been sleeping in the dark. All the same, he was dressed as I was in slacks and shirt. I amended it slightly. 'Waiting in the dark.'

'For you. I watched you start on your way round. Come inside, then we shan't have to whisper.'

Whisper? He was having to raise his voice against the thunder. I went with him into his room. He closed the door and put on his lights. I had not been invited in there before. It was an honour.

This was nothing like the guest rooms. This was where he lived. For one thing, the door was heavy and padded and it fitted snugly into its frame. The central light was a chandelier.

Bookcases lined one wall, the others displaying choice specimens of his own work, in his own style . . . along with one Manet, one Degas, one Morisot, one Sisley, and one Renoir. This was his collection of genuine originals, I knew at once.

I walked round, he politely putting on the strip lights above them.

'Bruno,' I said, 'you really are a double-dyed cheat.'

He was standing in the middle of his Aubusson rug and eyeing me with uncertainty, a weak little grin on his face. Bruno wasn't looking well. His confidence had been receiving a battering.

'Richard, I wanted to talk.'

I flicked my hand, indicating his Impressionists. 'You give people the idea that the genuine ones are mixed in with your own efforts, round the balcony. It's a lie. They're here.'

'I like to look at them.'

'You challenge people to pick out the genuine ones and they don't have a chance.'

'We're wasting time.'

'But it's immoral.'

'Nothing of the sort,' he said with a burst of spirit. 'Can't you see, it's my final fall-back in the case of burglars. I'd rather lose every one of those others, if I can save these.'

I sighed. Nobody ever told me the truth, not all of it. Did I inspire a feeling of guilt?

'We didn't come in here to talk about these,' Bruno complained.

'Right you are. What's on your mind?'

My eyes registered the rest of the room. He had a curved settee that Louis XV might have sat in, set in front of a low, graceful table. The desk in the corner deserved the title of escritoire, surely having come from the same salon as the settee. There was nothing plain and solid, like the furniture in the guest rooms.

'Sit down, Richard,' said Bruno, indicating the settee. I did so, and he tossed a number of sheets of sketching paper on to the table in front of me.

'Take a look at those.'

I examined them. Somebody other than Sam had been trying

his hand at portraiture. These were charcoal sketches, a dozen of them, the subject being Sam herself. And they were good.

'That's top-class work,' said Bruno. 'Far above the standard of anybody here, including me. The line's confident and the eye's true. The man can draw, Richard. He's professional.'

I looked up. 'The man?'

'They're by Lewis Hately.'

'Hmm!' I said, wondering where this was leading us. 'And where did you find them?'

'Amelia brought them to me.'

He said it apologetically, then looked away in case I was shocked. As I was. It told me two things. One, that she hadn't trusted me. I had disparaged the petal-painting theory but she'd pursued it and taken the result of her efforts to Bruno. And two, that I was still faced with an idea that I knew to be too wild for acceptance – that someone (who must now be Lewis Hately) had painted the petals on the pistol after having killed Roy Towers. Both thoughts I found distasteful but I took it a step at a time. I looked up at Bruno.

'And how did *she* get them?'

'She didn't say. But Richard . . . look.' He turned away to one of his shelves and produced a thin booklet. It was last year's programme of the annual exhibition at the Royal Academy. He had it open at the right page. Number 108: *Portrait of Woman in Yellow Hat*, by Lewis Hately, RA.

'The man's an imposter,' said Bruno. He was agitated. 'At the very least.'

'Suppose we take it quietly.'

'Suppose we take that programme and slap it under his nose,' Bruno countered.

'It wouldn't hurt to have a word with him,' I admitted, surprised at Bruno's aggression.

'Now?'

'Why not? Assuming he's awake.'

But now that a genuine clue stared me in the face, I wasn't happy with it. Lewis might be an impostor but I couldn't see him as a murderer, and what worried me was the attack on Samantha. I'd heard him talking to her and nothing he'd said explained a necessity for stifling young ladies in their beds.

I grabbed up the programme and the sketches and said: 'Right. Let's do it.'

Lewis's room being right next door, it wasn't going to require much effort. 'Better put your light off,' I said, my hand on the door knob, the other on the light switch. He nodded. I clicked it off. It was because of this and because the heavily padded door moved so silently that we did not disturb the person moving along the balcony just beyond my room. I put up a hand. Bruno stopped at my shoulder.

A sudden flash, followed immediately by a crash of thunder, solved the mystery. It was only Sam on one of her pilgrimages to the bathroom, though this time taking the shortest route. With the jolt of the storm she jumped, startled. In reflection, she stood up sharply, having just reached the bathroom door beyond Poynton's room. She would not need the assistance of the empty recess, although the space caught the light clearly.

It is not a pleasant thing to do, to stand silently in the dark watching a young woman going to the bathroom. Two seconds, though, and she would be inside and we could move. But she did not go inside. Not all the way. The door opened, she reached inside for the pull switch and stood for one frozen second as a silhouette against the bathroom light. Then she snapped off the light and jumped back. Her tiny 'Oh!' came to us clearly. Then she shut the door and stood with her hand to her throat. Hesitantly, she moved on around the balcony.

The next bathroom was the one between rooms six and seven, to reach it requiring that she passed Rex's bedroom. I had the sinking feeling that she was engaged in one of her fantasies, again persuading herself of a necessity to pass his door. Or perhaps not to pass his door. We stood, unmoving, waiting while the lightning chased her progress. It was now almost continuous, thunder rocking the house to its foundations. She'd have no excuse for failing to locate the 'bathroom' sign and we none for standing there silently, as we could have jumped up and down and still not have been heard.

She located the correct door. She reached inside for the switch, put on the light, nervously thrust the door fully open, then scuttled inside as the thunder shook her again.

'What was that about?' asked Bruno.

'Heaven knows.' I felt depressed. So many things I didn't

know and so many people I didn't understand. 'Let's go and wake him up.'

We tapped on Lewis's door and got no response. There was no light from beneath it or round the edges, as there would have been with the lights on since the doors fitted poorly. I tapped louder. Nothing. I opened the door. 'Lewis?' All was quiet. I ushered Bruno inside, we closed the door, and he put on the light.

It was a room such as I'd expected, the same furniture and curtains, the same low table. Lewis had scattered his impatient personality freely, spreading his possessions on all available surfaces and cluttering the walls with his paintings, each one leaning beside the other to dry or whatever. Or just to be stared at from the centre of the room, turning slowly, absorbing the impact of that childish and utterly false style.

Lewis was not there.

'He's not here, Richard.'

'So I see. We'll have a quick look round, shall we.'

Bruno was appalled. Search a guest's room? 'We can't.'

'He's an impostor, isn't he? Your own word. So hasn't he forfeited his rights?'

'What if he comes back?' demanded Bruno.

'Ask yourself – and this is perhaps more important – back from where?'

He made an impatient sound and went to stand with his back against the door. 'If he comes back and catches us . . .'

As he spoke, the door opened against his back. His nerves were tense. He gave a cry of panic, then grinned weakly. The intruder was Amelia. I groaned but managed to keep it inside.

'So Bruno's told you,' she said, closing the door.

'The drawings, yes.' I was very patient, very polite. 'Where did you get them?'

'I've been around, talking to people. I did tell you I was going to do that. He was working in the spinney and those fell out of his satchel.'

'Fell?'

She looked beyond me. 'Sort of. I picked them up. He didn't see me.'

'Well, that's something to be thankful for.'

119

She was disturbed by my attitude. I couldn't be angry with her, but she'd precipitated something that I believed to be a side issue. I was anxious to be free of it.

'There might not be much time,' I said, turning away from her pleading eyes.

Then I set to work. There is a method in these things, adaptable in accordance with whether or not the search has to remain a secret. This involves the careful replacement in the exact original tidyness. With Lewis, this did not exist. The wardrobe drawers were a tangle of underwear, sweatshirts, socks, handkerchiefs, even a few tubes of paint that had found their way in. The wardrobe was nearly empty. Surprisingly, there was a dinner suit he'd brought along in case we dressed for dinner. One lounge suit. An anorak, a pair of grey slacks.

There was nothing whatever to connect him with the killing of Roy Towers.

I dragged his suitcase from under the bed. It was large, rather larger than I'd have expected from the quantity of his clothes. It was carefully strapped, but not locked. I opened it up.

'There's this,' I said calmly, lifting it out.

It was a half-finished portrait, in oils, of Sam, the glow of artistic creation on her face and her hair flying in a breeze. This, then, was the outcome of his sketches. No doubt it'd be on the Royal Academy walls this year. *Young Woman in Ecstasy*, by Lewis Hately, RA.

'So where does it get us?' I demanded. 'He's an impostor. So what?'

'He could have painted the petals . . .' began Amelia.

'For God's sake! Can you imagine it?'

She bit her lip. But my exasperation was partly caused by his continuing absence and partly because I was being kept from doing my guard job, as I'd intended.

'I can't stay here,' I decided, and headed for the door, Bruno standing aside and Amelia watching me with big eyes.

It was just as my hand reached the door that the uproar broke out on the landing. For the past few minutes the thunder had been almost unbroken and yet I'd not really noticed it. This change in type and intensity of noise broke through. I flung open the door.

With the lightning flickering on them, giving the impression of an old film, a jumble of arms and legs belonging to two people was rolling on the balcony, just outside the bathroom next to room five. There were roars of anger and pain, thumps of heels pounding the boards, screams in the background as the women entered the audible part of the fray. I ran out, Bruno at my heels, and we dashed round the angle of the balcony.

Amelia rushed after us. 'Richard!' she screamed, assuming incorrectly that I was intending to join in.

They struggled to their feet, climbing over each other to get there first, Lewis panting, swinging his fists like a flail, Rex cold and dark, intense and vicious. I tried to put an arm between them and a toe caught my knee. I backed off.

'Lights!' I shouted, and Bruno rushed back to the stairhead.

'Murderous bastard,' Lewis spluttered, burying a fist in Rex's guts.

The lights came on. Amelia hung on my arm. From beyond the fighting couple, Rex now with his back to the wall and blood running down his chin, Samantha came running. She'd been a long while in the bathroom but now she was out and active. She had taken up the vase from the alcove next to the bathroom, the very same vase that had (or had not) been in its alcove on the Tuesday night. She was holding it, two-handed, above her head and screaming at the top of her voice. No fear in this scream, though. Nothing but fury.

'Don't you hurt him! Stop it, you pig!'

Bruno gave a shout of distress. 'No!' He threw himself past me, careless of flying fists and butting heads, straight at Sam and the vase, his hands lifted, imploring and groping. 'No!' he shouted again, and he caught the vase from her fingers a split second before it made contact.

The head it would probably have split wide open was Lewis's.

Moaning, Bruno clutched the vase to his chest. Lewis, startled right out of his stride by Sam's attack on himself, dropped his hands and stared at her.

Rex was not going to waste such an opportunity. I saw his face, then the expression that flowed over it and the translation of that expression to his limbs. I've witnessed gutter fighting at its worst but nothing, I think, faster and more precise. One, two, three. Fist to guts, knee to down-coming chin, elbow in the raised eye. Then a half step back and a right that almost took Lewis's head off.

He fell with a bang, face down on the balcony. Sam put her hands to her face and began to cry. Veronica said: 'Well, I'm not going to stand here and watch this,' having done so. Then she went to Rex and put an arm round his shoulders. 'Oh, you poor dear,' she murmured. He gave her what he could of his most charming smile, blood running from his chin, his lower lip already thickening.

From behind us at the stairhead Inspector Poynton spoke wearily. 'Don't you people ever stop?'

Marion was standing beside him. In fact, his hand was on her arm and in no way suggesting he'd helped her up the stairs. They were both completely soaked, limp and flabby and wind-dashed.

'I found her wandering in the grounds,' he growled, noticing my lifted eyebrows.

'Bruno!' Marion appealed. 'You didn't come. Haven't. And I . . . had to see you.'

It was all too much for Bruno. Previous painting courses had no doubt been peaceful. He stood there, mouth open, clutching the vase to his chest, and stared. Amelia pushed through to Marion, looking up at Poynton.

'And why shouldn't she?' she demanded. Then she took Marion's arm. 'You must get out of those wet things. Richard, you just knock before you come in. Now, Marion . . . at least a dressing gown . . .'

The door closed behind them.

Veronica had taken Rex into the bathroom to clean him up. It was fortunate it was right there. Sam stood out on the balcony, looking in, listening. I caught her eye. She glanced away.

The others were drifting away. 'Get some sleep, some time,' Bert grumbled. Poynton and I managed to carry Lewis into his own room, Bruno backing ahead. Lewis was breathing deeply but steadily. We took his shoes off and laid him on the bed. We looked at him.

Poynton shook himself. He was making a pool on the carpet.

'I'll go and get out of these clothes,' he said. 'Don't do anything – say anything – until I get back.'

He marched out. I heard him mutter something to Sam, so I nodded to Bruno and followed Poynton on to the balcony.

She was hovering, her own door wide open, so she'd got that far and come back. Veronica and Rex were still splashing around, he making groaning sounds to attract sympathy, she supplying it.

'What happened, Sam?' I asked quietly.

'I don't know.'

'Before the fight, I mean. You put the light on in this bathroom. Then you put it out and walked on. Why was that?'

'He . . .' she mumbled. She jerked her head towards Lewis's door. 'He was sitting in there . . . on the . . . on the seat, in the dark. We just looked at each other. And I . . . went on.'

'You tried to brain him.'

She twisted her head back and forth in agitation. 'I don't know. I just . . . did.'

I patted her shoulder. 'Get to bed, Sam, why don't you.'

I went back into Lewis's room. Nothing had changed. Lewis lay very still. The sketches lay face up on the table, the programme lay on the floor. The half-finished portrait leaned against the wall by the door. Bruno was standing where I'd seen him last, the vase clasped in his arms. There was a wounded look about him, his eyes staring into somewhere far beyond me.

'You can put it down now,' I said, grinning at his possessiveness.

'This?' He looked down at it.

'You went crazy as though it was the genuine one.'

'I didn't think. It was pure instinct.'

His eyes were focusing again but there was still a wild look in them. I laughed easily, trying to shake him out of it.

'A good job you grabbed it, I suppose. Our friend here would probably have a cracked skull if you hadn't.'

'I mean, just instinct,' he repeated. 'I knew the real one was downstairs in the studio.'

'Of course. Locked away. But you didn't get time to remember.'

'I've been looking at this, Richard,' he said in a faraway voice. 'It didn't register for a while. Then I had a closer look. I mean . . . I'm the one to know. I made every one of the copies. The trouble is . . . this happens to be the real one.'

10

I didn't get time to take this in. Of *course* the genuine Chinese blue and white vase was in the studio. Bruno had said it was the genuine one when Roy brought it down. From then on it had sat there, Roy gradually recording it and its flowers on canvas. And the photographs showed the canvas still matching the vase and the flowers. Still. Venables had sealed the studio, that was why it still looked the same. So the real one had to be in the studio.

Either Bruno had gone off his head, or I had. I could take no decision on this point because Poynton returned at that moment, bare legs sticking out from a vivid silk dressing gown with a red dragon on it.

'Has he come round?' he demanded.

'Not yet.'

He went to the bed and tried his cheek-slapping technique, not too effective when the beard's so thick. But it produced a groan.

'Coming,' said Poynton. 'Anybody like to tell me what that was all about?'

I jerked my thumb towards the bed. 'He,' I said, 'Lewis Hately, was doing a bit of guarding on his own account. Or so I'd guess. From what Samantha tells me, he was sitting in the dark in that bathroom. And somebody's already had one go at Sam. So he was guarding. I think. He didn't say a word when Sam put on the light and looked in.'

'Like bloody soft kids,' Poynton grumbled.

'With you being outdoors, somebody . . .'

'I've had a word with this Rex character,' he growled. 'Says he wanted to go to the bathroom but somebody was in the one on the other side of his room . . .'

'That'd be Sam.'

'. . . so he walked on down and this lunatic here pounced on him before he could get the light on.'

'Was going past,' said Lewis weakly from the bed. 'Not going in.'

'Not what Lightfoot says,' Poynton told him severely.

Groaning, Lewis elbowed himself up, his eyes out of focus. 'He's a lying bastard.'

I didn't say anything. I didn't think that Lewis knew about Sam's adventure with Rex on Tuesday night but he might have indulged in a little crafty eavesdropping. In that case, though, I couldn't see why he'd held his hand. No, his attitude had been protective, so that he'd have watched Sam's interest in Rex with slumbering anger. But he'd been on guard against a midnight creeper and Rex had been creeping at midnight. Lewis might have pounced too enthusiastically. Rex's expedition could well have been innocent.

Usually I liked to toss around such speculations but just at that time my mind was engaged with thoughts of a Chinese blue and white vase and a half-finished portrait of Sam.

'How're you feeling?' I asked.

Lewis put his face in his hands. He explored the inside of his mouth with his tongue and tenderly felt his jaw, his beard rather. 'Had a bit of padding,' he said, his voice thick. 'Comes in useful.'

'I suppose that means,' said Poynton, 'that you make a habit of these rough-houses.'

Ages since I'd heard that. Rough-houses.

'I do not,' said Lewis with dignity, trying to swing his legs down to the floor. He winced. He sat very still on the edge of the bed and his gaze fell on the exposed painting. 'Oh,' he said. 'Lor!'

'I searched the room,' I told him. 'I came up with that.'

'You searched this room?' Poynton demanded. 'By what right did you search his room? Even I couldn't, not without a warrant.'

'And quite right too.' I nodded. 'Invasion of privacy. We couldn't have that. But I'm retired now, so all he can do is sue me. I don't think you want to do that, do you Lewis?'

You could see it in his eyes. What the hell were we talking about – sue? 'Where's Sam?' he demanded.

'In her room.'

'Are you all insane?' He tried to get to his feet, but his legs weren't working and he fell back on the bed. 'You've got a murderer wandering around loose and nobody's watching out!'

We stared at him. The thunder was retreating to distant,

pettish rumbles. Bruno found a chair and sat down, but still he clasped his precious vase in his arms.

'Lewis,' I said, 'I've got bad news for you. I'm afraid the present showing is that *you* are the prime choice as murderer.'

'What the hell's this?' Poynton glared at me.

'Get her in here!' shouted Lewis. He clasped his head in his hands.

'This,' I told Poynton, 'can be explained through that.' I pointed at the portrait.

'It isn't even finished. What does it mean?'

'That's what I'm hoping Lewis can explain.'

Lewis threw himself towards the door and fell flat on the carpet. We helped him to his feet. He was shaking his head stubbornly.

'Not one word,' he said. 'Not one bloody word will you get out of me while Sam isn't being guarded. If nobody's going out there, then get her in here.'

Bruno was all sympathy. 'It's the shock.' He looked round.

'Will you all be quiet!' shouted Poynton. 'D'you want everybody in here?'

'I want *her* in here,' Lewis said. 'Where I can keep an eye on her.'

Poynton cocked an eye at him. 'If she wants to have another go at you, we're here to protect you.' Maybe the mood was getting at him and I'm sure it was intended as a humorous remark but Lewis stuck out his beard and bunched his fists. Not strong on humour, Lewis.

'I'll get her,' I comforted him. 'Give me a minute.'

I went out again on to the balcony. It was now almost as dark as it'd been before the storm, distant lightning doing no more than brush the windows. There was no movement. I tapped gently on her door. 'Sam.'

A pause. Then her voice, breathless it seemed. 'Who is it?'

'It's Richard.'

She drew open the door, her white face peering at me.

'We're in Lewis's room,' I said. 'He's going wild to get out here on guard again so it'd be easier if you'd come in there.'

She hesitated only a second. 'I'll throw something on.' Then: '*Was* he guarding?'

I told her he was. She disappeared and returned in her thin

housecoat. It was enough. She followed me into Lewis's room and his eyes fastened on her. He said nothing but she avoided his eyes after that initial contact. She found a seat in the far corner. Her gaze had brushed over the painting and she'd seemed to stiffen. She sat demurely, a faint blush on her cheeks.

'Right,' I said. 'Now, Lewis, can we please have an explanation of this painting, seeing that you've been turning out a lot of rubbish for the past ten days. And these . . .' I showed him the sketches.

'Not yet,' Poynton cut in. 'Not so fast. There's an explanation or two that *I'd* like to hear first. By what sort of reasoning did you take it on yourself to search this room? Take your time. But I want the truth.'

I took a deep breath and condensed the whole affair as much as I could.

'The petals still being on the pistol in exactly the way they're shown in the painting, and after the artist had been shot, meant that the one who painted the petals had to be some other painter but Roy Towers. Okay so far?'

'I don't follow your reasoning,' Poynton said flatly.

'It'll come. And as Bruno here seemed to be the only one who could have painted the petals, and as there was no reason for him to have done that, then we looked round for somebody else who might have the ability to paint the petals. You with me?'

Poynton shook his head. It was a gesture of disbelief. 'Go on.'

'And these sketches turned up, which gave room for thought, so I came here . . .'

'And searched my room,' Lewis complained bitterly.

'So all right,' said Poynton, waving Lewis to silence. 'You decided he could paint petals. Marvelous deduction. Always accepting, which I don't, that petals come into it.'

'He's a professional,' I told him. 'He's here under false pretences. That's suspicious, and you can't deny it.'

'That doesn't make me a murderer,' said Lewis plaintively.

'But it made you an impostor.'

Poynton jerked his head. 'Let's get on with it. We're not going to get any sleep.'

'I'm about finished,' I said. 'We searched this room – I searched this room – and found that half-finished canvas in a suitcase.'

127

'And that's the lot?'

'It's how far we'd got.'

Bruno cleared his throat to attract attention. 'And I found that this vase . . .'

'So now we're waiting for Lewis's explanation,' I said quickly.

'Now hold on.' Poynton put up a restraining hand. 'Quite apart from the fact that I can't see he owes you any explanations at all, do you usually think like this? Do you always whip up complicated theories by such weird reasoning?'

It was not the time to explain that the reasoning was not wholly mine so I fell back into my pompous style, which Amelia might have approved.

'When you've hammered away at the impossibles, what you've got left, crazy or not, has to be the truth.'

'And don't throw your paraphrases at me,' he snapped. 'Let's hear what he's got to say.' He turned to Lewis. 'Let's have it.'

Lewis was recovering well. His eyes were clear, and his head wasn't aching enough to prevent him from shouting.

'Don't talk to me as though I'm a crook! I'm not denying anything. Yes, I'm here as an impostor and the only one that's been hurt by that's been me. If you knew what it's like to turn out rubbish . . .' He met Bruno's eye and then avoided it. 'But you know how it is. Say you're coming – give prior notice – and everything gets prepared and polished.'

'It's *always* polished,' Bruno protested.

'You know what I mean. Things laid on, best face showing, and all that rot. All useless, when they do that. You don't see how things *are*. So I came as just another student. I didn't expect murder and criminal assault and fist fights. Not my line at all.'

He appealed to Sam with his eyes but she looked down at her hands.

'You came as what?' I asked. 'In reality.'

'The Arts Council asked me to make a report. Bruno Fillingley had applied for a grant. They wanted a recommendation.'

Softly, from behind my elbow, Bruno groaned. 'My dear chap . . .' he mumbled.

But Lewis was in full flow. Bruno's distress was not to be

taken into consideration. In fact, Lewis seemed to derive some pleasure from it. 'Well . . .' He spread his palms. 'Bruno Fillingley, RA. That didn't help much. I mean, you don't want to encourage an RA. Heads were wagged at the meeting, I can tell you. But the word was that he was a forger.'

'Let me explain,' Bruno pleaded.

But Lewis wasn't listening. 'A faker, a copyist,' he said with relish. 'That carried some weight. But nothing had landed on the market. No scandals or anything like that, no exposures, no television interviews in the street on his way from the court. That was bad. The decision was in the balance, but they decided to send me along and have a look. So I came. And . . . oh dear me . . .' He shook his head sadly, then winced.

'What?' demanded Bruno, his eyes glazed.

'You turned out to be a *good* forger, you see. I mean, you could paint. That would never do. I very nearly packed in, that first week, sent in an adverse report, but there were other considerations . . .' He mumbled to himself. We waited. His head came up. 'And then we had a murder and a criminal assault and though Bruno couldn't take the credit for it, a fight on the balcony. As far as I'm concerned that clinches it.'

Poor Bruno didn't know whether he was coming or going. He hardly dared to ask. 'Clinches?' he got out at last.

'In the morning I'll get on the phone.'

'You will?'

'Though I wish you'd just tell me one thing, first.' Lewis waited for Bruno's eager, breathless nod. 'Show me which are the real Impressionists, out there on the balcony. It's driving me mad.'

I watched Bruno's face. He wasn't certain whether to admit that his forgeries wouldn't stand up to close comparison and thus add to his status, or admit the truth and perhaps undermine his chances. I nodded to him encouragingly. Bruno sighed. His personal standards were being assaulted.

'Well . . . to tell you the truth, Lewis, there isn't one genuine original on the balcony. They're in my room, next door.'

'Where you can gloat on them in private?' Lewis seemed to approve. He was also relieved. 'I was beginning to doubt my own judgement.'

'Come and see them,' Bruno invited, still not sure how his

grant was going and trying to force enthusiasm into his voice. 'We could have a drink . . .' He stopped, tried a weak smile. 'Though I suppose that could be taken as attempted bribery.'

Then Lewis laughed, his confession seeming to have shed a great load from his shoulders. There was pain in his laughter but he was nevertheless more happy than the rest of us. 'Too late for bribes,' he said, 'but I'll take you up on it.' He tried his legs again and they held him fairly steadily.

'Too late?' Bruno placed the vase at his feet as he stood up. 'Yes . . . I suppose so.'

'I couldn't do anything else but recommend it,' Lewis said casually. 'It's not every painting school that's so interesting.'

Bruno was laughing now. He looked uncertain on his feet, still shaky from the relief. He slapped Lewis on the shoulder, neither of them really up to such violence.

'Then come along, old chap. The night is young.'

Then Bruno stopped. His eyes went from Lewis to Sam. 'You coming, Sam?' he asked. He'd realized he wasn't going to get Lewis without Sam.

She moved towards the door, where Bruno waited to take her arm. She paused as she passed me, a pert little smile on her lips, a glint in her eye.

'D'you think I'll be safe, Richard?'

'I'd watch Bruno if I were you, when he's had a few.'

Out on the balcony, Bruno laughed. I closed the door behind them. I knew we were not finished in that room.

'Now,' said Poynton, sliding the glasses up his nose, his voice crisp. 'Suppose you tell me one or two interesting things.'

I returned to the same chair and sat, waiting. He perched on the edge of Lewis's bed, assuming an attitude of relaxation, false as hell. I fumbled with my pipe, my fingers not achieving their usual ease in filling it, and when I lit up the taste was foul. I stared at it, wondering how long I'd have to wait before something went right.

'D'you think I could have that again?' he asked. 'That bit about the petals.'

'It's surely not a difficult mental exercise.'

'Oh, is that what it was? A mental exercise. A harmless puzzle.'

I sighed. 'I was there, on the spot. I found the scene of

the crime before anybody else could get at it and mess it about.'

'Not before the murderer,' he observed. But no smile accompanied the remark.

'I saw it as the murderer had left it. Roy Towers was on his back, and dead. I've seen dead people. I knew. And there was the pistol, just as Roy had painted it, leaning against the vase and with four petals on it. There were also three petals lying on the table, but *they* got blown off the moment your lot arrived. I could tell the gun had been fired.' He raised his eyebrows. 'Very well, I'll rephrase it. It was my opinion that the gun had been fired, and later your superior, Venables, seemed to get great pleasure from telling me that it *had* been fired, and that it'd been the weapon that killed Towers. Are we all right, so far?'

'It's the petals I want to hear about.'

'Ah yes. The petals on the gun. The fact that you're so interested in *them* suggests you didn't waste any time in disturbing those, too, and now you're kicking yourselves for missing it.'

He didn't look as though he was kicking himself. He lifted his feet on to the counterpane and stretched out, head on the pillow, hands beneath it. His eyes were expressionless, viewing me down the line of his cheeks, between his tan slippers.

'Not entirely, but go on.'

'If you did disturb them,' I told him, 'all is not lost. I happened to have a camera with me and got some very good shots. Would you like me to go and fetch them?'

'We'll try to manage without, I think. After all, it *is* only a mental exercise. A game.'

I lit my pipe again, but it tasted worse. 'The pictures show the petals there, on the gun. Now . . . if you can tell me how the petals on the gun could still be exactly as he'd painted them, when the gun'd been picked up and used, then I'd be very interested to hear it.' I was pushing this, as though fond of the idea, but really interested in probing for information.

He smiled. I think he smiled. It was difficult to tell because his chin got in the way. I noticed that one sole of his slippers was wearing thin.

'And for that,' he said, 'four petals that shouldn't have stayed where they were, you've worked out a theory that involves murderers crouching there and painting desperately! You've involved the whole household, brought on fist fights and searches and a whole complicated mess . . . just for one completely false farrago of bloody daft reasoning.'

I got to my feet. 'If you can't be constructive . . .'

'For God's sake sit down.' He waited while I did so. 'You're not in the force now, Mr Patton. You're not in charge of this case. Are you really telling me you went through all your career tangling your life in stupid theories and with not one atom of imagination! What grade did you reach . . . did you say?'

'Yours,' I jerked at him, none too pleased with his tone.

'You surprise me. And it never occurred to you to imagine what you'd have done, if you'd been Roy Towers, sitting at that stool and painting those petals! How long would it take? An hour? Two hours? And maybe with a break in between while you did one of your gormless tours in the guise of a security guard. What *would* you have done about the petals on that weapon?'

'I . . .'

'Go on. Flex the old imagination. Or is it dead? You wouldn't want the petals to move.' He inclined his head against the pillow.

A terrible suspicion seemed to obstruct my tongue. 'What . . . well, what I'd have done, I suppose, would be to fix 'em on, somehow. Glue them, if I could.'

'Ah now! That's better. And what if I told you that *that* was just what Roy Towers did?'

'But the ones on the table were loose.'

'Never mind the ones on the table. He hadn't started painting them. Maybe he wouldn't have done.'

What had Bruno said? That Roy wouldn't have painted the three on the table, it would have ruined the balance.

'But that was how it was,' said Poynton, sitting up now to hammer it home. 'He'd used some sort of rubber solution, an impact adhesive, they call it. Four petals, grouped along the top of the barrel and on the frame above the cylinder.'

'I know how they were.' I couldn't get any force into my voice.

'And d'you know something . . . when it got to the lab, in a motorcyclist's shoulder bag, the petals were still there. They fired four test shots and they were still there. Lord alive, man, the murderer simply went down to the studio while Towers was out on one of his patrols, loaded the pistol, waited in the shadows behind the table, waited till he'd sat down and taken up his painting stuff, then shot him. And put back the gun roughly where it'd been. The petals stayed with the gun.'

That was how it must have been. I saw that now. It was so simple it hurt.

'The tube of glue was in his pocket?' I asked.

'No. What does it matter where it was?'

'Did you search his room for it?'

'Now you listen to me!' He pointed a finger at me angrily, swinging his feet to the floor. 'You can cut that out. No more complications. No more theories. Get me? This is a straight killing. Motive and means and opportunity. Think about that, Patton. But only think, because if you start your funnies again, damn it all we'll throw you inside.'

He marched to the door. 'You coming?'

'I'll just sit here . . .'

'I ought to make sure you're shut away safe in your room.'

'A minute.' I stared at him. If he'd taken it one step further, I swear I'd have gone for him. But I had to sit there and take it in and absorb it until nothing showed all knobbly on the surface, before I could face Amelia. He read it in my eyes, gave me a grim smile, and then he was gone.

They hadn't said a word. I'd mentioned petals and Venables hadn't put me right about them. He'd let me fumble around, perhaps believing I'd stir things up and reveal something. All right, blame myself. I'd made a basic assumption, just on the fact that those three petals had been loose. Encouraged by Amelia, yes, but I'd made it. My fault. Assumptions were things you never made.

But that had been in the grand old days when I'd been in the force. Assumptions were not made because facts were unearthed and planted side by side to see whether they'd mate. Facts. Evidence. Ah, it was just the same as everything else in life. When it was there, you didn't appreciate it. And I'd grumbled at all the tiresome routine of ferreting for evidence and facts and hadn't known how lucky I was. Venables now! He'd be there, sitting at his desk, and it'd be pouring in on him.

Heavens, he probably had profiles of all these people at the house. Bert Inskip could be an international thief, for all I knew. Rex Lightfoot could be a Mafia hit man. For all I knew. I knew nothing, that was the point. Only what I saw for myself, heard for myself, theorized for myself.

But for the moment I could not face that word: theories.

It comes to this, Richard, I told myself, you're shut out of it. One simple item of forensic evidence not in your knowledge and you fall flat on your face. What you've been doing is wallowing in nostalgia – and for what? Nothing produced but upset and embarrassment. So . . . you stop. No more conjecture. Watch it all happen, from the outside.

I relit my pipe. Funny, it was drawing fine now. Got to my feet, stretched, and made for the door.

And I nearly kicked over Bruno's genuine and only Chinese blue and white vase which he'd completely forgotten. Which should have been in the studio, and wasn't. There was something strange about that.

Now – Richard! Lay off. Nothing to do with you.

I picked it up and went outside on to the balcony. All was quiet. No light shone from beneath Bruno's door but there wouldn't be with all that soundproofing. I decided to replace the vase for him. Safe enough there in its alcove. I wandered round the balcony with it and carefully arranged it in its recess between rooms six and seven. No sound from room six, Rex's room. No sound, either, from number seven, Veronica's room. Perhaps they separately slept. Perhaps they lay together in silent passion.

Conjecture, Richard! I moved away. But wasn't this permitted conjecture? Wasn't I destined to trail out my remaining years as an increasingly senile gossip? About all I was good for . . .

I remembered to knock on my own door, and waited.

'It's all right, Richard,' called Amelia.

They were having a perfectly happy old rattle together, Marion on the edge of the bed, Amelia using the smoking-chair, as I was beginning to consider it.

'Here he is now,' said Amelia, so clearly they'd allocated a task for me to occupy the otherwise pointless minutes. 'I couldn't let her walk back alone,' she told me.

Marion was smiling and relaxed. I didn't think it was up to me to point out that she'd come here in order to see Bruno and talk to him and so on, and had not achieved any of these. If she wanted to go back to the gatehouse, I'd escort her there. I wouldn't have thought that anything of Amelia's would have fitted Marion, Amelia being shorter and a little slimmer. But the slacks didn't look bad and a cardie looks well enough, even over a slip. There was a white plastic bag by the door, presumably containing Marion's wet things.

So they kissed each other on the cheek and we left and strolled back to the gatehouse. The manor was wide open, the alarms still being switched off. To hell with security.

We strolled, as I said. The night, after the storm, smelled sweet. Black, silver-edged clouds chased across the moon. Neither of the ladies seemed to think it strange that I should be walking through a dark estate with a very attractive woman.

There were, I was beginning to realize, certain advantages in being retired. The word 'retired' seems to carry a magic overtone. It is not exactly assumed that sexual activity has ceased, that it dies on your trip home with the presentation clock under your arm, but it is a safe assumption that it's no longer rampant. You are not, for instance, about to pounce. This leads to relaxation. Already I'd found that women, and the younger the better, would allow me closer to their confidence. They were no doubt taking a breather from the eternal sexual conflict, but what of it!

So we didn't hurry and we talked, Marion and I, she with a husband murdered only two days before.

'We intend to marry,' she told me. 'As soon as possible.'

'Decent interval,' I murmured past the pipe stem.

'Perhaps two months.'

'Lovely.'

'You'll come to the wedding?'

'Be delighted.'

Not, perhaps, as best man. Wasn't I well past my best?

I left her at her front door and waited until the lights went on, then strolled back. Short flashes of the moon, now, dripping trees and the rustle of the night predators. Life as normal. Death as usual.

'It sure is,' he agreed. Then his face crumpled again.

'Do you smoke?' I asked quickly.

He nodded to the dressing table. I twisted, reached, and with a swipe of my hand got cigarette packet and matches in one go, and tossed them to him. He made a sound that I thought was thanks but his eyes were down again, hidden. Then he lit up and looked round for an ashtray. Before I could find one he noticed his vase, set it upright between his knees, and dropped the match in it.

'This,' he said, glancing up, 'cost me thirty quid. I reckoned it was worth it. Could've meant a lot to me.'

'You bet.'

'If it'd worked out. But of course it didn't. Nothing ever does.'

He was silent, thinking about it. Feeling it might encourage him, I searched my mind for a compliment. 'You did a good job with the polystyrene jacket, Bert.'

'Yes. Great, isn't it! That's what we do at the factory – expanded polystyrene packing moulds. For delicate stuff, you know, hi-fi things and instruments. It's a growing market. So this . . . it was easy.'

I nodded, not being able to imagine Bert being able to handle anything complicated. I probed for details. 'Nobody caught you at it, then? I mean – it must have been unofficial work.'

His eyes fastened on mine. Sitting still, his mind now casting him back to the factory, he seemed more capable. It often happens. A man's personality gets involved with his work.

'Caught me?' he asked. 'There wasn't anybody to *catch* me. I did it after hours, with the full run of the place.'

A caretaker, I thought. 'But still . . . you could've been spotted.'

'I'm Production Manager,' he said. 'Nobody would dare question what I do.'

I jammed my pipe between my teeth to prevent myself from laughing. For one second he'd been firm and confident. What, I thought, our Bert!

'I'll bet they wouldn't,' I said.

He drew on the cigarette, his eyes dreamy, stuck out his lower lip, and directed a stream of smoke at the ceiling. This wasn't the Bert I knew. 'I'll tell you something, Richard. When

Amelia was sitting up in bed, waiting for news. 'What happened?'

'You mean – Rex and Lewis?'

'Of course.'

I told her: Lewis standing (sitting) guard over Sam and Rex unfortunately heading for the wrong bathroom (or past it). I told her that Lewis was now all right, very much so, and what he'd really been doing at the manor house. She pursed her lips at that and I omitted carefully to mention the sketches she'd found. I went into some detail about the subsequent interview with Poynton, not trying to slant it in any way in my favour. I allowed her a minute or two to absorb it.

'So you see,' I said at last, 'all the while those petals have been glued to the pistol. The petal theory goes right out of the window.'

She nodded, apparently not regretting the loss of a theory here or there. 'We'll have to give it more thought,' she decided.

I grunted at that. 'There's one thing I don't understand,' I admitted.

'Only one?'

'It's just . . . Samantha. You saw her. Why did she attack Lewis, when he's been so considerate with her?'

'Oh you fool, Richard. Of *course* she would. Of course.'

Which was no explanation at all, just female logic. And she criticized mine!

'Now do come to bed,' she implored.

'A second.'

I got out the brown envelope from the dressing table drawer, the one containing the photographs.

'Surely there's nothing left to see in those,' she said, disillusioned with their worth. 'We know now why one looks just like the other.'

I slid them out on my palm and spread them under her nose on the counterpane. 'That's really the trouble. I mean, it now appears that Bruno's genuine Chinese vase has found its way back to the balcony so that means the vases have been switched.'

'How strange,' she said wearily.

'And *still* the painting looks like the group, and there's one thing damn certain: they weren't switched after I took these pictures. So somebody went to no end of trouble to switch the vases and then arrange the flowers as they are in the painting. Just think what a job that'd be. And why? What was gained?'

'Don't you think we ought to sleep on it?' she asked.

I slid them back into their envelope. 'And there's another thing.'

'Oh no.'

'Why go to all that trouble to switch the genuine vase up to the balcony on Tuesday night when the odds were it'd be back in its old place, anyway, on Wednesday, because Roy had just about finished with it.'

She thumped the pillow. 'Oh damn you, Richard. I was all dozy, and about ready to get to sleep, and you've got me wide awake again.'

'But you like to keep in touch,' I reminded her, reaching for my pyjamas because it was now much cooler.

Then I lay beside her, wide awake, trying to make sense of it and if I slept at all it couldn't have been for long, because I remember the dawn, and when I swung my legs down to the floor my head was woolly and thick with wandering thoughts.

11

Friday morning. Our last night at the manor was coming up. Breakfast was a miserable affair. Rex and Lewis kept as far apart as possible and Carla was in a vile mood. She, if nobody else, she declared, was intending to go home that very morning, but I noticed later that she made no move to leave. It was the atmosphere that held her. Venables came and consulted with Poynton at around ten and there was general speculation as to whether an arrest would be made that day. After all, it was all so much more exciting than applying colour to a flat surface.

I tackled Bruno early but he backed off. 'No Richard, I don't want to hear any more theories.'

'Just tell me,' I asked him. 'Can you be absolutely certain it was your genuine Chinese vase that Roy brought down to the studio?'

'Didn't I say? Of course I'm certain.'

'I mean . . . you *said* it was a kind of act, you and Roy. Did you actually examine it?'

His lips were bloodless. 'I examined it and it was the genuine one.'

'Then do me a favour . . .'

'I'm not getting involved with any more of your ideas.'

I grimaced. 'I'm not asking you to do anything. Simply, not to do something.'

He eyed me with suspicion. 'What must I not do?'

'Don't mention that you know your genuine vase is back on the balcony.'

His eyebrows shot up. 'Is that all? I can do that.'

'Nearly all. Now, now . . . don't run away. I'd just like to borrow the key to Roy's room.'

It wasn't officially sealed, only locked. Bruno wasn't going to get himself arrested for allowing me the access. But he shuddered.

'I couldn't do that.'

'I just want a look around.'

'For what?' he demanded.

'A tube of glue.'

He absorbed that. His eyes went vacant. 'If you need glue, I've got some you can have.'

'I just want to look,' I told him, my voice even. 'Not touch. Look.'

He capitulated and led me to his office, found me a key, and pressed it into my palm. 'Don't lose it, Richard. It's a master key, and fits all the doors.'

Useful, that. I thanked him and wandered away casually. Or rather, I hoped I looked casual because inside I was tense and jittery. Somewhere just beyond my sphere of understanding was the answer to all this, and I couldn't quite reach it. In the meantime, I knew, Samantha was in danger.

I walked into the banqueting hall trying to look like a man who hadn't noticed the vase switch. My nerves were taut. I jumped when Bert said: 'Psst!' at my elbow. Never did anything right, did Bert. A cleared throat would have been enough. I beat him to it.

'No, Bert. There's no chance they're going to open up that

studio. Forget it, mate. You're not going to fire that vase this week.'

'You're not supposed to leave it too long.'

'Bad luck.' I tried to move away but he kept pace, almost skipping.

'I've had a look at that seal, Richard.'

I paused. Faced him. 'Now just you get those thoughts out of your head,' I told him.

'It's only a piece of wire with a lead seal. Could cut it easy.'

'They'd toss you inside to rot.'

'But not till after I'd fired it,' he claimed brightly.

I gave him a full-scale lecture on it, forbidding him from going near. With a bit of luck, I put the fear of damnation into him because he looked very downtrodden when he stumbled away.

Then I went and had a look at both the seals myself.

When a room or premises is sealed legally, there is no set procedure. Sometimes it takes the form of security, a warehouse, for instance, getting the full treatment of heavy chain and a high-security padlock. But in other cases it's purely nominal, more of a gesture, a tape across the jamb of a door as a symbol, and not much more. So I went to check.

From the corridor direction the door to the studio was of recent manufacture, the corridor having been built only as covered access when the barn became a studio. It had a strong lock. The seal was a piece of pink ribbon, the lock presenting the security challenge. There was no way through there, not without force.

I went out on to the terrace. The day was brightening, and smelt brand new. Painting outdoors was feasible. Sam was there, with Lewis at her elbow, both of them exclaiming at some game they'd invented. It involved each using alternate brushfuls of paint and working on the same canvas. Scrabble in colour. I grinned but did not intrude.

I began on a tour of the estate, hoping to make it last the morning, trying to locate everybody before I approached Roy's room. I found Veronica, struggling to get the Degas effect with wild poppies; Rex, flourishing his shaving brush, but with his back protected by a large rock, I noticed; Amelia, trying a change with quick sketches of a mallard and chicks, and all looking happy enough in their tasks.

Unhappiness, I decided, was a sealed studio, when you want to get in.

I'd done a circuit, my steps naturally leading me back towards the house by way of the cobbled yard behind the studio. This gave me the opportunity to study the seal on the yard door.

This door was part of the security system. I was well aware of this because I'd arranged it myself. It had an automatic lock, which dropped into place electrically when the alarms were set at eleven at night. During daylight hours it was therefore not locked, so that the official seal was the only barrier. A bit of wire with a lead seal, Bert had said.

They had taken two staples and hammered one each into the door and the frame. Then they'd linked a loop of wire through each staple, and where the ends overlapped they'd clinched on a lead seal. It was effective. But I could see that one of the staples was not fully home. A pointed instrument, such as the tang of one of the three files in my tool kit, could be inserted in the space and the staple could be levered free. Then the wire would lift off and the door swing open. Afterwards, the staple could be tapped back into its original holes, and nobody need know a thing.

This was purely academic speculation, you realize.

Strolling away from there I came face to face with Poynton, who gave a small grimace and said: 'It's still sealed.'

'So I see.'

'The Chief's here,' he told me. 'Wants a word with you.'

'Right,' I said briskly. 'The office?'

He nodded and left me to find my way there myself.

Venables was reading a report and did not look up, simply gestured to my usual chair. An old trick, that. It's supposed to impress but indicates a small lack of confidence. When he did look up it was with a smile, unexpected and rather sour, but a smile.

'I've got a confession to make,' he said. 'That first night, I told you a lie. I had not obtained your personal records.'

'I realized that. Far too quick and much too flattering.'

'But I've got it all now. Prone to irresponsibility, it tells me.

Prefers to improvise, it says. A reluctance to accept orders.'

'That sounds more like it.'

'But you got results, it seems. I don't have to tell you that you've been getting far too many results around here for my liking and it's going to stop. From now on, you *will* take orders. I'm not going to waste time framing charges against you, Patton. Obstruction of the police, blah, blah, would do for a start. But, if necessary I'll make time. So . . . put one finger wrong from now on, and you'll have me to contend with. Understood?'

'Understood.' I pushed back my chair. Made for the door.

'One thing,' he said. I paused. He gazed past my left ear. 'I understand you're quite close to Bruno Fillingley. I'd like your impressions . . .'

I stood there, nothing on my face I hoped. 'I can't help you with Bruno. We're *too* close.'

'You're an officer of the law.'

'Ex. Everybody's been telling me how ex I am. Out of it and past it. No, Mr Venables, you'd better leave me out.'

I saw that he realized he'd made an error. Still, he'd tried. He nodded, acknowledging his failure.

'All right if I leave now?'

'Of course.'

I had my hand on the doorknob when he spoke quietly, almost to himself.

'How wonderful to be retired.'

I turned. He had his fingers steepled, thumbs tapping his teeth, eyes on me dreamily.

'To be able to indulge yourself in personal loyalties,' he went on. 'I bet you never thought of it like that. No – you had to go rushing round. A rogue elephant who's shut off from the herd, crashing around and uprooting everything in sight. And I bet you've been treating yourself to all sorts of cynicism and bitter comment.' He raised his eyebrows, but I didn't interrupt, he was doing so well. 'And look at the benefits you ought to be enjoying. Your own decisions, your own actions, your own ideas . . . and taking your own risks. I envy you, Mr Patton, really I do.'

He stopped. 'Finished?' I asked.

'I'd just like you to think about it, and decide to leave me to get on with this alone. That's all. This is a straightforward case. Why complicate it?'

I wondered whether to mention switched vases. Decided not to. I smiled instead.

'Staying to lunch?'

'I don't think so.'

I opened the door, to find Poynton reaching forward the other side. I stood back for him. I'd noticed that Venables had brought sandwiches.

I now knew where everybody was except Bert. I wasn't worried about him; I could overawe him into silence. And Bruno I didn't have to consider because it was he who'd lent me the key.

I ran up the stairs and was round the balcony in seconds, into Roy's room in two more and locked it behind me.

It smelt stale. I had to resist the temptation to open the window, while I stood in the centre of the room looking round. He'd made it his own, but all the same he had not collected around himself the personal evidence of any specific personality. There was no TV set, no hi-fi record equipment, no row of books or pile of magazines. What the devil did he do with his spare time, I wondered. Or did he allow himself no spare time, packing his life with work, food and sleep, to give himself no time to contemplate the mess he'd made of his life?

I began to search the room. As the police had finished with it, I didn't have to worry about fingerprints. As Roy had finished with it, I did not have to leave his drawers and cupboards looking as though they hadn't been touched.

No particular strength of character was revealed by his possessions. He was an artist. That much was obvious. On the wall was hung a still life of fruit, glowingly real. Against the wall leaned his previous effort at *Still Life with Pistol*. It looked just like the one in the studio, complete with pistol and petals on it. Four petals. There were spare tubes of paint, brushes and canvases in the bottom drawer of his dressing table.

Nowhere did I find evidence that he'd kept any cartridges around. I'd have expected a cartridge box, even perhaps empty. And nowhere did I find a tube of impact adhesive.

I locked up carefully behind me and slipped the key into my

pocket, wondering whether to go and tell Venables that I'd found no glue. But I didn't think he'd be enthusiastic.

For the rest of the day I flaunted my good behaviour. Amelia tried to sound me out on my thoughts but sharing them with Amelia could have been difficult, particularly as they were disorganized. I sat beside her as she worked, saying nothing, and admiring her sketches. Poynton had nothing to complain about, either. Didn't I accompany him on his round of working painters and stand at his shoulder, explaining the various techniques, in so far as I'd learnt them? I couldn't fathom Poynton. His interest seemed genuine.

Bruno had no time for me. There was the following morning's show to prepare. He was worried about his criticisms, something Lewis had said making him uncertain about his approach.

'Encouragement, Bruno, encouragement,' I advised. 'Why else d'you think they come here?'

But he was not keen on accepting my advice.

'Did you get a word with Marion?' I asked.

He was holding one of Rex's watercolours at arm's length. 'Last night? Well, no . . . other things . . . you know.'

'Changing your mind?'

He turned on me angrily. 'Don't be ridiculous.'

'Then don't you think you should?'

'It's none of your business.' He averted his face, changed his mind and his tone. 'I just don't see it's a good idea for us to make too much show of it.'

'But Marion doesn't see it like that?'

'You know what women are, Richard.'

'Well no. A complete mystery to me. But if I were you I'd try to get down to the gatehouse some time tonight. I know that much. Not too late, I'd suggest. Around eleven. Dark enough by that time.'

He faced me again. 'If I go, it'll be when I decide.'

'Of course, Bruno. Of course.'

Dinner that night was quiet. Hardly anyone said a word. Venables was known still to be in the building and this rather destroyed Poynton's image as one of us. Anything we said would get straight back to Venables, the memory still fresh.

Afterwards, we all gathered as usual in the drawing room.

143

Poynton was the only one trying to make a social event of it. I sat beside Amelia in my bush jacket, the one with the large pockets. In one pocket was the eight inch file from my tool kit, minus its wooden handle. I'd filed its tang to a sharp point, which I hoped wouldn't work its way through the material. In the opposite pocket was my small flat torch, which I didn't expect to need, but you never know. Timing would be important.

Just before ten we began drifting away to our rooms. I didn't know what arrangement Lewis had made for Samantha's safety that night, but it didn't require my assistance. I therefore stood at our open window, looking out at a clear sky and the promise of half an hour's good light. The atmosphere between us was relaxed.

'Care for a stroll?' I asked, aware that she'd reached the pyjama stage.

'I'm rather tired, Richard.'

'Mind if I go myself? A walk round the grounds.'

'Why should I mind? But don't take too long.' A short laugh. 'You don't want to be caught outside when the alarms are set.' A brighter laugh when she realized what that would mean. 'And the gatehouse is occupied.'

I scratched my head with the pipe stem. 'I dunno. Could be a good idea.' And used that as an exit line.

I intended to be back well before eleven, though I'd laid on a fall-back with Bruno that might delay the setting of the alarms. Amelia didn't know that and was still chuckling when I left. Not too flattering, I thought.

I made nothing secretive about it but walked with manly strides into the distance until I could be certain that trees and shrubbery completely hid me from the house, then I made a circuit, using the route I'd worked out during the day, and came to the cobbled yard within five minutes. There I stood for a while in the shadows but nothing was moving. The windows of Rex and Veronica overlooked the yard but the lights were now on in both the rooms and the curtains were drawn. It was not too late, I thought, to cancel the whole thing but I had a strong yearning to get a look at that vase.

I crossed to the studio door and produced the file. The light was still good. I'd need all of it inside, anyway. The staple lifted out with surprising ease. I allowed the wire loop to dangle, loose staple hooked on it, pushed the door open, slid inside, and quietly closed the door behind me.

The roof windows were north facing, the sun lowering a little north of west. The light was a warm glow throughout the studio. It smelt peaceful, the dust having had time to settle and find rest, with overlying it the smell of turpentine. I moved forward. There was no necessity at that stage to use my torch.

They had not interfered with the group set-up, nor with the canvas on its easel. I could have repeated exactly my initial set of photos, except for the absence of the pistol. But now I had no interest in the pistol. The four petals had been explained into insignificance.

I didn't know what I expected to find. The vase was an excuse. This expedition was, I knew, more a gesture of defiance. What had Venables said? I could take my own risks.

What first attracted my attention was the fact that the flowers had not drooped. After nearly a fortnight, I'd have expected them to be shedding their petals. In fact, I'd assumed that the seven petals, four of which Roy had painted, had been shed by the flowers, three in excess of requirements, thus explaining the fact that he hadn't been intending to paint them in. If he'd picked them off, why had he picked seven? But the flower cluster didn't look droopy, in spite of the fact that the water Amelia had put in would surely have evaporated by that time.

Curious about this, I peered into the vase. This required my torch. There wasn't any water in there at all. What was inside was tissue paper, the soft kind that Amelia used to lay between her clothes when she packed. It had been thrust down quite firmly, so that it held each flower stem in position.

It was only then that I realized the flowers were artificial and made of silk. I searched for the three petals that had blown to the floor, found them, and checked. Yes, silk, and wonderfully made. I looked, then, at the flowers in the vase and could find no missing petals. Roy must have brought the loose petals there separately.

I had seen no spare flowers or petals in his room. This was strange because the implication had been, from the fact that the four on the pistol had been glued on, that Roy had glued fresh petals to the gun for each painting, removing them afterwards. Otherwise, why had he not produced the pistol with the petals already attached? And if he produced four each time, why had he made it seven for his last painting?

With awakening interest, I stood back and considered what it all meant. Roy had probably used these same flowers in every painting as he'd used the same vase and the same hunting horn. They were no doubt washable so that he could produce them, looking fresh, each time. I recalled his look of surprise when Amelia had put water into his vase but he'd been too polite to comment. No doubt, after we'd left him alone, he'd poured out the water and substituted tissue paper.

But had he? This was not the same vase. If the flowers had been switched from one vase to the other and tissue used to make sure the arrangement matched the painting, then it had been well done – and must have taken quite a time. And . . . done after the murder? If it had been done before, Roy would surely have noticed. But nobody wants to hang around after a murder especially when this vase switching business seemed to have achieved nothing. Certainly it had no influence on the hiding of the murderer's identity. So, the obvious, had it been done as part of a plan to steal the genuine vase? But the genuine vase hadn't been stolen. It had simply been taken back to the alcove next to Roy's room.

All this I found very interesting but it was getting me nowhere. It was then that I noticed something very strange about the painting itself. It seemed to be a finished work. Well, all right, he'd expected to finish it that night, but – and I bent close with my torch – he'd actually signed it. Roy Towers. In black on the brown background of table surface. Surely the signature was the artist's last action when a painting is proudly completed. And yet the reconstruction of the murder required that he should have left the studio on one of his patrols, giving time for the pistol to be loaded, and had been shot as he sat down to continue. He'd even had the palette on his thumb and the brush in his other hand.

And there they were, palette and brush, neatly laid on the table beside his container of paint tubes. I picked up the brush. Its sable hairs were stiff now with hardened paint, and it was a mid brown. The palette was liberally smeared with the untidy scramble of colours that artists always acquire but only one colour seemed to be solidified into sufficient quantity to suggest that he'd been using it. This was the same brown as on the brush.

So, what had he sat down to paint in his last few seconds? The canvas indicated he'd finished and all he could possibly have been intending to add to it could only have been the three petals. These were yellow. But he'd had brown on his brush.

I was unable to pursue the possibilities any further, because at that point I was hit on the back of the head forcefully with something heavy and hard and in those circumstances you're lucky if you get time for the single thought: will I wake up?

My first impression on doing so was that it was considerably darker in there. I put this down to depleted eyesight but as I groped to my knees and stood swaying it didn't become any lighter. My torch was at my feet so I scrambled for it and found it still to be working. I swept the paltry beam around.

Clearly, I'd discovered something I was not supposed to, because the possibility of any further conjectures had been removed. The canvas was a slashed and tattered mess, face down on the floor. The palette had been trampled to splinters and I couldn't see the brush anywhere. The flowers had been snatched from their vase and scattered, the hunting horn severely dented by the same foot and, worst of all, Bruno's blue and white vase was in pieces around my feet. How happy Bruno would be that his genuine one was safe upstairs. How much happier if I hadn't entered the studio at all.

It was then that the fact of the darkness entered my awareness. It must be late, later than I'd intended. I fumbled back the sleeve of my jacket and turned the torch on my watch. It was a minute to eleven when my eyes focused.

I had one minute to get out of there with the door shut behind me. I plunged for the door, not having realized how weak I was. My head swam and I staggered, found I'd run into the wall, blinked around for the door, felt my way along to it, and grabbed at the handle.

The two things came together. I swung the door open just as the electric lock operated. One was a micro-second before the other. The effect was appalling because hell broke loose. This I'd advised. The idea was to provide sufficient impact of sound to scare the hardiest of criminals. With my head already throbbing, it nearly forced me to my knees.

I pushed my way into the dusk leaving the door swinging behind me. It was much lighter out there, lighter than I'd have wished. I made a weaving lunge for the nearest shrubbery. For a full minute that hideous din went on, then it cut off abruptly leaving a second's vacuum of silence behind it, to be replaced by shouts and somewhere a woman screaming.

By that time I was well clear and recovering my senses. I'd instinctively managed an extended curve so that it was possible I'd be able to return to the house looking like an innocent man. Shapes were running between me and the house, heading round towards the studio. I joined them, not hurrying as they were but at a fast walk.

At that time I thought I was going to get away with it, my conscience not operating very forcefully. After all, the crime of physical violence had been done to me whereas I'd merely broken and entered. I considered I was still on the debit side. Walter Race would have approved this reasoning.

Just before I rounded the corner into the yard the shouts became louder and crystallized into the words: 'Stay where you are.' I burst into the yard. A number of shadows confronted me, silhouetted against the glare of two powerful torches. Fully caught in the light, backed into a corner, was Bert Inskip, his eyes wild and his hands extended in front of his face.

'I didn't do it,' he shouted. 'I didn't do it.'

If it had been no more than the breaking of an official seal, I'd have left him to it. What was he doing there, anyway? But there was also the question of destruction of property. I stepped forward.

'It wasn't him. It was me.'

Noble words. It was me. Never in my professional days had I encountered them. But I wasn't feeling noble, I was simply furious at the stupid bugger, lurking there in the yard.

They turned on me, the torches blinding me and sending pains shooting through my head.

'I might have guessed,' said Venables. 'What the hell have you been up to in there?'

'Richard!' cried Amelia from somewhere in the shadows, her voice full of distress, though whether because I'd been caught or because I hadn't taken her into my confidence, I couldn't tell.

And Poynton said: 'Let's go inside and have a look.'

With only the two of them there and pretty busy with the scene of destruction there was nobody available for crowd control. They all trooped inside and there was a general protest of horror that a work of art had been destroyed and a howl from Bruno when he saw his vase in pieces on the floor.

'That wasn't me,' I said, but a denial holds less force than an admission and this time I was ignored. Who else could it have been, I could imagine them thinking, who'd want to destroy all this? Who else but a heathen who doesn't even paint?

'Let's get back to the office,' said Venables savagely. 'Bring him along.' Meaning me.

Bert jerked at his sleeve. 'Mr Venables.'

'What is it?'

'Does this mean I can use the kiln now?'

I could've sighed for him.

'It'll be sealed again,' said Venables, raising his voice so that everybody was included. 'See to it, Inspector, and this time let's have a proper job. And we'll have this place cleared at once, please. Haven't any of you got beds to go to?'

Veronica was by the door, hands pressed to her face and eyeing Bert with what I took to be blank disbelief. She couldn't really have thought him capable of destruction, surely, but he wouldn't meet her eye with firm denial. Amelia peered round her shoulder with a stricken look. Carla was nodding to herself as though saying: isn't this just the sort of thing you could expect round here?

Bruno was collecting up the bits of his vase, each one precious to him. After all, he'd made it himself.

I led the way to the office. Nobody had enquired about my welfare so the first thing I did was have Poynton look at my bump. He said it didn't look much to him. But he was outside it.

'Evidence,' I explained to Venables. 'In case anybody gets the idea I did all that destruction.'

We were seated as before but this time with Poynton standing at my shoulder. Venables, seated opposite to me, was in a savage mood. 'You admitted you did it,' he reminded me.

'I was talking about removing the seal.'

'Didn't I warn you?' he demanded, knuckles white on the desk surface. 'Didn't I say?'

'I merely wanted to look at the evidence . . .'

'You were told about the weapon and the petals, damn it.'

'. . . in the light of what I'd been told.'

'And what good has it done you?' He didn't give me time to tell him. 'But you've gone too far, Patton. I shall be preparing charges against you for breaking and entering and for the wilful destruction of private property. Now laugh that off.' He sat back. I'd handed it to him. Pleasure blunted his anger.

'I've already denied the destruction bit and anyway, you know I wouldn't have done such a thing.'

'Know it? Do I?'

'No possible motive.'

'We'll see about that. You're forgetting you're one of my suspects for murder.'

'If we're not going to talk sense,' I said, 'I'm wasting my time.' He had gone a little red. 'I only wanted to check the evidence of my photographs against the present position after a lapse of three days.'

'And considering the place has been sealed until you managed to get at it . . .'

'I was intending to replace the seal.'

'. . . I trust you found everything the same.'

We had been talking through each other. There's only one thing to do about that: take a breath and wait. I did. He appeared to be waiting for me.

'Well, that's the trouble,' I told him. 'It *was* the same.'

'What d'you mean by that?' he demanded, leaning forward angrily. He held up his hand. 'No, don't tell me. For pity's sake, don't tell me. I've had enough of your theories.'

'I wasn't going to trouble you with it,' I assured him.

'Thank God for that.'

I turned my head up to Poynton. 'Don't you think you ought to be sealing that door?' I asked him. 'Seeing I didn't get around to it.'

'Oh my God!' Poynton gasped. He gave one apologetic grimace at his Chief, and dived out.

Venables and I sat and waited and continued to chat in the mood we'd established. He explored all the possible charges he could level at me, with me countering to the best of my ability. We both knew I'd been naughty but not really criminal. Then, belatedly, he asked me what had happened and I'd just finished telling him, but minus my observations, when Poynton returned with Bert's arm firmly in his fist.

'This stupid sod was back in there, playing about with that oven,' he said angrily, passing on his own guilt for not having prevented it.

'It's a kiln,' Bert protested, shaking off the hand. 'I was only checking how it worked.'

'What the hell for?' Venables demanded. 'You weren't going to be able to use it.'

Bert had only been window shopping, running his hand over the glossy new luxury car that wasn't going to be his. He'd been dreaming of great things.

'Just wanted to look at it,' he mumbled.

Venables caught my eye and jerked his head. 'I'll see *you* in the morning.' It was a threat. He'd come armed with warrants. As I was closing the door he called after me. 'And get to bed and stay there.'

I went slowly up to our room. Now my head was throbbing and I could have done with some sympathy. Amelia was settled in when I opened the door, head buried in the pillow, a sheet over her now that the air was cooler.

'Amelia?'

'Please get undressed and into bed, Richard. I don't want to discuss anything.'

'I'll be a few minutes, love. Just want a word with Bruno.'

I thought she mumbled something though it could have been a sob. I closed the door gently behind me.

I'd really annoyed her by getting into trouble without her assistance.

12

Bruno needed more comfort than me. He was as shattered as nis vase, the bits of which he was staring at on a sheet of paper.

'It could've been worse,' I said. 'It might have been the genuine one.'

He looked up from his chair. 'I *made* this. With my own hands.'

'So you make another. That's the point of originals, they can't be done again. Copies can be copied.'

He didn't lift his head. 'I don't want your philosophy,' he told me, quieter now. 'I don't want anything from you. Nothing. I don't want you near me, Richard.'

'But I didn't do the breaking, you know.'

'It wouldn't have happened if you hadn't *been* there.' He twisted to look at me over his shoulder because I'd been moving around restlessly. 'Don't you see that? Can't you see anything past your stupid theories and your fancy logic?'

I crouched down on my heels so that his face was level with mine. 'Wouldn't you like to know *why* your genuine one is safe, Bruno? Doesn't that interest you?'

'No, it doesn't.'

I straightened, my knees aching. 'I'm sorry for you, Bruno. Truly I am. But I've got a nasty feeling that the truth's going to be important to you.'

I waited but he didn't ask what I meant. I went out and closed his door behind me and stood silently on the balcony. I didn't know how long he had left so he might as well spend it in peace.

I couldn't see why Venables was holding back. Bruno had the right motive; he was in love with Roy's wife. It should be clear by now that she'd come to the manor house not to see Roy, not to try to force him to return to her, whatever hysterical performances she might put on at times, but to see Bruno. It was a little late for him to put on an act and refrain from visiting her. Everybody could see through that. And just as easily they'd see that a man such as Bruno would not have access to thirty-eight calibre cartridges. But Marion did. She was the widow of a pistol club member, who himself had been licensed to possess handguns and ammunition.

They have to have two safes, these authorized users, steel safes set in walls or anchored to concrete floors, one for the ammunition, one for guns, and in separate rooms, the keys to be kept secure in a third room. The police have to call round from time to time to check that these regulations are being complied with. This is a spot check, unannounced. Consequently, it saves a lot of trouble if the wife knows where the keys are kept or knows the safe's combination. So Marion would have access to ammunition if Roy had left any behind at his home. He'd claimed he had none at the manor house.

To a jury it would sound bad that Marion had brought to Bruno six of Roy's own cartridges, with which to load Roy's gun in order to shoot Roy through the heart.

Venables must have seen all this and yet he was holding his hand. He surely couldn't flinch at their alibi. Neither of us could have shot Roy because we were spending two hours in each other's arms! Oh, lovely. That'd convict them out of hand.

And yet Venables was holding off.

At that moment, Venables was interviewing Bert, hoping he'd explain what he was doing in the yard when they arrived, and of course Bert would be explaining that he wanted to use the kiln, and if somebody else could get in, then so could he. Venables, furious and frustrated, would vent his anger on somebody who couldn't fight back, and would go at him and at him, oh . . . for hours.

So why didn't I nip along to Bert's room and have a quick look at that wonderful vase of his? After all, I still had the master key. And didn't the throb in my head remind me that the Chinese vase, which Bert had said he was trying to copy, was apparently at the centre of things?

You can't go on asking yourself questions like this and do nothing about it. I found myself slipping the key into his lock, moving inside, closing the door behind me, and putting on the light.

There was no possible reason why the vase should not have been out in the open. Yet there was no sign of it. My interest sharpened and I went round the room quickly, opening anything large enough to contain it.

He had it standing in the corner of his wardrobe. I lifted it out.

One minute later I was back in our room. Amelia sat up as I put on the light.

'Whatever . . . what've you got there?'

'It's Bert's vase.'

'So, what am I to say?'

I went up to the bed, supporting the vase on my two palms. 'Just look at it, Amelia. Go on. It won't bite you.'

She tried a smile, then a frown. 'What's the matter with it?' Her interest broke through. 'Let me see.'

'I don't know what it's supposed to look like because I've never seen an unbaked one before.'

'I have.'

'But there's certainly something wrong with it.'

The basic vase was a matt white. On it was now crudely painted the three-clawed dragon pattern that appeared on Bruno's vases, this done in a dull grey.

'It looks all right from here,' she said.

'It's a bit bigger than Bruno's. I tried it against one of them.'

'It'd have to be because they shrink when you fire them. And he hasn't put on the glaze. Otherwise . . .' She shrugged, obviously wondering what I was talking about.

'And is it supposed to be soft?' I asked.

'Good Lord, no. Hard. Brittle. As delicate as an egg at this stage. Do be careful what you're doing . . .'

I bent a thumb over the top of it and applied pressure. She raised a hand in protest. My thumb sank in an eighth of an inch. The dent remained when I removed the pressure.

'This one's soft,' I told her. 'In fact, it isn't china clay at all, it's polystyrene, that light, soft packing stuff they use these days.'

'But it can't be!' Her world didn't include soft vases. 'It looks heavy, anyway.'

'Oh, it is, it is. Here.' I tossed it to her.

With an exclamation she caught it as though I'd tossed her a hedgehog, then she stared at it in her hands. She bent over and placed it in her lap and tried the surface herself. She peered inside it.

'There's a proper vase inside,' she murmured.

'So it seemed to me.'

I waited, not rushing her. There'd been a lot of conjecture flying around in the past few days and she was suspicious. At last she looked up at me, her eyes shining but her lower lip uncertain.

'I don't understand.'

I sat on the edge of the bed and took her hand. 'I nearly got it last night. I said to you: why should the vases have been switched when Roy had about finished and the genuine one would've been back on the balcony on Wednesday.'

'And a fine time it was to tell me that. I had the devil's own game getting to sleep.'

'But it wasn't, was it?' I asked. 'Going to be back on Wednesday, I mean. The switch just had to be after Roy was dead or he'd have noticed, so somebody who knew a few things about police procedure would have realized it would be sealed away.'

'The last chance to switch them.' She shook her head. 'It's kind of morbid.'

'Worse than that – what if Roy was killed purely to bring that about?'

She put her free hand to her mouth. 'But that's horrible.'

'Murders have been done for less.' I paused but she didn't say anything. So I went on. 'What the murder achieved was to make sure the studio *was* sealed.'

She couldn't accept it. 'You think that's what it's about?' Her eyes were huge.

I nodded. 'It all fits. Look at it. This place is burglar-proofed up to the hilt. There'd be absolutely no chance of walking out with that vase in the night even if you could tell which of the ten was the genuine one. Oh I know, there've been gaps in the security the last few days but that couldn't have been counted on. What *could* be counted on was that Roy always managed to drop on the genuine vase for his group. That could be discovered by sending one or two people for courses over a period of a few months. It's routine with this sort of thing. They'd have the thing thoroughly researched.'

'They?'

'Bert Inskip and Veronica. This pose of theirs of being separate and almost not on speaking terms – that'd be a blind to distract attention. But they would come here with the knowledge that they couldn't get the vase out at night and that it'd have to be in the open, in daylight, say on the morning they both left. And look how it's all worked out. Or rather, how they've made it work out.'

'It's quite cold-blooded.' She shuddered.

'Yes,' I agreed. Art thieves are not usually murderous. This time I'd met two who were. 'Have you noticed something about that thing? There's a join down opposite sides. Well, there would be, wouldn't there, or they couldn't have got that one inside. It's a polystyrene sleeve that opens up and I expect there's another Chinese vase in there. Probably you can get cheap copies all over the place. But Bert came here with the intention of walking out on the last morning with that thing under his arm, looking just like it is now only by that time it'd have the genuine one inside that sleeve. And Bruno would watch him go and shake his hand and suspect nothing.'

'It's quite diabolical. I don't think I want to hear any more,' she lied.

I patted her hand. 'But so clever,' I comforted. 'Bert would come here with half a dozen thirty-eight cartridges in his pocket. He'd know about the Smith & Wesson in the still life group. He'd go down to the studio as late in the fortnight as he could, which turned out to be the Tuesday, and while Roy was patrolling the building he'd load the gun and wait for him.'

I paused then. I had no explanation for the brown paint on the brush nor for the fact that Roy had apparently finished his painting. But maybe those three petals explained that. Comforted by the thought, I carried on.

'Then he shot him. The studio's the only place within the alarm system from where shots wouldn't be heard. I expect Veronica helped him then, bringing down any one of the vases from the balcony and assisting with the switch. The flowers had to look as they did in the painting. They did a good job. And then they left, replacing the genuine vase in the place from which Veronica had taken the copy. *Now* do you see what had been accomplished?'

Amelia saw. She'd been ahead of me, I decided, being patient out of a consideration for my ego.

'Being professional crooks,' she said, 'they'd know the studio would be sealed.'

'Exactly. And . . .'

'And Bruno would believe that his genuine vase was shut away in there quite safely.'

'So that when he saw Bert walking out with his unfired vase under his arm . . .'

She pounced in. '*Another* benefit from the sealed studio. Nobody would expect Bert to have fired it.'

'And Bruno,' I said, 'wouldn't question it for a second. Don't forget, tomorrow morning there's the show of work, with Bruno doing his criticism bit, and nobody would be surprised if Bert wasn't there.'

Amelia was delighted with the audacity and cleverness of it, clapping her palms to her cheeks, and completely, for the moment, forgetting the viciousness of the shooting.

'And where Bert would be,' she cried, 'is the balcony, where he'd leave his copy and take the genuine one. It's dark up here during the day. Nobody would spot it. Oh heavens, Richard, what a wicked and ingenious scheme.'

I watched her, smiling. She hadn't envisaged the next step.

'You'll notice,' I said, 'how Bert's been pretending that he wanted the studio opening up when what he really wanted was the opposite.'

She was immediately serious. 'Is that why he hit you on the head?'

'Must be. I'd opened it up. He destroyed all those things to create another crime and make sure it got sealed up again.'

She bit her lip. 'Is Venables still here?'

'He's downstairs, asking Bert a few questions.'

'Then you can take him this . . .'

'And have him throw me out?'

'He wouldn't!'

I stood up and reached over for the vase. 'There's a distinct lack of enthusiasm for my ideas,' I assured her. 'No. I'm going to take this back and watch what happens. Tomorrow morning, Bert won't be the only one absent from the show. I'll be watching on the balcony. See if I can catch him in the act. How's that?'

She was uncertain, not having missed the fact that Bert, if he'd brought cartridges with him, might also have brought a pistol into which the spares would fit.

'If you'll be careful, Richard.'

'My very best lurking-in-the-shadows act,' I promised her. I smiled, went to the door, put off the light, and opened it.

There I was, out on the balcony again, buoyant and confident that I'd at last thought it through. Or nearly all of it. But as I turned towards Bert's door I realized it was open and that his light was on. He'd returned. He was casting moving shadows.

Then I heard him moan, close to a howl, as he discovered his loss. I hurried forward to his doorway, realizing that my plan for the following day had gone up the spout.

'This what you're looking for?' I asked, offering up the vase and improvising wildly. 'Sorry. Just borrowed it to show Amelia.' Which was ridiculous.

He was standing with panic in his eyes, swinging his arms as though to reach in all directions at once. The eyes focused on his vase. He took one step back, tripped and fell on to the edge of his bed. Then my intrepid killer, my cunning con-man, my subtle and nerveless crook, buried his face in his hands and began sobbing fit to break his heart.

Behind me, Rex said: 'How you do enjoy your bullying, Richard!'

I turned on him. I was suddenly furious, not because of his accusation, not even because Veronica was hovering just behind him, but because he had the stupidity to intrude in Bert's distress. Not, I was sure, that Bert had heard him. But all the same in that second Rex was close to getting his jaw broken.

I thrust him back against the door jamb vigorously and stuck a fist under his nose. 'Get away from here,' I said softly. 'And now.'

I swung him out on to the balcony and slammed the door on him. On Veronica, too. Then I picked up the vase from where it had fallen on the carpet and tossed it on the bed. It rolled against Bert's thigh but he didn't seem to notice.

He was dragging his fingers down his face with hysterical little jabs as though to tear the flesh from his face. I fetched the padded stool from the dressing table and placed it in front of him, sat on it, and reached for my pipe. Behind him the door opened softly. I jerked my head up, but it was only Veronica, and alone, subdued and concerned and very silent. She closed it just as gently behind her and remained by the door.

Returning my attention to Bert, I said in a tough voice: 'You gonna come clean, Bert? The jig's up.'

Tears always upset my balance and I usually say the daftest things. In this case, I wasn't sure what the jig was as it didn't seem my theory had been valid but I appeared to have hit the right note. Bert raised his head and showed his teeth in what could've been a smile.

I drive through that factory gate in the morning it's like coming alive. I'm somebody there. I do a responsible job and I do it well. When I drive out I go to pieces because I'm driving towards . . .' He dropped his voice. '. . . Veronica,' he said hoarsely.

It took all my willpower to hold my eyes on his. Beyond him, she was peripheral and out-of-focus. I didn't see how she took that.

'But . . . at the factory . . .'

'I live a little.' He gave a tiny smile. 'Eight hours. A third of my life, that's all I live. And mind you – and I wouldn't tell anybody else – the job's not difficult. With everything on computers, the place runs itself. We load the machines as the computer tells us to. I don't do anything, just walk around pretending I'm in charge. Nothing can go wrong . . . well, not much ever does. Machine breakdowns throw the computer into a panic but I have a word with the lads and we work something out. Union trouble? Can't say we get much of that. Clive and me – that's the senior shop steward – we went to school together. I was a tiddler then and he used to look out for me. Still does, I reckon. And the buyers . . . well, you have to rely on the buyers but I trained them myself. So . . . the job does itself.'

But maybe wouldn't with a different Production Manager, I thought. 'I can understand why it suits you.'

'But you see what I'm getting at, Richard.'

'Perhaps a little.'

'I just don't *do* anything, that's the point. No achievement.'

'Now . . . come on . . .'

'Nothing I can hold up and say: I did this.' He dropped the cigarette stub in the vase, then turned in disgust from the pungent smoke rising from it. 'Like *that*,' he said, reaching over and putting the vase on the floor well out of the way. 'I make mistakes. It's nerves, I reckon.' He flapped his hands together, raised them, and rubbed his hair into a mess. 'Funny I don't get 'em at the factory. It's Veronica . . . I think it's her fault. Well, I know, really. Just trying to be loyal, I suppose. A man's not supposed to criticize his wife. But make no mistake, no criticism intended. She's a wonderful woman. Wonderful. And that,' he declared, 'is the trouble. Have you ever tried to live with somebody who can do anything and never makes a mistake? Have you? It makes you feel this high.' He reached down and nearly fell off the bed, trying to get his palm near the floor.

I caught his shoulder and hoisted him up. 'An active mind,' I told him. 'They can't help it.'

'All the same . . . here, I'll tell you. Shall I? Just a bit of it. She's got an Advanced Driver's certificate. It terrifies me to be with her in the car. She says she could scream, the way I drift along. So we bought two cars, the same, so as to be fair. If we're going anywhere, I simply start out an hour earlier. We go abroad a fortnight every year and she goes and takes evening language courses. Different countries every time and I have to sit there, Italy, Spain, France, Austria, and listen to her chatting to the waiters in their own language as though she was born there. It makes you feel like a spare part. You see what I mean. If we go in the winter, she's up the bloody ski slopes and racing the pro. In the summer she can swim the heart out of the life-guard round the bay. She walks on to golf courses and slams balls in all directions. She can shoot a bow and arrow and play bridge with the best people and chess with one hand while she gets a double top with the other. And me . . . me, I can't cope. I feel inferior. I cringe. I go to pieces.'

He snatched at the cigarette pack and tore it apart. He managed to scatter his matches so I offered him my lighter, bobbing the flame around in a wild chase of the cigarette he'd managed to capture.

'Just talking about it . . .' he said, taking a deep breath and choking. He recovered, his eyes red.

'Last year we went to a painting school in France where she knocked 'em sideways with her oil colours. Year before, Devon. Terracotta modelling, then. "Oh, isn't your wife clever, Mr Inskip!" they said. "Don't *you* do anything, Mr Inskip?" What can you say? No . . . I'm bloody useless? So . . . this time I could see it all happening again and I just couldn't bear the idea. You know, I thought maybe I'd have to strangle her . . . just for peace of mind. But . . .' He stared at his shaking hands. '. . . I'd only balls it up. So this time I thought something out.'

His eyes lit on me, shining. We're coming to the vase, I guessed. 'Something clever, Bert?'

'You listen, then you can tell me. We booked in this place.

You get a coloured brochure, and it had all this guff about the facilities – the kiln, it mentioned – and the usual come-on of a stately home, along with pictures. One of the pictures was his Chinese vase. So I got to thinking, see, and I went out and bought myself one like it. Didn't have to be special but it cost me thirty quid. Then I got a polystyrene shell made for it. Fred in Moulding did that for me, the foreman. And when I took it home – 'cause I had to do that – I conned Nicky . . .' He stopped, cocking his head. 'I used to call her that, when we were first married. Funny how things come back to you. But Veronica fits her better. Veronica who can do everything. Not Nicky. No.'

'The vase, Bert,' I said quickly, before she could say anything.

'Yes. Well . . . I took it home. I couldn't let her handle it, of course, so I had to lock it away, and told her I'd been attending evening classes in pottery. That was how the row came about. She said I'd make a fool of both of us and she said she wouldn't come here *with* me . . . oh, it's such a damned bore. Anyway, my idea was that I'd come here and pretend to put on the pattern . . .'

'You did a good job there, Bert. It's a good copy.'

He dismissed it with a wriggle of his fingers. 'It's nothing. I started off as a draughtsman. So – as I was saying – I was going to put on the pattern and cover it with glaze stuff . . . I *did* do a few nights at the pottery classes, 'cause you've got to make it look good. I was going to build up the suspense, you see. Everybody here waiting to see how it'd come out. I was hoping to get it in the kiln on the second Friday . . . Heh, we've just had that. And we'd all be gathered round when I opened the kiln up. But I knew the polystyrene would burn away to a black dust and take the pattern and the glaze with it. And there it'd be, my vase. *My* vase, Richard. Nobody would believe it. Bruno said he didn't think it could be done. But I'd have done it. And I'd take it home and stick it on the mantel, and she could see it every day . . .'

'You'd be proud, Bert. I can see that.'

'Lord – wouldn't I just!'

'Like a racehorse-owner, leading in the winner.'

'Just like him, yes.'

Like a racehorse-owner, I thought, who'd instructed an agent to buy a suitable horse, instructed a trainer to train it and to find the best jockey, and got his first sight of the horse on the day of the race. Yes, *he'd* be proud, leading it in, just a bit nervous in case the dratted animal bit off his fingers.

'And that blasted Roy Towers had to go and get himself shot,' Bert complained. 'And I've got myself all worked up.' He smiled. 'I made a right charlie of myself, didn't I?'

'I wouldn't say that.' The right charlie around there was sitting facing him.

'And it's all been for nothing.'

For the first time I risked a glance beyond his shoulder. Veronica was slipping out as quietly as she'd entered.

'I wouldn't say that, either.'

Poor Bert, I thought, he would never succeed in anything creative because he didn't understand pride. He could never feel the thrill of achievement because he couldn't imagine it, any more than I could understand a woman's glow when she first puts her hands on her child.

I gestured to the vase. 'So what will you do with that now?'

'Toss it in the dustbin, I reckon. No . . .' And he smiled a great, face-creaking smile. 'I'll give it to Veronica for her birthday and she'll hate it. Won't be able to get rid of it because it's a present so it'd be the only ornament or knick-knack or decoration, including the wallpaper, the paint on the wood-work, the curtains . . . half the damned furniture, even . . . that she hasn't done with her own clever little hands. And she'll *hate* it.'

When I left him he was still contemplating this tender thought. I made my way around the balcony. Or started to. Then I turned and went round the other way because I'd seen a dark shape leaning with elbows on the rail and staring down into the darkness of the banqueting hall. I didn't want to intrude.

I was passing Bruno's door. I paused, tapped. In pyjamas, he put his head out. 'What now, Richard?'

I dangled the key he'd lent me. 'Returning this.'

'It could've waited till morning, surely.'

'Sorry, Bruno. Good night.'

'Good night.'

Amelia was out of bed and pacing, her face shadowed with worry. 'You've been so long . . .'

I grinned at her. 'Sorry love. Been talking to Bert. Want to hear?'

'Of course.'

So I told her. Her expression hovered from disbelief to sympathy, to amazement. Finally she collapsed on the bed, stifling her laughter, because it was so late.

'Oh Richard . . . if you'd gone to Venables with it!'

'I hate to think.'

Then I laughed with her until she was silent in my arms. But really, you know, I was rather cast down over the failure of that theory. I'd liked it. Really liked it. I mean, it fitted so neatly into the background facts. So I didn't laugh wholeheartedly.

'Richard,' she whispered. 'Isn't it a good job you're retired.'

Afterwards, when she slept, I lay there and wondered what she'd meant. It hadn't sounded very complimentary to me.

13

The following morning was heavy with that deflation feeling when friends newly acquired were due to depart from your life and the after-breakfast packing seems to set a gloomy seal on it. I left Amelia to the suitcases and went down to see what was happening.

Bruno was in the banqueting hall where the show and criticism were to take place. I found him in a very puzzled mood.

'What am I going to do with these?' he asked me.

He had arranged a crescent of upright chairs and perched on them the various offerings, there being no wall board to hang them on, and had discovered that Veronica's selection of seven pastel paintings had disappeared, to be replaced by a fresh batch.

'Are they really hers?'

'They've got her initials on them.'

She had used a grey Ingres paper and brilliant red, yellow and green pastels. They were apparently flower studies but the style was childish and amateur. Scribble-scribble, as Bruno described it, very close to Marion's description of Roy's methods. But the end result was a mockery of Roy's results.

'Appalling,' he said. 'What can I say about them?'

'What comes first to the mind?'

'Rubbish.'

'Well . . . perhaps a little more charitable, Bruno. Why not: shows little talent, but one mark for effort?'

He grimaced. 'You think I should?'

'I imagine she'd expect it.'

She must have sat up all night doing those, I decided. Veronica had surpassed herself. Nicky was being reborn.

We had the show, then our last meal together, lunch, with an anticipated departure time of around two. But those final minutes of leave-taking always become extended. Addresses have to be exchanged, along with vows to keep in touch. It always turned out to be closer to three, Bruno said philosophically.

That would leave him two and a half hours to oversee the preparation for the arrival of the next group, preparing the rooms and his welcoming smile.

Amelia seemed eager to get going. We had everything in the Stag and there was no point in hanging around. I knew that she was anxious to have me away from there before I became involved again, but I lingered. I like to be last. Don't know why. But this time it didn't look as though I would be.

Carla had left first with only the most curt of leave-taking, Veronica and Bert next. Bert shook my hand with embarrassment and mumbled something and I smiled. Then he led off, Veronica following. Rex made a grand, gravel-thrown exit round the drive. But Lewis and Samantha seemed to be locked in an argument.

The show had been a success. Bruno had performed well so that everybody felt that the fortnight had been well spent, even Veronica, who'd taken Bruno's hard words, a little more polished than I'd suggested, with calm, straightforward nods. Bert had been there. Nobody had asked about his vase. Nobody had mentioned murder and attempted murder and assault with a blunt instrument.

It was a fine June afternoon, the last day of the month. I stood out front, with just a hint of headache, watching Sam and Lewis, he gesticulating with more and more emphasis. Then, throwing up his hands, he walked away from her and came stamping up to me.

'You have a word with her, Richard. She's having another attack of don't-think-I-coulds.'

'What about?'

'I want her to go in for some proper art training but she's gone all shy on me. It'd mean she'd have to come and live in London.'

I considered the fact that she'd handed out her present address to everybody and that the genuine vase *had* been switched from its table in the studio to its niche by the bathroom.

'Good idea,' I said.

'You approve?'

'Absolutely. She can't be allowed to go away and become all solitary again.'

'Too much talent,' he declared forcefully. 'But now she won't believe it. I think I can get her into the Slade.'

'You've got influence?'

'I teach there, damn it.'

'Ah!' I said.

So I went to have a word with Sam, she who would be so reluctant to abandon one leaking boat before she was sure the other would float.

'What's this nonsense I hear?' I asked cheerfully.

'It's not nonsense. I've got this little flat in Nottingham – high-rise – and I don't know I can afford to live in London.'

'With what I've seen of your painting, I don't think you can afford to pass up the chance.'

She drew a breath, summoning up all the paltry objections that she secretly hoped I'd be able to demolish, but we got no further with it. A large car was circling the lawn. Beside the driver was Poynton. In the rear, sitting beside Venables, was Marion. It was now clear why Venables had been holding his hand. He'd been using a little sensitivity not wishing to take Bruno away before the course was finished.

Venables got out of the car alone. It was clearly not expected that force would be required. The car had stopped well short so that Venables was able to adjust his smile before he spoke to Bruno, not triumphantly, but with sympathy.

'I'm afraid I'm going to have to ask you to come along with me, Mr Fillingley.'

Bruno shot one desperate, terrified look at me. 'But I can't.'

'You will be formally charged with the murder of Roy Towers and asked to make a statement. Your rights will be explained to you, and you may ask for a solicitor to be present.'

'And Marion?' Bruno asked in agony.

'She will be charged as an accomplice. Now, I'll come up with you and advise you about what you'll need . . .'

'I want to speak with her.'

'I'm sure we'll find time for that.'

With a kindness I would not have expected, Venables laid a hand on Bruno's arm. 'Shall we, sir?'

Again Bruno's bleak face turned to me. I nodded encouragingly. He could take that any way he pleased and I'd try to satisfy him.

Amelia said: 'Richard, what are we going to do?' She clutched at my arm. 'I must have a word with Marion.'

'You do that.'

'Will they let me?'

'Of course they will.'

She hesitated, her eyes moist. 'Can't you do anything for them, Richard?'

'I can't defend him in court, no. I can't wave a wand and produce evidence of their innocence.' I don't know why I said that. But she was asking too much and I'd already done all I could, all to no good effect. I was annoyed at my inadequacy but I managed to soften it. 'I'll see what he says, while you talk to Marion. All right?'

There was shock in her eyes though she must have expected it. 'How could they be so stupid?'

She meant the police, I assumed. I watched her go over to the car, taking small, precise steps. Poynton got out and held open the rear door for her.

'What's going on?' asked Lewis, coming over with uncertainty.

'They're arresting Bruno and Marion, that's what's going on.'

Sam gasped, and clutched Lewis's arm. 'But that's wicked.'

'Not pleasant, certainly. Can you hang on for a few minutes, Lewis?'

'Certainly. Be glad to.'

'And you, Sam,' I said. 'We hadn't finished what we were talking about.'

'But I couldn't go to London. Really.'

I didn't want them separated, Lewis and Sam. I wanted her well away from that high-rise flat as soon as possible. I hadn't forgotten that her little episode with Rex had been followed the following night by an attempt on her life. If necessary she'd have to be taken forcibly to London.

When Bruno came down with Venables carrying an overnight bag for him, he had obviously already mentioned his difficulties because Venables hung back so that Bruno could have a word with me.

'Richard. I'm so glad you haven't left.'

'I wanted to see you dragged away.'

He managed a sour smile. 'My guests,' he said. 'My new ones. They'll be here in a couple of hours. Oh . . . it's quite impossible. This is a ridiculous situation. But could you . . . well, kind of *be* here? They can't be allowed to arrive and find nothing.' His eyes were looking wild the more he considered it. 'I wondered . . . I know it's asking a lot . . .'

'I can be here,' I said. 'I suppose there's a list of allocated rooms?'

'In my office. Charles will know what to do . . . the catering . . . but I'll be back before it gets out of hand, once I've explained to Venables . . . Oh God, what am I going to do?'

'Give me a second. Hold on, Bruno. It'll be all right.'

I turned to Lewis and urged him a couple of yards away. I had to talk fast. Bruno was not fit to stand unsupported for long.

'They'll keep him in till Monday, Lewis. The magistrate'll probably let them out on bail, then. But his guests, they've come here to paint and I can't help them there.'

'I'll stay,' he said at once. He turned to Bruno. 'I'll see they're fixed up. I can hardly claim to be the lord of the manor but I'll have a go with the old charm and get 'em sharpening their pencils.'

Bruno smiled weakly. 'If you would.' He looked round in distress for Venables. 'I'm ready.'

'We'll hold the fort,' shouted Lewis after him, and Sam tugged his sleeve. 'You *are* a fool, Lew.'

Seeing them approach the car, Amelia got out quickly, put her head back in for a last word with Marion then walked towards me. I could see it was agony for her to face Bruno's distress, and her face was stiff. But as they passed she reached out and touched his arm.

'Are we going now?' she asked in a child's voice.

I watched the big car swinging away round the oval. 'I've promised we'll hang around for a while.'

She appreciated the situation in a flash. 'Of course. We'll do what we can.'

'And Lewis is staying to look after the artistic side of it,' I explained.

'Then everything's in control. I'd better find out who's coming and have a word with Charles . . .'

This was Amelia in her natural element, in charge of a household, a little larger than she was used to but that didn't deter her. I watched her hurry off in search of Charles and knew I could relax. I turned, lit my pipe, and stared down the drive, wondering what I could do to help.

The answer came back: nothing. I have never felt so useless. Amelia and Lewis were now in complete control and there was not one useful idea in my head.

Samantha was moving with uncertainty to her car.

'Heh!' I called. 'Where d'you think you're going?'

'Home.'

'You're not deserting us? We need you, Sam.'

'I can't see what for,' she said, watching Lewis who'd come back to unload his car.

'You can sharpen Lewis's pencils. You can go and help Amelia sort out bedrooms and things. Come on, Sam, you know you can't leave.'

With a slight blush, she began to take out her cases.

I was still there, in front of that studded door, when the new group began to arrive. I'd decided my role. I was the welcomer, the bag carrier, the one to display the banqueting hall and the balcony. I was the one to explain that their real host was delayed, but should be back on Monday, but meanwhile Lewis Hately, RA, would arrange the painting schedules. Etc. Etc.

To tell you the truth, I enjoyed myself, even to the point of phoning Venables and arranging to have the studio unsealed, seeing that he'd captured his murderers. It was only then that I realized I didn't know the code word for setting Bruno's alarms so that we had two more nights with the manor house unprotected.

This seemed to justify Amelia and me in moving into Bruno's apartment, along with the genuine vase, on the excuse of providing personal protection for all his treasures. His bed was very comfortable.

As I'd promised, the host was back on Monday.

I was in court that morning when Bruno and Marion appeared, expressionless, to answer a charge of murder. They pleaded not guilty. Their solicitor applied for bail which was granted. It was hardly likely that Bruno and Marion would abscond.

I drove them back in Bruno's Jaguar 4.2, having declared my confidence in this outcome by borrowing it. Neither of them spoke during the journey. Bruno refused to allow Marion to be dropped off at the gatehouse. 'They've legally linked us,' he growled. 'So we'll stay together.'

The three of us went up to his room, now cleared of our things, where he had a stiff drink while Marion indulged herself by finally giving way and weeping in gasping hysteria. Amelia knew how to handle that, too, breaking down in sympathy and crying all over Marion's bosom. Marion was forced into self-control. Lewis and Sam came in to sympathize.

When this was all sorted out Bruno became businesslike, asking Lewis what he'd got going on. 'I can't thank you enough,' he said at the end.

'Enjoyed myself,' said Lewis.

'And you, Richard.'

'I've done nothing.'

Eventually we got away. Bruno and Marion would have to appear in court each Monday for further remand until the case was ready to be presented in a higher court. A date would then be fixed for the trial at Hereford Crown Court. It sounded dreadful when I explained all this to them. They sat, side by side, her hand in his. I could offer no more.

We were heading for Devon, Lewis to London, Samantha to her little place in Nottingham. We swapped phone numbers. Keep me in touch, I instructed Lewis. He knew why it was an instruction; I had to know when he'd persuaded her to move to London.

Home at that time was a rented cottage in Devon on a summer lease. We would soon have to start looking for something more permanent. It was pleasantly situated near the cliffs and the steps down to the enclosed and isolated beach. Our life together was resumed. We went for cliff-top walks, I took photographs, we went for runs in the car, and she laughed again. Only occasionally did she ask what I could do for Marion and Bruno but I could offer nothing.

And I haunted the phone, tense when our trips took me away from it.

A week after the arrest, Lewis phoned. He'd found Sam a little bed-sitter and shown her work around the Slade. She was to be admitted on a trial basis, and she'd tentatively agreed to go to London and have a look at things. She was due there the next day. I told him to keep his eyes open but he already knew that.

We walked some more. Bruno and Marion had been remanded a further week. I suggested a trip to London to see the shops. Train, that would be, because I hate driving in London. We booked a night at the Piccadilly Hotel and Amelia had a grand time until the shops closed. On the morning after, I said I planned to search out a tobacco shop I'd always wanted to visit and suggested we should meet at Liberty's in Regent Street for lunch, where she could look at materials and dresses if I kept her waiting. She was suspicious but I did bring along a quarter of a pound of mixture to prove I'd found the place. This was deception which I hated having to use but I didn't want to raise any false hopes when I'd already displayed my talent for failure.

By the time I had the tobacco in my pocket I was only a few steps from Old Bond Street and all the art shops. It had promised to be a hard slog with a lot of luck involved but in practice it was easy. I hadn't allowed for the fame value of death. The second side street that I tried had a small gallery with a window display featuring a single painting. It was a still life group of a blue and white vase, a hunting horn, and a pistol with four petals on it.

'Yes sir,' he said. '*Still Life with Pistol* by Roy Towers. Very rare. The artist . . .'

'I know. He's dead.'

Even better, from a consideration of public interest, was that Roy Towers had been murdered. I didn't care for his effusion, his pleasure in that fact. He didn't admit it, this young man with the perfect suit and the huge spectacles. He merely blinked at me.

'What're you asking for it?'

'The one in the window? Two thousand, sir.'

'Oh,' I said. A fortnight's work and even that as a sideline. How Roy would have laughed! Or wept. 'The one in the window, you said. Are there any more?'

'We hold his entire output.'

'Less the ones already sold.'

'Of course.' A thin smile at my stupidity. 'Six sold, five left.'

'Six at two thousand?'

'No . . . indeed. Three before he, er . . .'

'Became famous. I see. And how much were they then?'

'I'm sorry, I can't . . .'

'I'm not trying to knock the price down. Just interested.'

'It's really not . . .' A jerk of his head at my expression. He cleared his throat. 'Two hundred.'

'I see. Could I see the other four?'

He shrugged. His interest in me was fading. 'They're very much like the one in the window.'

'If I may, please.'

He raised his eyes, put his palms together, then went away, to return with his assistant carrying three canvases, himself one.

They put them on little stands, side by side, even fetching the one from the window, and I examined them carefully. Each used the same props and the differences were minimal. Perhaps a varied aspect of the dragon design on the vase, a fractionally different arrangement of the flowers, but always the same yellow ones with the brown eyes. And all had the four petals on the gun.

'Did the ones you sold have four petals?' I asked.

'Most certainly.'

'And you've handled all his paintings?'

'We had faith in his work – yes.'

'Never with three extra petals on the table surface?'

He looked horrified. 'But of course . . . no. The balance . . .'

'I know, would've been destroyed.' I straightened. 'You've been very patient. Thank you.'

'If I could show you something else? We have two of his fruit studies.'

'I'm sorry, no.' I turned to leave. 'Oh, by the way . . . you couldn't tell me where he'd get the flowers? They're silk and very well made.'

He registered a distaste for artificial flowers. 'I do believe there's a rather chic boutique, farther up on the right . . .'

I gave him a small salute and went to find it.

They sold nothing real. Artificial diamonds in artificial gold settings. Artificial pistols that produced genuine (one assumed) flames. Artificial (I hoped) goldfish enshrined in balls of glass. And whole phalanxes of artificial silk flowers.

I spotted the yellow and browns at once. They were identical to the ones Roy had used. I asked the price. Ten times the price of real blooms. 'But they last forever, sir,' she said with pride. How sad.

I bought one, which I could put away in an inside pocket and later compare with the photographs. I asked whether they were the only suppliers and was assured they had the sole import licence. They were made by hand in Taiwan at no doubt a tenth of the price of real blooms.

I cut through to Regent Street and Liberty's where Amelia was examining a bolt of silk.

'My colour, Richard, do you think?'

'Matches your eyes,' I told her, noticing too late that it was a pale beige. But I had good reason. My mind was miles away. I now knew what had been done. What I didn't know was why it had been done, and therefore by whom.

We ate a leisurely and splendid lunch and had time to take a look at the ducks in St James's Park before packing and ordering a taxi for the station. We were in complete agreement that it had been a successful trip.

A week later Lewis phoned in agitation. Samantha had gone missing.

'I tried to tell her . . . Richard, you know she's good. But she saw some of the work being done by the others and, damn it, she lost her nerve. I've been round to her place three times but she's not there. What the hell am I going to do about her?'

'You have to tell her and keep on telling her. She has to have reassurance. All the time. It gets tiring but start the minute she gets back.'

'Oh hell . . . what about if she doesn't come back?'

'She will.'

It's all very well to speak with confidence but then you've got to deliver. I wasn't sure I could.

'I'll be away most of tomorrow,' I told Amelia, walking back into the sitting room.

'Away?' She looked up. 'Where?'

I walked past her for an ash tray. 'Nottingham.'

She was on to it at once. 'It's Sam! What's happened?'

'That was Lewis on the phone. She's disappeared from London.'

'But she's *left* Nottingham.'

I was trying to be casual. 'Well, you know Sam. Never abandon one boat until you're sure of the other.'

This was what I was hoping – praying. But it was only a chance. 'Want to come?' I asked. It would be a long and lonely drive but I wanted to be alone. Amelia didn't know what some of these high-rises could be like and I didn't want her in her dismay saying the wrong thing. Sam, even if she was there, wouldn't be easy to handle.

She frowned at my expression. 'I don't think so,' she decided. 'But phone me when you know.'

'I'll do that.'

With only the address that block of flats was difficult to find. More time finding somewhere to park, more finding a lift that worked. It was that sort of building, haunted by vandals and graffiti experts. The lift rumbled up. She failed to answer my ring. I tried again. Nothing. I put my head close to the door and shouted. 'It's Richard, Sam.'

I heard the chain rattle and then the door opened. She looked untidy and afraid. 'Oh. You'd better come in.'

I walked in. Bedroom, sitting room, bathroom, and a tiny kitchen. It looked dusty and there was no evidence of her painting. Not much furniture left, either.

'Lewis was worried,' I said, pretending not to notice that she hadn't even unpacked properly. 'Why did you run away, Sam?'

'I didn't run away,' she said, reaching for dignity. 'It was just . . . oh, I felt so hopeless. You should see what they do! And me . . .' She turned away and went to look at her view of identical high-rise blocks.

'Your rooms didn't suit you?'

'That's another thing. I couldn't afford to keep *both* going.'

'That wasn't really the intention.' I smiled but she didn't respond. 'You've got to make up your mind, you know. Here you're a nobody. There, you're somebody.'

'I'm a beginner there,' she said with scorn.

'No. You're an artist. That's more than you are here. What do you expect? There a week and you expect to be best girl in the class? It doesn't do to turn your nose up . . .'

'I never did!' She was aghast that such an accusation should come her way.

'. . . until you are. And you will be. Not just a painter but an important painter. Lewis is sure of it. Then . . . well, then's the time to go all modest and pretend it's nothing.'

I knew she was weakening when she tried a back-up. 'I've got friends here.'

'Many?'

'The phone was ringing the minute I had the door open.'

'One of your friends?'

She shook her head. 'They hung up,' she said in a whisper. 'The moment I gave my name.'

'Not a very good friend, then. Have they rung since?'

'No.'

'Then there's nothing to stop you from getting moving, is there? Did you bring your car?'

'Yes.'

'Got to pack anything?'

'Not much.'

'I'll help you carry it down.'

She nodded, biting her lip. It was a reluctant abdication but not too reluctant. She enjoyed being bossed around. I hefted her case and carried it round to the garage.

'Been out since you got here?' I asked casually, standing beside her car.

'Once. Shopping. Oh, they're mad here. Mad drivers.'

'Worse than London?'

'Somebody actually tried to force me off the road. Lucky I wasn't going fast.'

I said nothing. I watched her pull away and waved to her. She seemed more peaceful. I hadn't asked her where she'd managed to get the small hole in the bodywork, just behind her seat. It was around the size of a thirty-eight bullet.

I dug out the Stag and followed the route she would have taken. After ten miles I spotted her up ahead. I gave it another twenty, varying the separation, until I was certain nobody else was having a go at following her. Then I peeled off for Devon.

As promised, I stopped at the nearest phone box and called Amelia. 'She's on her way home.' I meant London. Then I phoned Lewis. 'She's on her way home.' I didn't have to tell him where; I wanted him there waiting for her.

'It wasn't a waste of time, then,' said Amelia when I arrived.

'In no way.' The bullet hole had confirmed my thinking, but had increased my concern.

She was silent then. Something was wrong. I wandered after her into the kitchen. 'Had a good day?'

She moved away when I came up behind her and tried to slide my hands round her waist. 'I caught up with the washing and got a few things ready for dry cleaning.' She turned to face me, her lips thin and bloodless. 'Richard, why is there one of those silk flowers in the inside pocket of your best suit?'

'Because,' I replied honestly, 'I forgot to throw it away.'

'You're up to something,' she decided.

I smiled. 'I discovered where Roy bought the flowers.'

'And you didn't *tell* me!'

I shook my head, looking rueful. 'To tell you the truth, my self confidence isn't working too well. I've been a bit wary of committing myself to anything positive.'

I should have trusted her. Her face crumpled as though she was about to cry, then she flung herself in my arms.

'And I thought you'd given up. Now admit it, there *is*

something positive?' She held herself away from me, searching my face.

'There was a very positive bullet hole in Sam's car.'

That quietened her. 'Oh heavens.'

'But it confirmed what I know.'

'And what's that?'

'I know what was done but not why. So of course I don't know who.'

'So . . . now what?'

I shrugged. Now there was nothing. I had a feeling that I was waiting for inspiration, some new clue. It was irritating that I couldn't reach out the truth from what I already had.

Two days later Bruno phoned to tell me that his trial and Marion's was set for mid-September. Hereford Crown Court. He sounded quite nonchalant about it. Shock, that was. He simply could not accept it.

'We'll have to go,' I told Amelia. 'I expect they'll subpoena me, anyway.'

Clearly, the idea of seeing Marion and Bruno in the dock was distressing to her. 'You'll have to think of something before then,' she decided, rather in the same voice as she'd use to tell me I ought to have the car serviced.

On the first day of September we were idly watching the news, neither of us really registering it, when the name Walter Race had us sitting up and paying attention.

'The Home Secretary is considering new evidence that is said to have a bearing on the three-year-old murder of Griffith Pierce, for which Walter Race is serving a life sentence. It is believed that a pardon will be recommended.

'On the industrial front, efforts continue . . .'

I dived at the set and switched it off.

'What does it mean?' Amelia asked.

'God knows.'

'Carla will be thrilled.' Light was now in her eyes. 'She always maintained that Walter was innocent.'

That wasn't strictly correct. She had maintained that Roy had rigged the evidence. But I didn't argue.

'We ought to give her a ring,' I suggested.

'You think so?'

'As a friendly gesture.'

It took an hour to get through by which time Amelia's enthusiasm had evaporated. But Carla soon revived it.

'My dear!' she screamed. 'Isn't it exciting? The phone's never stopped ringing.'

'We were so pleased to hear about it,' Amelia assured her.

My ear was close to Amelia's so that I could get both ends. Carla's voice cracked on.

'It came completely out of the blue. This man came, last night. From the Home Office or something. New evidence, he said.'

I mouthed: what new evidence?

'What evidence, Carla?'

'Oh, I don't know. Something about the pistol. Roy's, that is.'

'But do you *know* it's all right? The pardon, I mean.'

'From the way he spoke . . . oh, I'm sure. Amelia, they've been at my door now for hours. It was on the radio earlier. Everybody's so pleased. Walter was always very popular. They're talking about a welcoming party.'

Invite us, I mouthed, but Amelia shook her head.

'Richard and I are very happy for you, Carla.'

'A street party. Banners. I just don't know where I am, head or my heels.'

Ask her to invite us, I almost shouted.

Amelia laughed. It sounded empty, my end. 'If there's a party, I hope you won't forget us. Richard loves parties.'

A dig at me, that was. I hate them.

'Of course. *All* of you,' she cried.

All except Marion and Bruno, I mouthed, but I didn't mean her to say that, and she didn't.

After a few more words, Carla burst in: 'Sorry, dear, the door. I'll have to . . .' And rang off.

'Have you ever been to a street party?' Amelia asked, her lips crimpling.

'Got to start some time.'

'Cold sausages on chairs in the street. What's on your mind, Richard?'

I shook my head. 'I'll have to find out what's behind it.'

'It'll be in the papers tomorrow.'

'Not all of it. I'll go and see Alf tomorrow. Alf Peters. I

worked with him – I think he's Deputy Chief Constable, now.'

'He wouldn't have time for you.'

'I'll give him a ring and make sure.'

'Who is he, anyway?'

I reached for the phone. 'The big boss of the district where Roy Towers used to operate, where Griff Pierce was killed. Like to come?'

She nodded vigorously as I picked up the phone and dialled Directory Enquiries. She went to make a pot of tea.

'Tomorrow morning,' I reported. 'And lunch afterwards.'

'For three?' she asked tentatively.

'He wants to meet you.'

In the morning I felt tense with an excitement I couldn't analyse. Amelia was pale and kept glancing sideways at me, sensing my mood. But she allowed me to concentrate on my driving. I was wondering whether he'd changed, Alf Peters, who used to patrol with me in the good old days, who'd outstripped my progress through the ranks, and could now flaunt a fancy cap with his uniform. But he turned out to be the same old Alf.

'Richard,' he said, his hand thrust out. 'It's grand to see you. You're looking well. And this is Amelia.' He beamed at her, and bustled round finding us seats.

Then we had all the lead-in chat you'd expect, with his eyes not once wavering towards that piled in-tray

'And what's your interest in this?' he asked at last.

'I was there, Alf, when Roy Towers was shot. I found his body.'

He pursed his lips, eyes twinkling. 'Haven't I heard a little something about interference with the course of justice and wild theories?'

'Have you, Alf?' I didn't smile.

'You've changed, Richard. Why so serious?'

'I know a lot about Roy's death but next to nothing about this Griff Pierce business. Why this sudden switch – Home Secretary and new evidence? What new evidence?'

'It'll be released to the press . . .'

'And come out all garbled. I know. I thought I'd rather have the facts.' I grinned at him. 'Not that I'll get 'em all.'

'That's more like it. And for you – the facts in full. You know about the original case, the evidence of the bullets in the sandbag, and how they matched the murder one?'

'I know about that. Seemed a bit shaky to me.'

'To us, too. Once removed, you could call it, because the actual gun never turned up. So the sandbag was all we'd got. We weren't happy about the conduct of Towers, either. There'd been murmurs before then – you know how it is. But nothing definite until this business of his personal interest. Damn it, the man'd been having it off with that hot bitch, Carla Race. Sorry, Amelia! But I ask you! So . . . we were not happy even when we got a conviction from his bullet evidence. You with me?'

'Ahead, Alf.' Amelia was nodding beside me.

'And now . . . another murder in another district with Roy once more involved but this time as the corpse. Nothing to concern us, you'd say. Not our county. But about a fortnight ago we got a registered package. Inside it was a fired bullet and a short note, unsigned and printed. It said: This is from the sandbag. Check it with Towers's gun.'

'Ah,' I said. 'Yes.'

'Well, as you know, there's nothing fed into the computer about matching bullets – no known classification – so nobody would have picked it up. I got in touch with the chap in charge of the Towers killing . . .'

'Venables.'

'Him. Yes. And we sent the bullet along. It matched the one that killed Towers. We cross-checked, and fortunately Forensic still had the bullet that killed Griff Pierce. That matched, too. So there we had it. Towers's own gun killed Towers, and had also killed Griff Pierce. A right turn-up, you can see.'

'And the note? Any trace who sent that?'

'Posted in Birmingham, not a sign of a fingerprint.' His eyes went vague. 'This bit's pure conjecture. There was a sergeant, Finch, who worked with Towers on the Pierce case. It was Finch who went along to the clubhouse with Towers and sorted out the sandbag. Now I suspect that Finch wasn't happy about it either and kept a bullet back and, now Towers is dead, sent it along. I've tackled him on it – he's retired now and hating it – but he says it wasn't him.'

'So, what's the theory now, on Pierce's death?'

'That Towers shot him with his own gun. Must've gone crazy, over Carla Race. He hung on to the case because that was the only way to protect himself and he remembered Walter Race firing those two dozen shots into the sandbag so he simply went along there on his own, quietly, and put two dozen from his own gun into a fresh sandbag and switched them over. So simple, Richard, and absolutely diabolical.'

'So Race gets his freedom?'

'The Home Secretary's got it now but what else can he do? A pardon, and the poor bugger's lost over two years of his life and probably his professional standing.'

After lunch with Alf we drove away from there with me feeling a little sick. Amelia had been very silent. After a few miles I said: 'Penny for 'em.'

'Isn't it strange,' she said, 'how things turn out. If Roy hadn't been shot with his own gun this would never have happened.'

I drove another mile. Then I commented: 'What's even stranger is that he should have kept a murder weapon all this while and even flaunted it around.'

14

We were late arriving at the party, having been held up by a pile-up on the motorway. As we sat there waiting in the car fumes, Amelia tried to probe my thoughts but I needed to speak to Walter before things would come together so I didn't commit myself.

'But I want you to remember,' I said, 'that only you and I and Bruno know that the vases were switched.'

'Uhmm!' she said. 'And you think that's important?'

'The fact that they were switched is the most important point in the whole thing. And don't forget, Sam's the only person who can say when they were switched.'

She gripped my knee. 'And Rex, of course.' But she was smiling.

I had to park out on the main road, as the cul-de-sac in which

Carla and Walter lived was temporarily banned to traffic. The residents had their cars in the drives and garages, leaving the short length of straight tarmac and the turning circle at the end free for non-contact dancing and, later, for contact sports.

Already the canned music was thumping out as we walked into the confusion. Above our heads a banner was strung across the entrance. WELCOM HOME WALTER. Hastily prepared, no doubt. They had tables put together along the centre of the roadway, tablecloths draped, the ruins of a buffet feast still lying around. Someone had wired it for electricity because table lamps of varied designs stood in a row down its centre, already lit. The three stark-blue streetlamps were flicking into life.

Walter was seated in state in an armchair in the centre of the turning circle. It was his house that dominated the cul-de-sac, being directly behind him. I had the impression that he was longing for full darkness so that he could sneak out of that chair and back inside.

'I'm Richard Patton,' I said. 'And this is Amelia.'

Except that it wasn't. She'd drifted behind, appalled, I decided, by the din and confusion.

'Darling,' screamed Carla, rushing up, and half-cut I thought. 'You'd better grab something to eat, they'll be clearing the tables away soon. Any champers left, Walter?'

'God knows,' he said in despair.

I'd never met him so couldn't say whether his complexion was to be blamed on prison pallor or the blue lights. He seemed gaunt, sitting there, the image of a man just out of prison and longing to be back.

'Noisy,' I said.

'It was at least quiet,' he told me, 'inside.'

'Will you excuse me for a moment,' I asked him. 'I've got to find Amelia.'

He raised his eyebrows at that. My implication was that I intended to return for a lengthy chat. He nodded, his eyes wandering past me to Carla, who was now flopping about with abandon, very nearly in the arms of a willowy man who, I saw as they turned, was Rex.

So the invitations had gone out. We'd received ours, a scribbled note, but we hadn't known who else of the manor group had been invited.

I discovered Amelia talking to Lewis. She turned to me at once.

'Isn't he looking well, Richard?'

And indeed he was dressed more smartly, his beard was trimmed, his attitude was confident.

'Lewis, how are you?' I said. 'How's the painting coming along?'

He bobbed his head at me. 'I've at least got Sam working on something.'

'And Sam, is she settling down?'

'She's around somewhere,' he said, looking right and left. 'You can ask her yourself.'

'You mean you brought her here! Of all the idiots . . .'

'I got an invite so I brought her.'

'Don't you understand the danger she's in?'

But it was like shouting at a thick fence. He waffled a bit, then fingered my arm. 'But it's all over, Richard.' He waved embracingly. 'With this . . . isn't it all over?'

'Then who killed Roy? Do you really believe it was Bruno?'

'Lord no.'

'Then go and find her, Lewis. And stay with her.'

I watched him go, looking haunted. Amelia asked: 'Shall I go and help him look?'

'I'd prefer to have you within reach. Have you seen any of the others?'

'Rex . . .'

'Yes, I spotted him.'

'And Bert's here.'

'You haven't seen Veronica?'

'In this crush?'

It was clear that the welcome home was drawing outside interest. The cul-de-sac was a compressed pack of jostling humanity. Walter could never have known so many people.

'I've got to talk to Walter,' I said. 'Come on, you can hardly hear yourself think around here.'

I knew where Samantha would be. A street party was not her thing. She would be quietly retreating into the background and all the available backgrounds were rapidly becoming dark. I wished I had time to join in the search.

We went back to Walter. It was no longer his party. He sat

isolated and miserable. I stood beside him, Amelia still hanging on my arm.

'Nobody,' he said, glancing up with a twist of his lips, 'has asked me to dance. A pity, that is, because it's the only one I could do. Standing still. Let's get away from here, for God's sake.'

We followed him into the house. The front door was wide open, the sound wafting in after us.

'Why the hell do I have to be subjected to this?' he demanded. 'I need a drink. Come on through.'

The house was larger than I'd thought it. He opened a door into a commodious and well-appointed sitting room. The lights were on, and Veronica was sitting beside Sam on a sofa, patting her hand. Sam was sobbing.

'What's this?' I asked.

Veronica looked up. 'She was looking for somewhere quiet. The garden at the back seemed a good idea. It wasn't, apparently. Somebody attacked her.'

'Not . . .' Sam gulped. 'Not attacked. Just sort of watched. A shadow.'

Another of Sam's shadows? She was an attractive girl, I told myself. It could have been a local Romeo on the prowl. I told myself. But I wasn't convinced.

'She screamed and I found her there,' Veronica said. 'Half passed out.'

I looked at her. Veronica had more life in her face, less assertion in her voice.

'I don't know what this is all about,' said Walter, 'but a brandy usually does the trick. Here.'

He offered a glass. Amelia held it for Sam and I turned my attention to Walter.

'Did they tell you why the pardon was granted?'

'Oh yes.' He sipped at what was apparently a whisky. 'Want one? No? Oh well . . . Yes, they told me. I still don't believe it. About Roy, I mean.'

'But all the same, you didn't argue.' I grinned at him. 'You're out. You're free.'

'That's fine, that is.' He'd already had a few whiskies. 'My career gone and all my capital in legal costs but I'm free to enjoy what's left.'

'You'll get compensation.'

'Not to cover . . .' He stopped. For a moment he'd spoken violently but he controlled himself. 'Every day, Mr . . . what was it? . . . every day I told myself that during the next one I'd try not to go mad. And the next day, and so on. Stalling it off. Who the hell *are* you, anyway?'

'I was at the manor when Roy was killed. The name's Patton. I found his body.'

That distinction granted me special benefits, it seemed. He raised his glass to me, then his eyebrows.

'Roy,' he said. 'To Roy. But I still don't believe it.'

'What don't you believe, that Roy killed Griffith Pierce?'

'If he had, he wouldn't have arrested me,' said Walter simply.

Samantha whispered something. Amelia looked at me. 'She needs some fresh air, Richard.'

'I'll take her outside,' Veronica offered.

I shook my head. 'Why don't you go and find Lewis?' I asked her. 'Bring him here. Can we have a window open, Mr Race?'

He nodded, walked across the room, swept aside the tall curtains, and revealed a double french window. He threw the two halves apart.

'Come and stand over here, my dear.'

Samantha did so. She stood with her back to us staring out at the dark garden. Amelia hadn't taken her eyes from me. I hardly noticed when Veronica went off to look for Lewis.

'What did you think, then?' I asked Walter. 'You trusted Roy?'

Walter shrugged. 'You'd have to know him. I *knew* him. He was as straight as . . . as a balance sheet.' He laughed shortly.

So straight, I thought, that he was having it away with Walter's wife at the time. He curled his lip, reading my mind.

'Oh, I knew about Carla. Knew about all of her men. She made sure of that. But I always pretended it wasn't there and after a while it wasn't. There are two ways of dealing with these things, you know. You either go mad with jealousy or you wait it out. I waited them all out . . . but they kept coming. It would've been so much easier if I hadn't loved her. So bloody much easier.' He jerked his head towards the street. 'I see it's started again. Already.' He was referring to Carla and Rex.

'So Roy was straight?'

'As a policeman, yes. Completely. I reckon it broke his heart when they asked him to resign. Personal interest, they said, and that was supposed to be Carla. But his real personal interest was me. He was trying to find some reason for not having to arrest me. But there were those bullets in the sandbag. I didn't understand that. But believe me, if Roy had killed Pierce it would've been in blind anger. The following day he'd simply have gone to his superior and told him the truth.'

'Surely that's a bit naïve,' I suggested. 'In view of what's happened.'

'It's just . . .' He shook his head. 'I don't understand it.'

'Do you really want to understand?' I asked. 'Or does that idea scare you?'

'What *is* this?' he demanded. 'All I need to understand is that Roy's pistol killed Griff Pierce and three years later it was used to kill Roy.' He spoke in disgust, bitterly. 'Those are known facts, are they not?'

'They are accepted facts. Would you prefer to leave them undisturbed?'

The eyebrows lowered and his eyes seemed to go darker. But before we could go on with it Lewis came bursting in, closely followed by Veronica.

'Sam!' he shouted. 'What's been going on?'

There was a short break while everything was explained and Lewis went dashing out into the garden to explore. When he came back he got a chair and placed it by the open window and sat there, apparently on guard, then he remembered his manners and fetched another for Sam. They whispered together. Amelia stood by the door into the hall, whilst Veronica wandered around trying not to be noticed but all the same intensely interested.

'What do you mean – accepted facts?' demanded Walter, who hadn't allowed his mind to be diverted for one second. 'The Home Secretary's accepted them. That's enough for me.'

'It's just . . . well, don't you think it's rather strange that Roy should have kept a murder weapon for three years and for the past eighteen months even went to the lengths of putting it on show in his still life pictures?'

Amelia pricked up her ears. We hadn't taken it any further in the car.

'Over-confidence,' decided Walter.

'It's all backwards, you see. His guilty pistol out there in the open and your innocent one disappeared without trace – for no apparent reason.'

There was a tiny smile lifting the corners of his mouth. 'Go on.'

'Particularly as Carla brought to my attention the fact that you'd included in your statement an open admission that you'd fired shots into a new sandbag the night before the murder.'

'Hah!' he said in contempt. 'I could hardly deny it. Roy was with me.'

'But all the same, you needn't have *said* it, on paper. Could've let 'em prove it, as any solicitor would have told you.'

There was silence in the room. It seemed that everybody was listening carefully. Amelia seemed to feel the silence oppressive and asked Veronica where Bert was and Veronica replied lightly, something about enjoying himself. In that space, Walter refilled his glass.

'I don't get your point,' he said.

'Carla offered that fact to me as proof of your innocence on the theory that you wouldn't be so simple as to go to the trouble of disposing of your gun and then openly admit the bullets-in-the-bag business. It was almost as though you thought your pistol would be available to the police. But it wasn't. Your innocent gun *did* go missing, and the killer gun's been kept openly. How strange, then, that yours is still missing.' I allowed my gaze to roam round the room. 'I suppose it *is* still missing?'

He gave a flat laugh then he took me over to a bookcase with a false set of books which masked a small, square safe, spun its dial, and opened it up.

'My pistols. The Colt twenty-two match,' he said, handing them out. 'And my twenty-two Ruger.'

There was, of course, no Smith & Wesson thirty-eight. He had known that and known that I had not expected it to be there. But he had realized I knew the truth and it was as though he had reached the end of a long journey. His release from prison had not meant the end of anything, it had been nothing more than a continuation. I felt that he was relieved that he did not have to travel on alone. He offered me his weapons with a bleak smile, a surrender.

I took the Ruger in my hand. It came to my fingers as though it belonged there. Such a beautiful piece of engineering and so deadly! I tried a line on a vase across the room.

'Careful,' he said casually. 'It's loaded.'

'Loaded! Good God man, you're supposed to keep the ammo separate.'

He gestured the regulations into space. 'Burglars,' he explained. 'I've always believed in using my weapons to protect my weapons.'

'I'd have thought you'd had enough of guns.'

He might not have heard. 'I always leave it loaded.'

'You're not safe to have around.'

He smiled, not a pleasant smile merely a sour twist of the lips. 'I'm a marksman, Patton. I wouldn't kill anybody. Nick him a bit. Kill, no. Unless I intended to, of course.'

He placed it down on the sideboard casually. He'd been lying. He hadn't left it loaded for over two years. That pistol had been loaded since he'd come home. That very day.

'You know the truth, don't you?' I asked softly.

He raised his eyebrows. 'What *is* the truth? Roy killed Griff Pierce. They can prove that now. His pistol was used to shoot him. The same pistol fired the shot that killed Pierce. They matched it against the actual bullet. So simple. Can you prove anything different? Is that what you came here for?'

'Not prove,' I admitted. 'The only item of proof is known by that young woman over there. And even that could be argued.'

Well aware of that loaded pistol, I drew him away from the sideboard. Amelia moved to face me. She'd realized what I intended.

'You can't do this,' she whispered, her face pale. 'Please stop, Richard.'

'Stop? Aren't you forgetting Marion and Bruno?'

Her lips moved but no words emerged. Then she shook her head angrily and simply turned away.

Walter waited patiently, looking sardonic and challenging.

'Let's hear this proof of yours,' he said.

'No,' I decided, trying to avoid it if I could. 'Let's try looking at it the other way round. We can't dispute the fact that the same gun killed Towers and Pierce. Bullets from each body have been matched to the pistol. That much is positive. But what proof is there that it *is* Roy's gun? Of course, he fetched it from his room. He placed it himself in the group. His pistol. I picked it up and examined it. It wasn't loaded at that time.'

'His thirty-eight?' asked Walter.

I nodded.

'We bought twin guns at the same time. We were friends.'

'Sure you were. It was *his* thirty-eight pistol he put in his group. It sat there for over a week while he got to the point of painting it in on the canvas. I saw the gun half finished. Can you imagine he wouldn't have spotted the fact if it had suddenly not been his gun? Of course he would. So it was still his. Up to that Tuesday night it was still his. Now, just look at what convinces us that the situation was still the same when I found his body. The petals, of course. Those four stuck on the top of it, they meant the gun was still his. He'd hardly glue them on and not know he was doing it to a gun that wasn't his. And seeing that *he* painted them, exactly as they were, attached there to that gun, then there can't be the slightest argument that the gun that killed him was *his* gun.'

'Then what are we talking about?'

'We're talking about substitution. I'm saying that on that Tuesday night, the gun that was found there was no longer Roy's.'

'The petals, though.' He smiled.

'Yes. The big snag. We – Amelia and I – tried to argue all round it. But, you see, they were glued on, and then painted on to canvas. It's just too much to suggest that the murderer did that after killing Roy. But there *had* been one substitution and that was the vase. That can be proved or, at least, can be shown with some sort of reasonable assumption. It's the only piece of evidence and it's Samantha over there who can tell us how it wasn't in a certain alcove at a certain time.'

I waited. Sam had heard me quite clearly, I knew. She had wandered out on to what seemed to be a patio and was smoking a cigarette. It was the first time I'd seen her smoking. The noise out front was increasing. They were at the community singing stage now. But she'd heard me. She turned slowly, very pale.

Clearly, Sam had not told Lewis about the episode with Rex.

She saw me waiting and her face was very still. She stared at a spot just above my head.

'Must I, Richard?'

'Either you or me.'

'No, you must not!' Amelia burst out.

'It'd come better from Sam,' I said quietly. 'Sam?' I asked. 'Please.'

In a dead flat voice she said: 'I went to the bathroom . . . *that* night. I didn't put on the balcony lights because I could tell which was the right door by the vase missing from the recess.'

'The vase Roy was using in his still life group,' I explained quickly to Walter.

'But at that time,' Sam ploughed on, as though I'd not interrupted, 'there was another vase not in its place. So I went into the wrong room, by mistake.' She stopped, staring at the cigarette in her fingers.

'Whose?' I asked gently.

'Rex's,' she whispered.

'For how long, Sam?'

'What the hell!' shouted Lewis.

'It matters,' I said tersely, my jaw muscles fluttering.

'An hour,' Sam whispered. 'More.'

Lewis expelled his breath as though somebody had punched him.

'And the vase, Sam?' I asked.

She drew in a deep breath. 'It was back in its place when I came out.'

Lewis croaked: 'Sam!' and took a step forward. It was one step too many. Sam turned and ran out into the garden, with Lewis galloping after her and shouting: 'Sam, Sam!' He shouted back at me: 'Now look what you've done!'

I took a deep breath. 'So you see what we've got.'

'That was quite unnecessary, Richard,' said Veronica stiffly.

'It was necessary,' I said simply, then I turned back to Walter and went on. 'It was necessary that Mr Race should understand.'

'What am I supposed to understand?'

'Why an attempt was made on Sam's life the following night and at least one other since then. Look at it. Sam, on that balcony, saw a shadow she told me she didn't recognize. But that shadow couldn't be confident of not having been recognized and probably didn't know that it was Sam, either. By waiting, though, it would be seen that the shadow that was Sam went into Rex's room. The following day Sam painted her only portrait. It was of Rex. So now, Sam being a rather impressionable young lady, it was possible for anyone seeing that portrait to make a reasonable guess that the shadow that went into Rex's room was Samantha.'

Amelia was staring at me blindly. She was trying to reach me with her opinions but I didn't want them at that time.

'And what significant fact had Sam noticed?' I asked. 'That vase was missing from its alcove at the time she went in and was there when she came out. That doesn't sound very important, does it? But Sam, if she'd been questioned later, would have been able to confirm that this vase business happened at around the time Roy was killed.'

'Even so . . .' Walter shrugged.

'The point is that it wasn't the same vase. The one from the alcove had moved down into the studio and the one from the studio up to the balcony. *That* was what was so critical about it, the fact that the substitution of the vase was linked with the shooting.'

'But what have you really got?' asked Walter lightly. Yet his eyes held mine with painful concentration.

'Roy was shot when he sat down at his easel, apparently after one of his patrols, to continue with his painting. His palette was on his thumb, his brush in his hand. But he'd only just sat down otherwise he'd have noticed that somebody was there, behind his group and in deep shadow, holding a pistol. But *what* had he sat down to continue? Looking at it, the canvas seemed to be a completed work, even to his signature. The pistol was there, on canvas, with the petals perched on it. The only things that weren't painted were the three loose petals on the table. But, was he really intending to paint those? For one thing, he'd never done so before and everybody told me he wouldn't have done it because it would've ruined the balance. And anyway, he had brown paint on his brush and his palette seemed to confirm that what he was about to paint was brown. The petals were yellow. So, those three loose petals gave the wrong impression. They made it seem that he was working on *that* canvas. And I calmly dismissed them as irrelevant! By heaven, what a fool I was. You see, it means that not only was the vase substituted but also the canvas itself. Vase *and* flowers, I should have said. I was rapidly coming to the conclusion that every damned item, except the hunting horn, which would be easy to position, had been switched. Including the gun, Mr Race. *Your* gun. The one that killed Griff Pierce.'

'Ah,' said Walter. 'We come to it.'

'We do. But of course, I couldn't understand what it was all about. I saw that the gun was what really mattered but not until the news of your pardon. It was only then that I realized what had been achieved. Very important, that, the question of what's achieved.'

'And in this instance?'

'Your release from prison, the apparent proof that Roy Towers killed Pierce, and of course the fact that Roy was dead, so wasn't in a position to dispute anything.'

He winced. Amelia gave a shuddering sigh. But Walter was still fighting. He'd seen another bolt hole.

'Such a large undertaking,' he murmured, 'when it would've been much simpler to shoot Roy before he began to paint the petals, and simply place the substitute pistol on the table.' He smiled bleakly, apologetically. 'Why not?'

'Because it wouldn't work. I've already mentioned one objection: the immediate thought would be that Roy would never have kept a murder weapon in his possession so long. It would never convince the top brass of the police – who'd sent you to prison – because they're very chary of admitting mistakes. It's one thing proving a case to a jury but a very different one to disprove the same case to the Home Secretary. They'd say that there was no proof this was the same gun that Roy had produced and painted on canvas even if it looked the same. They'd be suspicious. But if it could be *seen* that it was the same gun . . . what then? If the gun in his painting looked exactly the same as the one that killed him then there'd be no arguing it. And it was the four glued-on petals, *exactly* as in the painting, that clinched it.'

I stopped because there was an interruption. Samantha had rushed in from the garden, panting: 'There's somebody . . .'

'It's me, damn it,' shouted Lewis. 'For God's sake, stop running, Sam.'

He burst in behind her, grabbed her arm, whirled her round, and made sure she stayed still by holding her so tightly that she had no breath left with which to protest.

'And you're saying this was done?' Walter asked. He hadn't noticed the episode.

'With the use of your pistol, yes. You signed a statement. The inference from it is that you expected your pistol to be found, otherwise why be so outgoing about the bullets in the sandbag? It was almost as though you were resigned to it. But Carla must have hidden it away.'

He pursed his lips but there was pain in his eyes. 'She might have thought it would help me.'

'That was what you believed?' I challenged him, but he turned away.

'All the rest,' I said, 'could be obtained. A painting of Roy's, a previous one, featuring gun and petals, that would have been available and, not so very far away, some of the same artificial flowers that Roy always used. The vase . . . there was a choice. The basically important point was the timing at the end. It had to be done when Towers was just about finishing his present painting. There's another point here, by the way. He had to have time to reach the end. No interruptions . . .'

'Oh!' said Amelia, clamping her hand to her face. Her eyes were huge above it.

'Exactly,' I said. 'So that when Roy's wife . . .'

'Marion,' murmured Walter, his eyes softening.

'When Marion made a hysterical attack on Roy's canvas, after he'd done a whole night's work on it, Carla went crazy and attacked her. No harm was done. The painting wasn't really delayed but for one moment it must have seemed that the whole plan was ruined.'

'Carla?' Walter cocked his head. It was the first time I'd made a definite accusation.

'I believe that Carla, apart from myself, was the only one who saw Samantha's portrait of Rex. I also believe that it was Carla who sent a bullet to the Deputy Chief Constable to make sure it was all checked up. She'd have to fire that bullet from *your* pistol, Mr Race, before she took the gun to Fillingley Manor. It was all very carefully planned, you see.'

'She surely didn't go as a painter,' he said, his voice dry.

'No. She was busily laying on the background of a person who wanted to break down Roy's resistance and get some sort of confession from him. Then, when he died, she was left as the one person who had apparently needed him alive.'

'I hadn't realized how very clever she must be.' He laughed bitterly. 'It's not true. Brains *can* go with beauty.'

'Indeed.' I glanced at Amelia. She was nodding and I didn't think she'd heard what Walter had said. 'But apart from that, she had very little to do during the first ten days. It gave her plenty of time to stick her petals to the gun – the one that killed Pierce – in exactly the same way as they were in the painting she'd bought. Exactly. Then, on the night, it would be necessary to borrow a vase from the balcony. It couldn't be before, of course, and that flower arranging would have been too risky and tricky to leave until after the killing. Sam noticed that the vase was missing. It was missing because Carla had taken it into her room in order to arrange her flowers in the same way as they were in her painting and pack them firm with tissue paper. She then took the lot down to the studio, the painting, the vase with the flowers in, the gun, already loaded, with the petals stuck on, timing it for when Roy was in some other part of the house on one of his patrols. Then she waited. She shot him as soon as he sat down and had taken up his brush. I'd guess that at that time he was working on the last bit of the brown table surface. The rest would take her no more than five minutes. She arranged the vase, with the hunting horn and the fired pistol against it, to match her own painting, which she put on the easel . . . and scattered three loose petals on the table surface.'

'Neat,' said Walter in grim appreciation.

'There'd been time to work it all out and a very big incentive. But the three petals were a mistake. They *had* to be used because she was working with an apparently finished canvas. They were meant to create the impression that Roy was actually working at the time of his death and that he'd decided to add three petals. Otherwise, it would not have seemed real. Then she hurried upstairs with the vase that Roy had been using and placed it back in its alcove. Sam saw it had come back. The flowers from Roy's vase could be hidden away in a suitcase. The canvas Roy had been working on . . . well, when she arrived she gave a vague impression of having come as a painter. She had two canvases, tied face to face. One was the Roy Towers painting she'd bought. The new one was taken away in the same manner. If you can locate it the thing's worth two thousand quid.' I thought about that. It was the one he'd actually been working on when he died. 'Much more than that,' I decided.

Walter managed a laugh which I thought he intended to be casual but it was a sour and miserable affair. 'You've got her chasing round carrying canvases and flowers and vases, and a pistol with petals stuck to it . . .'

'I never did find that tube of glue.'

'. . . as though she's some sort of athlete.'

I scratched my head with the pipe stem. 'Well, you see, she didn't expect to have to do it alone. Why d'you think Rex was sitting up in bed, awake, when Sam went in there?'

'Was he?'

'Oh yes. As though he was waiting. I believe he was supposed to help with the carrying around. He was probably waiting for Carla to tap on the door and say she was ready, having done the necessary flower arranging. But Carla had seen Sam go in that room. She'd seen somebody go in. And not come out again. Rex isn't the type to refuse gifts in the night – he wouldn't be able to resist. So Carla was stuck and had to manage alone. Sam told me Rex *did* leave the room, but not for many minutes. He was probably wondering how Carla was managing. In practice, she was managing very well.'

'An answer for everything,' he said sourly.

'I wonder what she promised him. I did think it was strange he didn't chase after her at the manor. You can see why. Whereas now . . .' I shrugged. 'You can see yourself what it's like now.'

It seemed that his term in prison had drained all emotion from Walter. Even at that point he was calm, as though he'd spotted a wrong entry on a balance sheet but knew how to reconcile it.

'And all this was done to achieve, what?' he asked, but for a moment his defences were down. He'd said it with disgust.

'To fabricate proof that you did not kill Pierce.'

'You're saying Carla shot Roy in cold blood – to prove that?'

'Perhaps she loves you as much as you do her.'

I said this in a neutral voice, not believing she loved him at all, but he missed the double meaning. She needed him as a background to her life. Without him, her love affairs would be empty and pointless and perhaps, behind it all, she feared him just a little. Spice, that would be, to her precarious existence.

'You can't prove any of this, of course,' he said.

'My only witness is Samantha,' I admitted, not failing to notice that he was moving closer to his target pistol. He'd left it there for a specific purpose.

His hand was reaching for it when the first shot rang out. I stared at his hand. It had not reached the Ruger. I turned quickly. Sam and Lewis, who'd been clutched together, were sagging. For a moment I could not see what had happened, then I realized that it was she who was supporting him.

'Lewis!' she screamed.

'My shoulder . . .' he moaned.

I ran forward, thrusting her aside urgently. The second shot from the garden plucked at my sleeve. Walter was beside me.

'Carla!' he shouted into the darkness.

A third shot came and something shattered across the room. He raised the Ruger and took one snap shot at the other pistol's flame. He was a marksman. No trouble for him to hit the pistol.

But there was no cry of pain. No sound. He waited. Lewis was crawling away across the room, Sam whimpering above him. Then Walter moved forward into the garden.

I looked round for Amelia. She came running to me and I caught her shoulders.

'Get in that corner and stay there,' I said. 'Now. Please.'

She nodded and turned away.

I could hear Walter calling out for Carla. There were no more shots. I followed his voice, his crashing feet. With the light now behind me I could see more clearly – his shadow, bending, then hers, stretched in the bushes. He crouched over her as the seconds ticked away. Then he straightened.

'She's dead. She's dead, Patton. My hand . . . oh dear God, I'm out of practice.'

He appeared to be utterly confused and made no reaction to the rustle of movement a couple of yards to our right.

I said: 'Go inside. Put that gun down and don't move.'

As Walter moved blindly away, I pounced sideways, got a sleeve, an arm, and flung myself on to the scrambling, panic-stricken figure of Rex. As his head came up the light from the house slipped across his face, like a cold, white slap, with his eyes staring blackly.

'I heard shots,' he whispered. 'Shots.'

'You bloody fool,' I said softly. 'Get away from here. Carla's dead. She's the only one who can involve you. Just run, to some place I can't find you. Get going, damn you.'

I thrust him away. Rex was a useless complication we could live without. Probably he'd never be anything more to anybody.

I went back inside and headed for the phone. Sirens would soon break up that party. While we waited, I got Lewis's jacket off and we had a look at his shoulder.

'Not too bad,' I said. 'You'll live.'

He gave me a sickly grin. 'Not my brush hand, thank God,' he said and Sam kissed his beard. How would she ever find his lips?

Walter was shaking when I went to him. I sat beside him, taking a full glass with me.

'Can they withdraw a Queen's Pardon?' he asked, his teeth chattering against the glass. 'When they know about my pistol.'

'I think they can. But why should they? Nobody will say you shot Griff Pierce. It'll be clear now that it was Carla. Maybe Pierce was threatening to come to you . . .'

'Did,' he said gloomily.

'And she was furious with him. He wasn't keeping to the rules.'

He thought a while. 'And . . . this?' He gestured towards the garden.

'Carla's death? An accident. Self-defence. You were defending Samantha and yourself and you *did* fire for the gun.' I paused. His hand was now more steady. 'Didn't you?' I asked gently.

'Yes.' He buried his nose in the glass.

I gave him a couple of minutes. We were alone in the corner. Amelia was whispering to Veronica and sirens were distantly probing the night.

'You knew, didn't you?' I asked softly. 'In the end, you had to accept that your pistol had killed Pierce so it must have been Carla.'

There was a long silence. At last he put his head in his hands as the sirens moaned to extinction. I sat looking at his bent head as feet pounded in the hall.

Much later, when Lewis had been patched up and the police had been and taken their preliminary statements, when Samantha had driven Lewis home to London . . . very much later, the dawn not so far away, we went out to the Stag.

I had the hardtop on at that time so I wound down the window before I lit my pipe.

'It's cold, Richard,' said Amelia, hinting that I should get started.

'I was thinking about Walter.'

'Poor man.'

'He'd loaded that pistol with magnum twenty-twos, you know.'

'What are those?'

'High-powered stuff. And the shot got her between the eyes.' She shuddered. 'Pure chance . . .'

'Do you think so? But when his pistol couldn't be found he must have known she killed Pierce. Known. Yet he said nothing, waiting for her to take some action. And when she did take action at last, he would know she'd also killed his friend Roy. He wouldn't understand it but he would know.'

She was staring at me, the stark streetlamp ghastly across one cheek. 'You surely can't mean . . .'

'He intended to kill her. The flash from her pistol would light her face and he fired at the after-image. A marksman, was Walter. But he wouldn't be able to forgive her that, whatever he might have forgiven in the past. Not forgive the fact that she killed his friend in order to save Walter from paying for the murder she'd committed herself.'

She was crying into her hands. I scattered sparking ashes outside in the street, wound up the window, and started the engine.

'I just hope,' I said, 'that he never realizes that his very good friend Roy probably guessed that Carla had killed Pierce but nevertheless used the bullet-in-the-sandbag evidence to put Walter away.'

198

I drove away from there, not even glancing in the rear-view mirror for a last sight of the house.

It was a long drive. I told her about Rex, in the garden, and then she slept, her head on my shoulder.

Once she woke, alert and abruptly lucid, as though reality and dream had come together.

'Why did you let him get away?' she asked.

'Who?'

'Rex. You could have done something.'

'He's not all bad when you come to think about it. Carla had to use Sam's painting of Rex in order to discover who'd been to his room. That means he refused to tell her. It also means he knew the danger telling her would mean to Sam. You'll notice he ignored Sam from then on and concentrated on Veronica. On the night of the fight, Rex and Lewis, I think Rex was guarding Sam, too.'

She laughed. 'Two guards?'

'I think Lewis will do it better, don't you. That's why I sent Rex away.'

ROGER ORMEROD spent many years in the
British Civil Service. He is the author
of more than twenty crime novels and
lives in Wolverhampton, England.